The Minders

M. Max Boroumand

The Minders is a work of fiction. Names, characters, places and incidents either are the product of the author's imagination or used fictitiously. Any resemblance to actual persons, living or dead, events, or locales is entirely coincidental.

A 2018 *boroumand – A MediArt Company* edition
(For Reviews: Go to bit.ly/boroumand)

Published in the United States by
boroumand – A MediArt Company

Cover Design: M. Max Boroumand

ISBN: 978-0-9969496-1-3
eBook ISBN: 978-0-9969496-0-6

For my wife, boys, mom, and sisters:
I love you and thank you.

Map of Iran

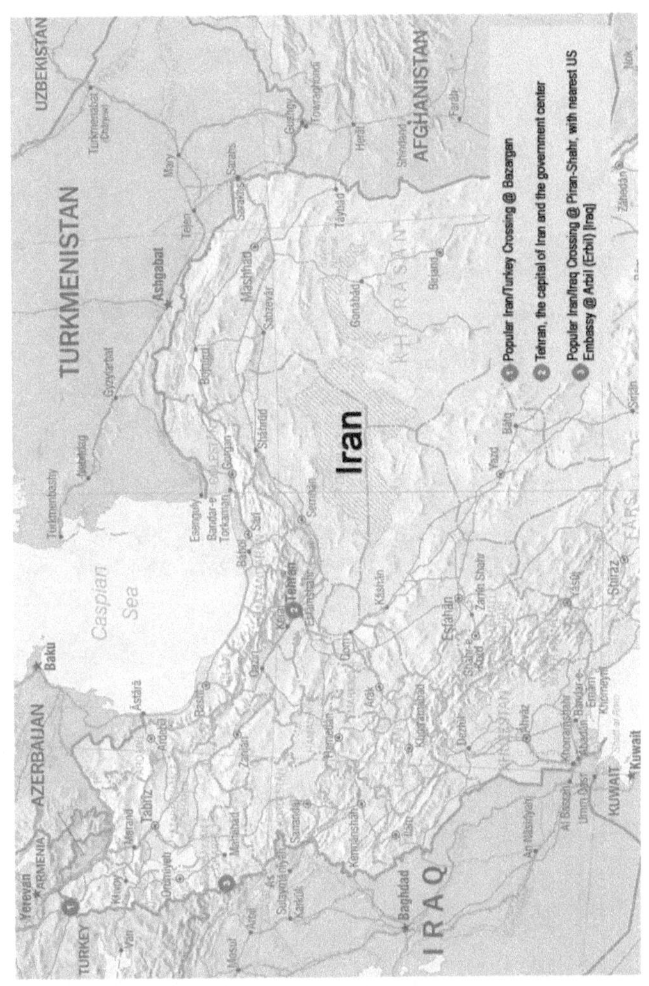

TURKEY
ARMENIA
Yerevan
AZERBAIJAN
Baku
UZBEKISTAN
TURKMENISTAN
Turkmenbashy
Nebitdag
Gyzylarbat
Turkmenabat (Chärjew)
Caspian Sea
Ashgabat
Mary
Telen
Van
Khvoy
Merand
Tabriz
Ardabil
Astara
Orumiyeh
Esenguly
Bandar-e Torkaman
Gorgan
Bojnurd
Sarakhs
Sarahs
Mosul
Mahabad
Zanjan
Qazvin
Babol
Sari
Shahrud
Mashhad
Sabzevar
Arbil
As Sulaymaniyah
Karkuk
Sanandaj
Karaj
Tehran
Eslamshahr
Semnan
Guchgy
Towraghondi
Iran
Hamedan
Qom
Kermanshah
Arak
Kashan
Gonabad
Taybad
Herat
KHORASAN
Baghdad
Ilam
Khorramabad
Esfahan
Dezful
Shahr-e Kord
Zarin Shahr
Yazd
Birjand
Shindand
AFGHANISTAN
Farah
IRAQ
An Nasiriyah
Ahvaz
Bafq
Al Basrah
Umm Qasr
Khorramshahr
Abadan
Bandar-e Emam Khomeyni
Yasuj
Shiraz
Sirjan
Zahedan
Nok
KUWAIT
Shatt al Arab
Kuwait
FARS
Popular Iran/Turkey Crossing @ Bazargan
Tehran, the capital of Iran and the government center
Popular Iran/Iraq Crossing @ Piran-Shahr, with nearest US Embassy @ Arbil (Erbil) [Iraq]

CENTRAL INTELLIGENCE AGENCY
WASHINGTON, D.C.

OFFICE OF THE DEPUTY DIRECTOR

MEMORANDUM TO: Director, Iran Clandestine Division
SUBJECT: Iran's ███ Clandestine ██████ *The Center / The Minders*
DATE: January ██████

This is a preliminary report on and analysis of th███████████████
████████ The Center ██████████████████████████████████████
██ Biologicals ████
████████ World Health Organization ████████████████████████
████████████████████████████████ Tehran, Iran ████████████
██████████

The Center ████████ Silicon Valley ████████████████████████
████████ California. ████████████████████████████████████
████ Tehran ██
██
██
████████████ MOSSAD. ████████████████████████████

A more detailed analysis will be forthcoming.

Warren Spencer
Deputy Director

Enclosures: ████████████, ████████████, IRAN_477.xls

1 | A WHITE ROOM

Bobby Shams woke up with a metallic taste in the back of his mouth. He felt woozy, his vision was blurred, and he still felt sleepy. He blinked rapidly to clear his vision. Somehow thinking he was still in the cab, he spoke to the driver. Several seconds into the conversation, he realized he was nowhere near a car. He was in a room. Maybe he was now in his uncle's house, though he was unaware of how he got there. He slowly sat up in bed, looking around for clues. The room was clean, with white walls, no windows, and a white door with a small round window. Along with the bunk bed Bobby was in, there was a metal desk with two metal chairs, and against the wall, a one-piece metallic sink, and toilet. On the wall above the sink, a reflective metal square served as a mirror.

"Is this a hospital? Was there an accident?" Bobby thought.

He inspected himself, looking for bandages and wounds. There were no signs of injury. He got up, wobbling towards the sink, and inspected his face in the metal square. There were no bandages, cuts or bruises. He walked to the door, only to find it locked.

His heart pounded.

"Is this a jail?"

He looked through the thick glass of the window and saw a similar door on the other side of the brightly lit white hallway. The other door had the Arabic number six on it. Looking left and right as far as he could, he counted five rooms across the hall and guessed at another five on his side. The window glass had an embedded wire mesh that seemed to be shatterproof. The door itself felt thick and unyielding.

There was no movement, no sound, no one around. As his strength returned, Bobby pounded on the door, watching through the window. He saw no one and heard nothing. He still wore his street clothes and checked his pockets for his cell phone and wallet. Finding his pockets empty, he went back to pounding the door. A minute into it, he heard a booming voice coming from a speaker in the ceiling.

"Please stop that noise. Be patient. We will be with you soon," the voice said in English.

Frantically, he began mulling all sorts of questions. Filled with despair, frightened and numb, he slumped down in one of the chairs.

• • •

Bobby was not alone along that hall. A few doors down, in a duplicate of his room, a middle-aged man, beaten and bandaged, was lying in his bed, crying quietly.

Across the hall from him, in another room, was the man's daughter. She was playing with several dolls. On her table was a half-finished puzzle.

All the other rooms were empty.

This was level B2, of The Center.

2 | ARRIVAL

Frankfurt, Germany | 18 Hours Earlier

Bobby began his trip to Iran with a flight out of Germany. He was on his summer break, having just graduated from MIT. His final semester and a grueling internship had taken their toll. His planned six-week European vacation would end with four weeks in Iran, his parents' native country. Born in the United States, he had never been to the old country. But, he had heard all the family stories and gossip, loved the food, the art, and the music, so he had long wanted to explore the sights and sounds first hand. He considered it a well-deserved break before starting his new job as a software engineer. He arranged through his mother and father visits to relatives in several cities. Before he left the states, the plans were all in place for a non-stop four-week, feast of food, family, and Iranian immersion.

Iranians occupied every seat on the Lufthansa flight #1120 to Tehran. In reality, a few brave non-Iranians filled some seats, but the rest were Iranians from all around the world. Intermixed with Farsi, you could hear several other languages. Yet, the closer you got to Iran the more Farsi you heard as if the passengers were practicing for a foreign language exam.

"Dad, how do you say 'my condolences for your father's death'?"

"Son, do you know what to say when someone asks 'what do you do for work'?"

In short, some combination of asking for something, replying to someone, or starting a conversation. Bobby too was quietly practicing. Although Farsi had been a household language for him as a child, after years away from home, his skills had dwindled. He had to practice pronouncing some harder words, the guttural sounds, sounds you don't hear in English, sounds that seemed to come from a sore throat. He practiced the greetings, return greetings, and basic chitchat, followed by recalling names and places. The first ten minutes of any conversation would be easy. The difficulties would come in conversations about career aspirations and related technical terms. It was hard enough to explain in English.

"How does one translate assembly code embedded in microchips supporting BUS speed optimization?" Bobby thought, smiling and shaking his head.

Adding to the difficulty were decades of linguistic changes since his parents had last lived in Iran. Early in the revolution, the Iranian government changed all Arab and Western words to Farsi. Bobby's vocabulary learned from his parents, came from the old dictionaries. He only knew a few of the changes. Soon enough, someone would correct him on many words, singling him out as an old school Iranian. Most native Iranians born after the revolution knew little of the old language. This created a gap between those born before and after the revolution. Each had a specific language with different cultural nuances.

Flight #1120 held a full load of colorful and happy people, many drinking their cocktails, reading their glossy European magazines, magazines filled with fashionably dressed, or seductively under-dressed, women and men, with advertisements for colognes, perfumes, or jewelry, all violating rules of modesty according to *Sharia* law. It was the last chance to enjoy soon to be forbidden sins before the inevitable final call one hears on all flights into Islamic countries.

Bobby finished his second Bloody Mary. Feeling drowsy, he pressed his seat button to lean back and to nap, thinking about experiencing his heritage, his lineage, his parent's homeland. What adventures lay ahead, he wondered.

• • •

An hour later, the sobering PA announcement in English woke him.

"Ladies and gentlemen, we are now crossing into the Islamic Republic of Iran airspace, and as per regulations we have to collect all alcoholic beverages, foreign magazines, and headsets." The same announcement followed in French and German. Over the next few minutes, the crew collected the now-taboo items.

Once the aisles cleared, pandemonium erupted, triggering a complete transformation of a kind that Bobby had never seen in any of his travels. Women lined up to use the restrooms, which became makeshift changing rooms. They would enter in their western clothes and emerge as *babushkas,* looking as modest as required by their final destination or household religious levels.

Once back in their seats, some put on headscarves to hide their hair, while others bobbed their heads to make sure their scarves wouldn't slip. Others removed fingernail polish and wiped off the lipstick. The transitions complete, everyone eventually calmed down. They were now ready. Colors had all but disappeared. Bobby felt as if he were drowning in a sea of black and brown. The pervasive palette one only sees in Middle Eastern countries, or in New York subways.

The plane landed at half past noon at the Imam Khomeini International Airport, fifteen miles outside Tehran, Taxiing took quite a while, adding to the air of prevailing apprehension. Flights were landing and taking off by the minute. Finally, the plane arrived at the gate and came to a final stop. The air inside the cabin seemed thick with uncertainty. Everyone took one last deep breath as if to relieve varying degrees of anxiety.

When the signal came that the door was open, people got up and moved into the aisle. Companions checked each other to make sure they were presentable, modest, and safe. They collected their belongings and began the walk forward. Bobby grabbed his backpack, checked his seat pockets, and followed the line of people disembarking.

. . .

Lines in the customs area were long. A cousin would arrive to pick Bobby up, so he hoped to get through easily, but lightly dressed in jeans and a t-shirt, carrying only his backpack, a fleece jacket, and his laptop, he knew customs wouldn't be a problem. He had nothing to declare that might be a problem. The line seemed to take forever, but finally, his turn came.

A large and chiseled customs agent in a dark blue uniform glared at Bobby, and then asked, first in Farsi, then German, then English, "Good day, sir. What brings you to the Islamic Republic of Iran?"

Glad to have the long wait over, Bobby happily handed the man his Iranian passport and all other paperwork, including his approved military exemption form.

"*Salam*. I'm here on vacation and to visit relatives," Bobby replied in carefully practiced, near perfect Farsi.

The military service exemption form and fees were a function of one's education level while in Iran. The more educated you were when you left Iran, the more you had to pay in fines for not having fought in the Iran-Iraq war. Having been born outside of the country, Bobby's fines were minimal and he was happy to have the exemption.

The penalty for draft dodgers was severe. Of course, Iran's version of the draft was to drive around neighborhoods picking up boys twelve and older. These boys were taken forcefully while their distraught parents were reassured with a martyred child living happily in a world filled with heavenly goods. During the war, most of the youngest boys, untrained, were used as living mine detectors, forced to run across open fields to clear a path for tanks and soldiers. If each wave of children running across a field resulted in a dozen dead and many dozens maimed and mangled, it was still far cheaper than having a tank destroyed.

The customs agent opened Bobby's passport, noting the line indicating U.S. citizenship.

"Very good sir and do you have your American passport and *Cart-eh-Meli?*" the agent continued in English. Apparently, he wanted to practice his English, as Bobby was practicing his Farsi.

Bobby handed the agent his U.S. passport and his Persian ID card, surprised that the man spoke English with no accent at all. The customs agent typed into his computer, clicking the mouse, moving between tabs on the screen, staring at each page for a bit. He suddenly frowned and walked to a supervisor several cubicles away. They chatted, facing away from Bobby. Minutes later and after a phone call made by the supervisor, the customs agent returned to his podium. Scanning the American passport and stamping the Iranian passport, he handed both to Bobby, along with all other documents.

"Welcome to the Islamic Republic of Iran," the agent said in Farsi.

Bobby took his documents, placed them in his backpack, smiled at the agent and walked by the podium into a much larger hall filled with arriving and departing passengers. The people departing seemed a much happier group and were moving a great deal faster. He slowly worked his way through the crowds, walking through the double automatic exit doors, stepping onto the hot concrete sidewalk. The heat and smog were instantly oppressive. The air hit him like a sucker punch. He adapted to the heat quickly. But, the smog was another story. Every breath was a hot mix of fumes and gasses floating in the air, replenished by countless exhaust pipes. He felt as if he were swallowing acid.

All around him, people were getting in and out of cars, taxis, and buses. As hot as it was, no one was wearing shorts, t-shirts, flip-flops, or any of the hot-weather outfits one would see in the States or Europe. Colors consisted primarily of dark earth tones and a lot of black. Children were the only ones with colorful garments as though color after a certain age was also against *Sharia* law. Bobby's first impression was one of a vast funeral.

• • •

He found a shaded spot, under a sign and against a wall, and waited for his cousin, who had been sent pictures of him. He waited for an hour, but no one came. He chalked up the delay to traffic. After several unsuccessful calls, he took a taxi. Furnished with directions, distances, city maps, painstakingly educated about fares and tips, he hailed the next taxi in line. A taxi from across the street squealed its tires, made a U-turn, and pulled in front of all the other waiting taxis, right next to Bobby. The other cabbies jumped out to protest, yelling, hurling insults and curses, waving their arms and hands like windmills. The rude cabbie calmly waved his ID, a badge of sorts, and within seconds, all the other cabbies stopped shouting and meekly got back into their cars, like mice scurrying back into their holes.

As odd as that looked to Bobby, he took the cab. Plus, none of the other cabbies even looked at him or in his direction after the incident, and he was sick of standing in the heat, breathing the foul air.

His cab driver was very polite. The cab, a Mercedes-Benz, was ultra clean, chillingly air conditioned, with a thick glass partition between Bobby and the front seat. On the partition, there was a speaker, a microphone, a drawer for exchanging money, the driver's laminated and framed license documents, and a clear view of the meter. The meter read 5000 before the cab even moved. The inflationary numbers reminded Bobby of his dad's travels in Italy where vendors would regularly add the year, 1980, printed at the top of the bill to the 230,000 *Lira* total, and no one would be the wiser.

"Do you speak English?" Bobby asked.

"Yes. I also speak German, French, and some Chinese!" The driver's voice came through the speaker as the cab pulled away from the curb. "Where are we going?" he asked in English.

Bobby leaned towards the glass partition, reading fluently in Farsi from a piece of paper. He gave the driver directions as though he had been there many times.

"We can practice my Farsi or speak English," he said as he leaned back in his seat.

"Or, we can practice Chinese," the cabbie replied, smiling.

The highway was expansive and in perfect shape, with large, clear signage that echoed American standards, large green signs with white reflective lettering, in English and Farsi. It seemed clear to Bobby that foreign-educated engineers, with proven standards of safety and efficiency, had built the highways. Yet, people drove like maniacs. Lane markings were treated as mere decorations. A four-lane highway could easily have six to seven lanes of cars and motorcycles moving on it. Traffic lights were an invitation to stop, not a requirement. If you could beat one or dart across before the light changed, drivers would, and clearly thought they should.

Fender benders were everywhere, with almost every car having some scarring. Cars consisted of Japanese, German, and many of the local builds. The driver pointed to all the locally made cars, mentioning their brands, and using the new Farsi words to describe them. The *Khod-Ro*, loosely translated, "goes-by-itself." The *IKO Samand*, the first national car, and *Saipa*, the second, were the two most popular brands in the country, and their manufacture employed nearly three percent of the population.

The cabbie was quite proud of the country's accomplishments since the revolution. He went a little beyond pride, becoming slightly preachy. Bobby took it all in as any good tourist would.

As the taxi entered the city, ongoing construction and infrastructure were the biggest changes Bobby noticed as he compared what he saw to what his parents had described. There were modern high rises everywhere, mostly apartment buildings, with the bottom several floors occupied by retail stores or commercial businesses. Sidewalks were rivers of people moving in every direction. People would run across streets through traffic and pour over the curbs to get around logjams on the sidewalk. It was chaos, even compared to New York City's pedestrian madness. Harried was the best word to describe everything.

"It's a long and slow drive, why don't you rest a bit." The cabbie suggested.

Bobby nodded at the cabbie and turned to rest his head while looking at the views. Quickly, he dozed off.

• • •

Once Bobby was deep into his slumber, the cabbie picked up his cell phone. "I have him. He's asleep and I'm bringing him in."

3 | SUNDAY

Colorado | Two Days Later

In a wealthy suburb of Denver, at the beginning of a long private road, stood a tall modern gate, spanning two brick columns, made of thick iron bars, six inches apart, painted in a black matte finish. Behind the gates were moveable in-ground mechanical barriers so that no vehicle could crash through the gate. In a gatehouse sat a large man with unblinking eyes, broad shoulders, brawny arms, holstering a pistol on his belt. Closed circuit security focused cameras all over the property. From the gatehouse, the curving road led to the main house.

The drive passed through a lushly forested property, over rolling hills, and finally up a long hill that ended at a spectacular home designed with two offset, crescent-shaped levels. On the inside curved edge, each level had floor to ceiling glass walls of a material that dimmed at a flick of a switch from clear to opaque. Technology was embedded everywhere, inside and out. Everyone who lived in the house carried or wore a digital ID pin that could, on a walk through the interior, trigger favorite music, adjust room temperature, unlock doors and cabinets, and display preferred digital artwork. The interior décor, combining unpainted concrete, steel, cherry wood, modern furniture, and Persian art, created a futuristic yet warm and inviting ambiance.

Mike Shams designed and built this dream home, a dream home created as a gift to himself and his family after decades of hard work, a home he deserved, satisfying every wish and need. It was purposely nothing like the home in which he'd grown up in Iran.

His childhood home back in Iran was a stuffy, formal old house with high ceilings, classic Persian chalk and mirror plasterwork on the walls, filled with uncomfortable Louis XVI furniture in every room. It had been his grandfather's house, given to his parents as a wedding gift.

Mike had hated that place. He hated the large, dark rooms with their small windows and doors on each wall that led to adjacent rooms. He hated the garish parties his parents gave, with all the furniture pushed against the walls, the many guests creating a cloud of cigarette and hookah smoke that lingered for hours like a low hanging fog. He vividly recalled walking through the smoke to get to the appetizers, always centered in the middle of the room. Through the entire walk, elders would shower him with questions, all asking the same things.

"How is school? What do you want to be when you grow up?" Each question followed by some demands. *"Fetch us that fruit and those sweets! Fetch us an ashtray!"*

The personal inquiries just masked the embarrassment of asking him to do something. After all, the true answers hardly ever changed so over the years the children in the family would practice making up fanciful answers to see who would remember and pass them along the gossip grapevine. Answers about ambitions for the future varied, from surgeon to garbage-man and from doctor to a mother of seven.

For Mike, one interesting aspect of those stifling parties were the culturally revealing seating priorities, with elders in the more comfortable seats at the upper section of the room, and the younger guests on the hard narrow wooden seats at the lower part of the room. This arrangement optimized the greeting process as each new guest arrived. Proper etiquette called for greeting the eldest first, then working your way down the age ladder, stopping at your station and then waiting for the younger guests to greet you.

The ranking by age could become an amusing game of sorts, as some ladies insisted on a seat farther down in the room to lower their age. This would invite loud ribbing and some public embarrassments as other guests called out a woman's actual age.

Finally, since there were always more guests than seats, there was an understood reservation system. Should elders get up to get something, their chairs would remain empty unless an even older person arrived and needed to sit. Therefore, the oldest person had a guaranteed secure chair, with the odds of a saved seat decreasing, as you got younger. These unwritten rules and strict hierarchy made your life hell if you greeted out of order or if you forgot to greet someone. Decades later, social errors would still be recalled as the worst kind of betrayal.

Someone would ask, *"Do you remember that one year when you sat in your uncle's chair"* And then would ruminate with pleasure on how you made a fool of yourself long ago.

The parties were not without entertainment value. The lower part of the room had the best jokes while the upper part had the best political discussions. A child had to learn to navigate a room to minimize silly conversations and find the interesting ones. In the end, though, the social lessons became very useful in Mike's career as a builder in America. As the founder and CEO of Towers Construction, it helped him network at trade conventions and architecture shows. Mike was both genetically predisposed and trained in the art of small talk, glad-handing and doling out compliments.

. . .

In his new house, Mike had built a combination sanctuary room and office. It was the perfect place to relax on his Sundays off. He had pictures of his family, his award-winning projects, and some beautiful Persian miniatures on the walls. His intricately carved walnut desk looked out on his well-manicured gardens. To the side, a large, matching walnut file cabinet held hundreds of design and construction projects his company had completed over decades. Placed in the middle of the room were a coffee table, a leather couch, and his favorite leather chair. He angled the leather chair just right so he could see his landscaped property.

On that particular Sunday, the morning sun was beaming across the room, warming the leather chair, a perfect invitation to sit. His reading glasses were on the coffee table, next to the newspaper, awaiting his arrival.

Mike banned all calls and messages on Sundays until well after noon, with no exceptions. Running a multi-billion dollar construction company took so much of his time he had to preserve a few precious hours on his one and only day of rest, even if this more accurately amounted to a three-hour break. He needed that time to reflect, a mental and physical escape from his daily work routine, a way to replenish his emotional currency.

He finally arrived in his office and softly sank into his chair. He had his drink, an aromatic cup of black tea with a splash of rose water and two cubes of sugar melting unstirred. He reached for his glasses, putting them on as he took a sip of tea. He picked up the Sunday New York Times, methodically separating the sections he liked and discarding those he didn't. Among others, the sports section would go into the recycle bin. Although his construction company had built three of the largest domed stadiums in the U.S., he had little interest in reading about sports. Ironic, he thought. As always, he kept all the sections orderly for later reading by his wife Parisa.

Deep into an article, and enjoying his tea, he heard a knock. Looking up over his reading glasses, slightly annoyed, he saw Parisa at the door.

"Honey, your cell phone keeps beeping!" She walked in and handed him the phone.

"Thanks, Love." Mildly annoyed, he put the paper down and took the phone.

He had to assume there was an emergency since his family and employees strictly observed his Sunday morning rule. He saw a text message, from a local number he did not recognize. He opened the message.

WATCH THE VIDEO. FOLLOW THE LINK. DO NOT TALK TO ANYONE.

Leaning back in his chair, he took another sip of his tea. The video loaded and he began to watch. Seconds into it, the teacup fell to the Persian carpet. As if pressed down by a great weight, he sank deep into the chair, unable to move.

Shocked, overcome with fear, he could not hear a single word of the audio message. All he saw was his youngest child Bobby tied to a chair. The boy's lips were quivering, saying something. He watched, over and over, finally he heard Bobby's faint gasping voice.

"Dad … help me … they've taken me … I don't know why!"

• • •

Half a day earlier in Copenhagen, Finland, the World Health Organization (WHO) liaison to the United Nations for Vaccines and Biologicals received a similar text message. A message from a local number read the same as Mike's, but in her video, the official saw her husband and young daughter tied to chairs. The child was bound but unharmed, but the husband had been beaten, bruised, and was in obvious pain as he spoke.

In Palo Alto, a week earlier, a Stanford mechanical engineering Ph.D. graduate received a letter inviting him to join a new stealth start-up, offering great pay and benefits.

In Denver, the head of City & County Permits & Projects received a text stating his gambling debts were due immediately, no exceptions, and no extensions.

4 | THE WATCHED

Tehran, Iran | Three Months Earlier

The business park, one of a few in Tehran, was a bustling ecosystem that could survive on its own, without the surrounding city. It contained a mix of ground floor retail stores, restaurants, clothing stores, repair shops, dry cleaners, and electronic stores, above which were the offices of professional businesses. Surrounding the buildings were green parks and walking paths. One of the few community-oriented and green business parks that were becoming popular, the place offered a relief from persistent congestion, smog, and traffic.

Surrounding the park were typical metropolitan high rises, all crammed together, and each competing for some piece of the sky. A nearby subway station pumped people out as fast as it sucked them in, a continual cycle of walking drones, ants on a mission before winter sets in.

In the middle of this park, was a building called 'The Cultural Center,' indistinguishable from all the other buildings in the park. On closer inspection, however, it was nothing like any of the other buildings. There were no retail stores on its street level. The entire building contained only the Center. There were just two ways in, the main entrance and a small door that opened on the private parking lot, a rarity in a city where most parking lots were public and operated on a first come, first served basis. There were no side entrances, nor were there any receiving platforms.

For anyone curious enough to look, other clues showed how different this place was from its neighbors. The windows had layered panes, probably bulletproof and definitely soundproof. The corners of each window showed subtle signs of electronic sound and vibration masking, preventing laser eavesdropping and frequency leakage. The parking lot had a magnetic card slot and license plate readers that, for authorized vehicles, would trigger a heavy sliding gate to open. The walls surrounding the parking area were twelve feet high and made of concrete.

To most passers-by, the building looked like a typical cultural center found in almost every city in the Islamic Republic of Iran. It was one of three satellite offices of Tehran's main cultural center. And, the only one that had little if anything to do with culture.

On the inside, the differences were even more glaring. The building was a technological and security marvel, electronically masked from floor to ceiling to deter outside eavesdropping. The computer systems were as high-end as anything at the National Security Agency (NSA). They assembled all servers and desktops in-house, to assure untainted hardware and software. The tech staff sourced components from a variety of vendors from many countries. All items that eventually made it to this facility were checked for any malicious code and integrated backdoors. All machines lacked USB ports and CD drives to dissuade data transfers. The software was custom-made or open source and further modified on site.

Each employee had a clone-proof, cryptographic RFID chip, with rolling codes, surgically implanted in one arm. The chip allowed for access to sections, rooms, files, and computers, as their projects or roles required. RFID rights management avoided all the pitfalls of lost, stolen, and expired keycards. Not to mention, the dangling of key-cards as one walked off premise. There was no need to draw attention to oneself.

Employees entered the building through the unassuming main lobby or from the parking lot. They continued to a secondary, closed processing area, where they walked through special body scanners on the way in and out. Across from the scanner was a large black metal disposal box. You did not leave with any documents or files, for risk of thermal incineration. Phones were randomly confiscated, checked for photos and scanned files, and delivered to their owners during the following day. All frequencies were jammed while on the inside.

Unauthorized communications never entered or left The Center.

Most astonishing of all was the use of languages. Center employees and agents could not speak or use Farsi, the national language, in the building. The only exceptions were in the main lobby, and the accounting and administration offices, all located on the front facing section of the main floor. In all other areas, the only languages allowed were any two or more of several foreign languages, with English mandatory.

For the people working there, The Center had nothing to do with culture, but everything to do with national advancement, power, and influence. It contained some of the country's most valuable intellectual property, both in tangible designs and deliverables. Moreover, it oversaw those people, globally, who had created them. They collected extensive information for each of those people: their weaknesses, strengths, career paths, relationships, friends, family, assets, and current locations. And, most importantly, any information that could be used to manipulate or influence them. Everything was cataloged, indexed and stored. This was Iran's largest and oldest Big Data project, in the truest sense of the concept.

• • •

The Center and its staff were one of many replacements of the SAVAK, the original Iranian secret police and intelligence services founded with help from the CIA. From 1957 to 1979, it focused only on Iranians within Iran and was the most hated and feared institution, infamous for torturing its citizens. In stark contrast, The

Center focused exclusively on Iranian expatriates and their children, outside of Iran, collectively known as 'The Watched', where it opportunistically and secretly raised the value of the people it watched. The Center housed a collection of analysts, highly educated professionals, and field agents, known as 'The Minders.'

At the beginning of the 1979 revolution, SAVAK disbanded, with departments and infrastructure converting into a new internal security and spying organization. One offshoot group became dedicated to expats and tracked those who left Iran. As more people left, it became clear that the magnitude of the brain drain was catastrophic, that vast knowledge and expertise were to be lost to other countries forever. Something had to either stop or recapture that loss.

Hessam Rezadad, an up-and-coming commander in SAVAK, educated in the U.S. and fluent in several languages, became Project Architect and Strategist. Eventually, he rose to the top at The Center, with a force now numbering in the thousands and revenues in the billions of dollars.

From the start, Rezadad's vision was to create one of the world's most sophisticated big data projects, one that could keep track of every person and can help, manipulate, or destroy the paths on which he or she traveled. He developed a culture of immersion. The Center hired only those who themselves had been educated abroad, were not Islamists, and who could blend seamlessly into varying cultures.

The Center believed in matching their people with the ebb and flow of the future world in which they had to live and work, which explained the rule that no one was to use Farsi while at The Center. The mandatory language was English and at minimum one of the following: Mandarin, Hindustani, Spanish, Russian, Arabic, French, or German. Everyone working at The Center was wholly fluent in his or her chosen languages, with no accents whatsoever.

The Center library contained digitized magazines from all around the world. Reading country-specific local periodicals helped acclimate agents to cultural and current language nuances and helped them adjust to living and working in those countries. Deep cultural immersion assured a low profile, better decision-making, and the avoidance of major strategic and tactical errors. Such errors had repeatedly marked western failures in Iraq, Afghanistan, and the Middle East for decades. Underestimating his opponents, at any level, was not an accusation Rezadad wished to hear, ever.

As much as it benefited his organization to see the bearded Iranian politicians roaming the political halls of the world, and to hear their asinine diatribes filled with religious dogma and factual denials, Rezadad hated the way it portrayed his people around the world. He hated to see the world perceive his people as it did the rest of the region as rag-headed peasants living in tents and eating dates by the oasis near grazing camels. Then again, this stereotyped visual was what allowed him to succeed beyond any of his dreams. The more normal and accepted his minders were and the more different they seemed from the crazies portrayed on Fox news, the better it was for The Center. The best place to hide was in plain sight, holding a bottle of beer, talking smack about sports and politics in a typical American style.

So successful was Rezadad that the Supreme Leader and Guardian Council of the Constitution had renewed their approval of The Center year after year even though they violated many tenets of *Sharia* law and used tactics the Assembly of Experts fully opposed. The Assembly had noted and documented well over three thousand violations over the decades. However, given The Center's protected status, many agents avoided the mandatory punishments including floggings by a copper wire and in rare cases execution by hanging. Nevertheless, success and privilege came at a price. Occasionally the president, under executive order, would use The Center's knowledge base and resources to make tactical or strategic moves against other countries, during war or peace.

As distasteful as that was, it was non-negotiable, and occurred more often than not, though few at The Center knew about it.

• • •

The remainder of the main floor and the floor above was where the data-entry, logistics, banking, international law, program management, and R&D sections were located. All departments either started projects, ran projects, or finished them, enabling The Minders to optimize the short, medium and long-term value of The Watched. Everything was project-driven and managed within a portfolio. There were no hierarchies, and everyone worked within and moved around a well-defined matrix structure. There was no single functional head to the beast.

• • •

Level B1

The Center's main conference room was large, well-stocked with drinks and snacks, and filled with varying and comfortable seating arrangements, with breakout rooms and phone rooms adjoining. During the day, light tubes and mirrors brought sunlight into the entire space. At night, LED wall lights illuminated every inch with a warm white hue. On each screen of dozens of monitors hanging on three walls, data was scrolling constantly, all of which meant something to someone.

A glass wall, entirely covering one long wall, faced the twenty thousand square foot server room and cooling towers.

The server room expanded beyond the floor plan above and under the parking lot. Servers, floor to ceiling, were blinking like a nighttime cityscape. Every so often, you could hear the faint humming of the backup generators that stood outside in the parking lot at the back of the main floor. These were must-have pieces of equipment for those random and ever-present citywide blackouts. Each time power went out for the rest of the people in Tehran, the lights at the Center would flicker slightly, and a second later all was well again on this floor.

Level B2

This level was reserved for special guests.

• • •

On a weekly basis, in the main conference room, the business-intelligence group leaders analyzed the weekly simulation reports, project status, and forecasts, and reviewed delivery and value assurance reports on existing projects. In this room, new vectors died or came to life. Each new vector numbered sequentially, would become either a one-off project or a continuing endeavor.

Vector #12 was the longest running project to date and involved all manner of legitimate local and international money-making schemes. Early on, Rezadad had decided the Center's scope would be so vast that the organization needed to support itself. In addition, it must have means to move funds globally to support other vectors. In over 30 countries, this portfolio had under its umbrella hedge funds, venture funds, small banks, brokerage firms, real estate firms, manufacturing, pharmaceuticals, biotechnologies, and numerous other businesses.

Vector #15 was one of the most interesting projects. Its sole purpose was to shape or accelerate the path on which The Watched traveled. Rezadad envisioned helping to position them in better and more important roles in their respective careers. On the legitimate side, Vector #15 supported scholarships, educational programs, and training in all areas of science, technology, engineering, business, and medicine. On the darker side, it helped manipulate others through bribes and coercion, to select, promote or otherwise make decisions favoring a particular candidate.

Vectors #1 to #10 were highly classified with few having knowledge of any details.

• • •

The weekly meeting started typically. It was early, with the smell of coffee and tea wafting through the air. Rezadad came in, chose a seat at random and sat, a cup of a dark red Darjeeling tea in hand that gave off a rose water aroma in the trailing steam. Stacked on the table were the weekly reports and project requests.

"Let's start with the visa applications," he began, taking a long sip.

It was important to know who was visiting Iran. This was a great source of intelligence from both the willing and the not-so-willing visitor. Most cleared customs with ease. A select few had to endure a longer Q&A session, all the while having their phones cloned, and their electronic equipment reconfigured. Center agents would upgrade every computer BIOS or system with an exploit and copy all hard drives for later decryption and access. They would install a new battery for some laptops, containing specialized microchips, firmware, and embedded Wi-Fi in the casing. They would tag all devices while the recent arrival sat patiently, or nervously, or angrily, at times scared, in adjoining waiting rooms. After a long delay, guests received a box of Persian sweets, as an apology, and sent on their way.

Looking at a stack of reports several inches high, Rezadad continued the meeting. He grabbed the cover sheet and noticed eleven new possibilities put out by the simulation and analytics programs, three having the highest scores. He took the second highest scoring choice.

"We've been eyeing this man for some time. I see his son has applied for a visa."

"Yes!" Ali Najaf replied with intensity. "His visit overlaps with another high-value target and her family's visa request. Look at the first file!"

Najaf was always excitable, especially when probabilities were favorable. It amused him when seemingly obscure things came together. No one was sure if he was a pessimist or an ever-hopeful optimist. Rezadad was never sure of Najaf's true religious beliefs. He always seemed a little off and a little narcissistic. Everyone suspected Najaf was a mole put there to spy, and would often show his colors via his Islamist remarks. It was a slight bother to Rezadad, but one he knew would happen no matter what. Distrust was a common trait amongst Iranians and something that might take generations to deracinate.

Rezadad read both profiles and instantly recognized a project that had come across his desk several times. A project that always had missing parts and one Rezadad hoped he would never implement. Nevertheless, he was under orders to implement it, if possible.

"But, do we have a delivery mechanism as yet?" he asked, reminding every one of the proposed vector.

"I believe we have one." Najaf shuffled through a stack of documents that went with the simulation output from earlier that day.

"Here it is." He slid a folder towards Rezadad.

"His education was funded by us. He recently received his Ph.D. in mechanical engineering, from Stanford, and his dissertation is perfect." Najaf pinged Rezadad's laptop with a link to the candidate's two-hundred-page thesis.

"How much did we pay for his education?" Rezadad asked quietly as he read.

"We paid nearly $500,000 for undergraduate and post-graduate work. He's a genius and well worth it."

Rezadad got up, poured himself another tea, and returned to read the dissertation titled, 'Inoculations and the Zigbee Matrix - A Sub-Saharan Panacea.' He read quickly, made notes, sketched a diagram or two, and then pinged an engineer upstairs to come to the conference room. He then asked Najaf to conduct several more searches, handing him new search criterion and asked that he immediately execute several new vector simulations.

The summoned engineer arrived and sat at the table. She was a tall, elegantly dressed woman, with flowing blond hair and blue eyes, having none of the traditional headscarves and covers, yet another benefit of working at The Center. Rezadad handed her a drawing and asked if the design was achievable at any of their injection molding facilities in the U.S. She took the drawings and went back to her office. Twenty minutes later, while Rezadad was still drafting project plans, she pinged a message.

"Yes, with some minor modifications we can easily manufacture the piece."

• • •

Soon after, the requested simulation results arrived. Rezadad walked over to a phone room, notes in hand, closed the soundproof door and made a call. He was on the call for a good thirty minutes, hands waving, yelling, agitated, with cheeks red and flushed. The only time Rezadad looked and sounded like this was when talking to the President, a call he always hated and a conversation he always regretted. Every call to the president was in support of something he didn't want to do but had to. As successful as he was, he knew he was still expendable.

This particular project was necessary, and one of several projects to help distract attention from nuclear talks and reviews. To the Iranians, the process of talking and reviews was a way to buy time. They knew that promises would fade by the month, and they needed to create a cushion and to buy more time via a distraction, one that would give them a year or two and would divert attention back onto the Arab Islamists.

• • •

Rezadad stepped out of the phone room, beads of sweat dripping down the side of his face, still fuming from the call and boiling on the inside. He sat back at the conference table and began to lay out the plan.

By late evening Vector #187 had been initiated.

5 | HANDICAPPED SEATING

Mike Shams revisited the painful text message dozens of times. He read, re-read, watched the video, and watched again. It made little sense.

Why would they take my son? What do they want?

He was afraid to tell his family. He didn't know what to say. He had no answers for the hundreds of questions that would follow. Sunday dinners were when everyone got together, all his kids and their respective loved ones. That Sunday dinner would be the hardest in his life. He so much wanted to confide in Parisa. She was his rock. She always was steadfast and gave him the strength he needed. The news of Bobby would crush her. This was her little boy. Mike had to keep quiet and look as normal as possible. At least until he had more answers. He knew the calls from Iran would pour in over the next day or two, with people asking about Bobby's whereabouts.

Parisa served dinner, classic Persian fare, on time. It was a nicely mounded platter of dill rice with fava beans, chicken in tomato sauce, and a selection of homemade *torshi*, a Persian relish, along with a side of raw onions cut up into chunks, fresh greens, and toasted pita bread. Bottles of Dutcher Crossing and Diamond Creek wines sat at each end of the table.

Mike sat through dinner barely eating, deep in thought. He smiled occasionally, nodding his head to comments and answering questions. When asked what was wrong, he merely brought up client issues. Soon enough, dinner was over, with everyone scattering around the house for after dinner activities. Mike could not take the pain of keeping it all in. He excused himself and went back to his office. Once again, he opened the text message, but this time, not wanting to watch the video, he followed the link.

This took him to a page that instructed him on how to install several specific apps on his cell phone, including further instructions, and told of a second link to follow once the apps downloaded. The apps allowed anonymous access to the web, messaging, and email, without the risk of interception by third parties or governments. This was an application and network infrastructure used by legitimate safety conscious users and the seedy underground to keep themselves and their actions anonymous. Mike installed the apps and worked his way to the URL link with an *.onion* host suffix, which he had never seen or even knew existed. He knew of *.com*, *.net*, and other dot-something endings, but *.onion* was new to him. He clicked on that link that opened a new page in the newly installed app with more instructions.

The page had only one detailed order and carried an ominous warning. The order, simply stated, was to replace all the handicapped seating at the Denver Super Dome, the first stadium built by Mike's company. The designs for new seats were included as an attachment, which he downloaded. The instruction then continued: He should have the seats manufactured by a certain date, then store them at his company warehouses between two given dates, and finally, install them by a certain final date. All dates and locations were specific and prescribed. The senders of the strange instructions would handle all permits and paperwork.

Handicapped Seating, Why? Mike thought, pounding his head with both fists.

He printed the seat designs sent by the kidnappers. He then looked through his file cabinets for the original stadium plans. Finding the CD, he popped it into his computer and looked at the blueprints. He jotted down notes as he kept looking through the CD. He found the final and signed Disabled Access Advisory Committee (DAAC) plans, reading those he took more notes. On a quick review, he counted 120 plus seats. A pittance, he thought, for saving his boy.

He printed the original seat design and laid it side by side with the new design. There were only minor differences. The armrests were slightly thicker. There was a solar strip in one armrest, including a small lithium battery, and a 360-degree blue LED light placed at the top of the backrest. A great idea, one he might have included in the original specs, without the kidnapping. The entire job was possible with most parts remaining unchanged. The existing seats were code compliant, top of the line in design, by all measures perfect.

Why make the change?

The web page ended with a short warning that put a chill through his body.

YOU TALK. HE DIES.

• • •

It was a night with no sleep for Mike. He was up by 4:30 a.m. He took a shower, dressed, and was gone before anyone else woke up. He needed to get out, to start on a plan. Sunlight was brightening the horizon. It would be a clear and nice day, but for Mike, it felt like a dark, desperate day. He drove to his favorite coffee shack, ordered his regular breakfast, but could only order a takeout coffee before paying and driving off. He needed caffeine in his body to survive the morning.

It was a fast drive at that hour. He reached his company's office complex, drove through the multi-level parking structure at the base of his building to the executive area where a sign clearly marked his space. He passed no more than a dozen other cars in the lot. He parked, walked over to the express elevator for a straight ride to his floor, coffee in one hand, his briefcase in the other. There were a few lights on. Some early arrivers greeted him and he responded in kind. He was in no mood to be his normal talkative self. He went directly to his office, sat at his desk, emptied his briefcase, and loaded the plans and designs onto his computer. He brought up schedules for several fabrication facilities and tracked down some available down time. He shot off several quick, inquisitive emails to supervisors and managers around the country and waited, his mind wandering all over the place. He was alone and afraid for his son.

An hour and a half later, his secretary cheerfully walked in and handed him the daily mail and paperwork, all neatly sorted. After some pleasantries about their weekends, she left him alone. At the top of the pile rested a courier-delivered package from the City and County of Denver. The large yellow envelope was bursting with form letters, renewal permits, and copies of the original contract between Tower Construction and the city, along with references to those contract sub-sections covering maintenance and repairs. Added to the mix were strongly worded references to existing errors and oversights. Substantial fines were forthcoming if those were not corrected by a certain date. All the paperwork he needed to get the job done was included, signed, and ready to go. The installation dates and deadlines perfectly matched the dates in his instructions.

Mike had never seen permits delivered this way. Usually, one went to city hall with plans, paperwork, and a checkbook in hand, and pride in check, for a day of torment. You would sit in some small, hot office where a government employee would scrutinize every construction spec, for conformity to their codes. That day of eating shit preceded more days just like it, more time, more checks, until eventually, you might get your permit to do something or part of something. It was hell on earth for contractors and engineers, a legally sanctioned mugging. Whoever was behind this thing had great influence. Government offices never finalized paperwork that quickly or cleanly.

Where else do they have people? Who else is in their pockets? What other influence can these kidnappers' bring to bear? Mike could not stop wondering.

He thought the task of manufacturing the new handicap seats would be easy. However, getting his boy back was something he had no confidence in, and he felt completely powerless. He did not know how to get help, whom to trust. On the drive in, he had fully intended to call the police or FBI. Now, even more, scared for his son, he'd decided to remain silent.

He would comply. Yet the what-if scenarios terrified him. He had to talk to someone. He needed an ear, some help, and some advice. He needed his best friend, Gordon Caius, someone he played squash with several times a week. He was afraid to call or to see him outside his normal routine. He waited until their scheduled squash game at six that afternoon.

• • •

This was the longest Monday in Mike's memory, but he finally found himself at the club. The place was crowded and active, with people coming in and out of games. The squash courts were busy, with the regulars chatting about the day's events, their weekends, their knee pains, and the round-robin tourney standings. It seemed whenever you got a bunch of men together around sports, the competition went on at all levels: who had the newest, fastest car, the new and better cell phone, or the highest yielding mutual funds. It was the modern-day version of chest beating. Mike had always thought this was a funny American quirk, a by-product of the consumerism culture. He loved watching it unfold, especially since he had nothing more to prove, since he was wealthy beyond his dreams, beyond most people's dreams.

When he and Gordon were finally on the court, with the glass door shut and no one hovering nearby, they warmed up, volleyed for the serve order and began the game. After a minute or two, Mike leaned close to Gordon to hand him the ball.

"Gordon, we need to talk after this, in private, and I mean *really* private. I need your help."

Gordon had never heard the sound of fear coming from his friend, and for the first time, he felt worried for him. He thought it might be cancer, or some other major ailment, threatening him or someone in his family.

"Sure, do you want to call the game and go right now?"

"No! We must finish the game. We need to act normal."

Gordon became worried. This was definitely a life or death issue. They both played as badly as they could just to finish the game. They walked casually to the locker room, grabbing a couple of robes and towels. They changed and walked into the steam sauna. People came in and out, but they waited until finally, they were alone. Gordon got up to look through the glass door. As if standing guard, he turned back toward Mike.

"No one is coming. I'll stand by the door, and you start talking. What's going on? What's with the 'act normal' shit? Are you being funny? Because you're really scaring me."

"They've taken my son," Mike said. "They've kidnapped my boy." Mike trembled as he spoke.

"Who the fuck kidnapped Bobby? What are you talking about?"

"You know that Bobby went to Iran. He went after his European trek. You remember, right?"

"Yes, I remember."

"Well, yesterday I got a text message with a video."

Mike told him all about the video, the URL link, and the demand to have stadium chairs replaced. He continued, telling him about the permits delivery to his offices. And, he told Gordon about the death threat. Having unburdened himself, he sobbed uncontrollably.

Gordon sat down and placed his hand on Mike's shoulder. He was willing to help in any way he could, he said. He then paused for a moment and then shouted angrily, "Fuck them! I'm calling Jason. I know how to get him here. I know how to keep it secret. We'll fix this."

For the first time in over a day, Mike felt a slight sense of relief. Finally, someone else knew. He was not alone anymore.

6 | PHONE CALLS

Jason Caius was on the last mile of his daily five-mile run. He loved the Monterey Peninsula trail, with its refreshing ocean breezes, salty air, and the sound of waves hitting the rocky coastline. Running was a habit etched into his genome by years in the military. Though hard on his knees, the runs always felt good. It made him glide through his daily chores and work with renewed energy. This day's run seemed a little long. He was eager to get home to chat by Skype with his son, Sean, who was now on his second tour in Iraq, a pilot, like his dad and his grandfather.

At the end of his run, he cooled off, patting himself down with a towel. Leaning against his car, he drank from a gallon jug of cold water. Finally, dry and hydrated, he began the drive home. The road and scenery were beautiful, with rolling hills on one side and the ocean on the other. He drove past the Defense Language Institute -

Foreign Language Center, where he worked as a specialist in Farsi and Arabic languages and cultures. He'd been teaching at the school since leaving his last job. His love of everything Middle Eastern came from living in Iran with his family as a child. His father, Gordon Caius, worked for Bell Helicopter as a pilot instructor for the Iranian military. Bell Helicopter had hired Gordon after the Vietnam War with a great pay package and a signing bonus. Taking advantage, Gordon took his whole family on the new adventure to Iran. Jason had loved the adventures that came with being in a new country, a place so foreign that everything was interesting, enticing, and even forbidding for a child. Those years as a child in Iran, and an eventual marriage to Amitis, an Iranian woman he met in Colorado, turned him into a willing expert on that whole region.

Jason pulled into his driveway, drove straight into his garage, and ran to his office, with a quick good morning to Amitis. His computer was up and running. Skype was on and ready to receive the call. His wife quickly followed him into the office.

"Is he on yet?" Amitis said, sitting next to Jason while handing him a cup of coffee. Black and bitter, just the way he liked it, or the way he'd got used to drinking it in the military.

Time drifted, glacially as always, as they waited for Sean to call. At last, Skype chimed with the incoming call tone. At first, it connected with no video and then reconnected with no sound, and finally, after a third time, it was all good, until it disconnected again. On the fifth try, it connected with video and sound.

Fucking Skype, it never works, Jason mused.

"Can you see me? Can you hear me?" Sean yelled into the laptop he was using. You could see people moving in the background, electronic gadgets piled up high on tables and all manner of commotion surrounding each table.

"Yes. We can hear and see you. How are you?" both parents said in unison.

"Everything is great, busy but safe, nothing to worry about."

They knew better. There was always a danger. Fortunately, Sean was in the northern Kurdish Region, dealing mostly with friendly Kurds. The three chatted for several minutes, the limit for each call before his or her allotment was over. The calls were mostly small talk, just enough to see that their child was alive and well.

Sean jokingly closed with, "So, I heard Bobby is next door in Iran visiting his relatives! Do you think we'll bump into each other?" They had been best friends since they were toddlers. The families' connection went back to when Jason and Bobby's parents became best friends in Iran.

"I don't know. Although, if you do, say hi for us. OK, son … I guess this is goodbye … we love you." Jason and his wife sent air kisses to the screen. The call ended and the video disappeared.

It was so difficult for them to see the image on the screen fade to black. It always seemed so ominous. They held each other closely, happy their son was fine and alive, a daily worry, no, an hourly worry.

Jason had not thought about Bobby or his dad in quite some time. It was difficult being so far away from Colorado. They spoke less often and saw each other even less in the months since he'd taken the teaching job. While living in Colorado, the two families had visited each other almost every other weekend for barbecues and dinners. Besides being social fun, the gatherings were a way for Jason to practice his language skills, to chat about politics, and to play backgammon with Mike. Part of every game was the mock insults about how each player rolled the dice or the errors they made in moving the pieces. They half-jokingly kept score. When Jason left for the West Coast, his number was something like 1910 to Mike's 2850.

When Gordon first moved to Iran, with little Jason and his mother, they met Mike at a Bell Helicopter meeting covering housing arrangements. Mike had just finished his degree in architecture at Cornell. He was a newly hired construction manager in *Shahin Shahr*, a master-planned city 20 kilometers north of Esfahan. In addition to the normal housing units, there was an American School stood for the children of American expats working at Bell Helicopter, Northrop Grumman Corporation, and other U.S. companies. Gordon and Mike hit it off right away, with their love of the same football teams, the same politicians, and Mike's fluency in

English. Mike became a guide, a friend, and a teacher to Gordon's family. Jason spent hours learning Farsi and backgammon in Mike's household.

The two families became so close that after the Iranian revolution of 1979, when Mike migrated to America with his wife, he moved close to where Gordon lived in Colorado. Mike's move to America caused him and his wife to delay having kids so he could spend his first decade building a career and starting his own company. He eventually had two daughters, and lastly his youngest, his son Bobby.

Mike's only boy and Gordon's only grandson Sean were born several weeks apart. Jason became Bobby's godfather, and Mike became Sean's godfather.

• • •

Feeling nostalgic, Jason picked up a photo album and went into his backyard with a second cup of coffee. He looked through pictures of the families. Birthday pictures, where all the kids were present and the dates were clearly marked, were his favorite. They were a good way to compare one year to another and to measure how fast the kids grew. It was also a sad reminder of how time affected the adults. He was well into the second coffee, staring at the photo album when his wife came out to sit next to him. She took the album from him and flipped the pages. She smiled, pointing to one picture.

"This is one of my favorites of the two boys, with their Halloween football costumes," she said, then added,

"Oh, by the way, your dad called my cell and left a funny message."

"What did he say?"

"Oh, something about a green ball changing colors or something like that." To which Jason jumped to his feet.

"What did he say *exactly*? What were his exact words?" Jason said, raising his voice.

"I don't know." She reached for her cell phone to check again and then put the voicemail on speaker.

"Hi it's me, Gordon, can you pass a message to Jason. Tell him, the GREEN ball has turned RED. Thanks."

Jason was stone-faced as he hurried to his office. He called his secretary at the language institute, telling her to find a substitute for the last week of class, that there was an emergency. He then packed a duffle bag with clothes and, from the garage, a leather daily planner. He topped it off by tossing in what looked like a radio. He zipped up the duffel bag and was ready to leave.

Something horrible has happened to my dad or mom, or both, he thought.

"What's going on?" his wife nervously asked following him around. "Where are you going?"

"Remember that story I told you about balls changing colors."

"No!" she said with a look of utter confusion.

"You know the story about my dad and his emergency codes. Codes like the ones we have."

"Oh, that story!" Nervous understanding crossed her face.

"Well. It's never happened before. All my life I was told if the ball turns red, drop everything and come home, it's an emergency. Well, it's red now. The ball is *red* now!"

"What emergency? This is so childish! Why not call him?"

"No. If anyone asks, I'm on a research project, and it doesn't matter. When the ball turns red, I have to go home, no matter what. That's the rule. It's always been the rule."

His wife continued to follow him around the house, begging him just to call and find out what is going on. At least, she said, call your mother.

With three generations in the military, the family always had rules established for emergencies, not to mention everything else. Each generation drilled these rules and procedures into the next generation, insisting they be used only when appropriate, with abuse never tolerated. This was serious. Something was very wrong. Jason knew he had to go home.

Jason had tried to instill the same rules in his son and his wife, but clearly, he had more work to do. He vowed to fix that upon his return.

He anxiously contemplated what could have prompted his father's call as he finished preparing for the trip.

7 | THE MEETING

Jason grabbed his duffle bag while his wife prepared to give him a ride to the Monterey regional airport. On the way, he unzipped the leather planner, switching all of his credentials with items he took from the planner. Then he called the airlines and booked a round-trip flight under the name John O'Brien. He didn't know when he would return, but he knew weeklong round-trip tickets caused less attention. Those trips always looked like business trips. Almost two-thirds of all flights in this country were business people working elsewhere weeks at a time.

"What's in the planner? And, who is John O'Brien?" his wife asked nervously.

Jason was torn between keeping secrets and confiding at least something to his wife.

"It's from my old days working those special projects!"

"I see, and which projects would those be?" She frowned, knowing he would never say.

"Look, honey, I really can't tell you now. Someday, I'll tell you everything, when it's safe and when it's the right time. For now, just know this stuff will help whatever trouble dad is in."

At the airport, he asked her to go past the terminal entrance before stopping. At the curbside, he gave her a hug and a kiss and then jumped out, with a casual wink.

"Goodbye, my love. See you soon." With a forced smile on his face, he walked away, looking back once again.

Amitis wasn't sure if this trip would be dangerous. However, knowing her husband, she tried not to worry. He was good at everything he put his mind to. He was always careful. He always had a plan B and C and every other letter in the alphabet. Years of being with him, watching him leave on his special projects, and always returning unscathed, she was sure he could handle whatever his dad's problem was. Jason was a great strategist and tactician. No situation ever came up without his thinking dozens of steps ahead of everyone else.

Once at the ticket counter, Jason handed the clerk his ID and mentioned the flight to Denver on which he was booked. She typed his name in, asking for his credit card, and the answers to security questions.

"Yes, I did pack my own bags. Yes, they have been with me the whole time." Handing the credit card over, he answered her questions. Several minutes later, he received the boarding pass and his personal items, never meeting the woman's eyes.

No, if I were a terrorist, I would still tell you the truth, you obtuse creature, he thought to himself.

He thanked her, grabbed his duffle bag, and walked towards the gate. It was an hour wait before take-off. On the way, he stopped at a booth and bought several AT&T GoPhone SIM cards, for which he paid cash. He bought a cup of coffee and sat by his gate, waiting, thinking, and worrying.

He hated flying, especially on flights that were now nothing more than buses manned with bitter and angry employees, who, in turn, had to deal with bitter and angry customers. He remembered his first flight, a Pan Am flight to Tehran via London. It was so memorable and so classy. He was a young boy, traveling in first class with his mother and father. The second floor of the jumbo jet was a luxurious lounge, with comfortable furniture, tables with chessboards, salted almonds in bowls everywhere, and bottomless sodas. You could sit in any chair in the lounge for as long as you wanted. The food was superb, served on real plates with metal silverware, and crystal glassware. He'd felt as if he was a guest in some rich person's home. The travelers were elegantly dressed. The flight attendants, all women, were beautiful, happy, and nice. Pan Am designed its flights to be special, and they were.

For Jason's flight to Colorado, special did not apply. The seats were narrower, packed tight, and cramped at a time when people were fatter and wider. The food was crap, plastic-wrapped dog food served in shoeboxes, with enough preservatives to last a generation or five. Watered down drinks were served in the plastic cups used for urine tests at the doctor's office. Everything was cheap, yet priced as if it were gold. And, everything was for sale, including the shoebox of dog food, the pillows, headsets, and blankets. Nothing was free anymore. Checking bags cost money as though anyone could travel without a change of clothes. Jason laughed to himself, bitterly, imagining hotels charging you for bringing a suitcase to your room.

• • •

When the PA system had made the call to board, Jason had stood in line waiting his turn, finally the line moved. Because he'd booked late, he hadn't been able to get into business class. His seat, row Hell, seat E, would be tight and uncomfortable. Walking the main aisle, he found his middle seat, placed his duffle bag above him. He squeezed his 6'2", 200-pound well-muscled frame into his row and sat in his narrow seat. He prayed for good row mates. He dreaded sitting next to anyone wider than the seat, or a loud talker, or someone unfamiliar with deodorant. He kept staring down the main aisle watching the crowd move towards him. No one smiled.

He kept a critical tally of the passengers. *That one could be good. Please, not that one.*

It was always a crapshoot. Finally, a petite young woman squeezed to the window seat.

Thank you, he said silently to the gods of flight.

A gigantic sweaty man was next, twice the width of any seat, holding a bag of food, standing by Jason's row.

"Hi. I'm sitting here. Can you hold this while I put my bag up?" the fat man said, handing Jason the paper bag.

Jason held the greasy-bottomed bag, no doubt fast food purchased at the terminal, while the man placed his carry-on, jamming it in multiple directions, smashing what was already up there. He sat heavily, and Jason was sure the plane tilted ever so slightly! Jason handed him his food.

Fuck me! This is going to be a long flight!

"Thanks. My name is Jake." He reached over to shake Jason's hand, with a hand the size of catcher's mitt, yet soft and squishy.

"I'm John," Jason replied, shaking his hand, wanting to practice a bit of the persona he had chosen for this trip.

The flight was long with one stopover in San Francisco, but overall the conversation with Jake wasn't bad and included the offer of a burger. At the very least, Jason was able to practice his back-story and role-playing skills with someone innocuous. It had been a while, but assuming another persona came back in no time.

The plane finally landed and taxied to the gate. Jason patiently stood in line, shuffling forward, still chatting with his new friend. Ten more steps and he would be off.

Once on the ramp, he said goodbye and picked up the pace as he walked towards the train to the main terminal. From there, he caught the first shuttle to a car rental lot, got a car, and while still parked, called his dad. No one answered. He left a message.

"Sir, I'm calling from the diner. Your order is ready for pickup!"

The diner was a pre-selected location to meet. He hoped it still existed. Worst case, he would just stand outside whatever now stood on that spot. He started the rental car, which smelled of pine mixed with perfume and cigarettes and began his drive.

• • •

Forty minutes later, he was at the diner, relieved and surprised that EATS was still there. He parked and walked in. The same waitresses were still at work, serving people with a frown. They'd looked a hundred thirty years before, and they still looked a hundred. Jason had always thought someone built the diner around a group of grandmothers playing bridge and then offered the women jobs for the inconvenience. The ketchup and mustard jars were the same as he remembered, just re-filled. The mustard was the bright yellow color used to paint median stripes on roads. The ketchup was just a little too brown to be fresh. The place reeked of fried food. Heart attacks were the daily special.

In and out went, the regulars, seeming like the waitresses, to be unchanged after three decades. Starved looking or fully stuffed, depending on direction. The door opened again. It was his dad. He got up to greet him. They gave each other a manly handshake and a quick hug. Jason had not hugged his dad since he was a child. Hugging was not something his dad did. He saw him visibly shaken, trying to be strong, trying to be the dad Jason had always known.

"You want something to eat?" His lips were tight as he sat down, picking up a menu.

"Sure Dad. Let's get something to eat." Jason knew it would be bad, whatever it was, but he could stomach a little greasy fried food for his dad.

"So, Dad, what's going on? I've never seen you like this. Is everything OK with you and mom? Are either of you sick? What's up?" Jason asked in a low, anxious voice.

"We'll take two lunch specials and two coffees, black," his father told the waitress.

"I'll tell you, just wait, don't rush me!" He put the menu back behind the condiments holder and looked around. Just looking, but not for anything special. Jason was patient when it came to his father. He said nothing more and waited. His dad sat there looking around again, playing with his fork and knife, getting his poise back. Then he suddenly looked up at Jason.

"OK. First, we're fine. We're not sick and we're not dying. And, no, we're not in any trouble." He leaned closer to Jason, pulling him in as he whispered just a few sentences. Jason sat straight again, his eyes focused on his dad. He waited for the meal and said nothing.

The food arrived and they both ate without a word. They drank their coffee, no refills. Jason paid in cash and walked his dad to his car. He then went to his rental car, grabbing his duffle bag, walking back to his father's car. He opened the trunk, dropping the duffle bag in and pulling out running clothes. He changed from his street clothes to his running outfit.

"Dad, I want you to drive to Mike's house," he said while quickly looking around and, just as quickly, dropping his pants and switching to his shorts. He finished putting on his running shoes and a t-shirt. Zipping up the duffle bag, he slammed the trunk shut. They both sat in Gordon's car, leaving the rental behind.

"Drop me off at the fire station. I'll run the last few miles. I want no one to see us arriving together, just in case. Please, Dad, don't talk about anything until I get there."

They sat quietly as Gordon drove, both feeling more determined with every mile. Jason's being there gave his father renewed energy. The last thing either man wanted was to appear worried in front of Mike and his family. When they arrived at the fire station, Jason got out, looked at his watch compass to get his bearings, and then shut the door waving his father off. He started running. His dad drove the rest of the way alone, feeling better now that his son was involved.

Gordon knew his son had done certain work he never spoke about, things that should never be spoken of or about in polite conversation. He also knew the things his son did were always for the good of his country and that he had raised an honorable person, a good man. He trusted his son. He knew his son's background, training, and language skills would all be of great use getting Bobby back. To Gordon, his son was the only solution.

• • •

Gordon arrived at the gate of Mike's compound. Inside the gatehouse sat a man with a clipboard, looking official, as usual, even though he knew Gordon was a friend and a regular visitor.

"Do you have an appointment?" he asked sarcastically, pausing briefly before opening the gate, winking at Gordon.

Gordon loved the drive up to Mike's house. He loved to see the house suddenly appear on the final turn through the trees. The house was indeed beautiful and peaceful looking, but what the family must endure now was unimaginable. He drove around the circle and parked in front of the main door. Taking Jason's bag from the trunk, he walked to the door and rang the doorbell.

• • •

The door opened remotely. Gordon entered and went towards Mike's office, where he'd enjoyed many games of backgammon. He walked in to see Mike at his desk, with one of the desk monitors showing video feeds from around the property. He dropped the duffle bag inside the door.

"Where's Jason?" Mike said, standing to shake Gordon's hand.

Newly cautious, Gordon placed his finger to his lips and gestured Mike to be quiet. "Oh, he's still in Monterey and won't be here till his fall break."

Gordon took a notepad and pen from the desk and wrote.

RUNNING AROUND THE TOPSIDE. SHOULD BE HERE SOON.

Mike sat back behind his desk, turning the monitor towards Gordon, so he would see his son arriving. Gordon continued writing.

HE WANTED TO MAKE SURE NO ONE SAW HIM COMING.

They both stared at the monitor, lost in thought. Eventually, they saw Jason running past the back garages and to the side entrance. As he got closer, Mike clicked several keys on his computer and the door opened for Jason. He stopped in the kitchen for a glass of water, then grabbed a kitchen towel and walked to the office.

He entered the room, and before anyone could say a word, he took a small radio from his bag, put it on the desk, and turned it on. It was a broad-spectrum frequency scrambler and jammer.

"It's okay to talk now," he said.

He then gave Mike a big hug, promising that everything would be fine. Bobby, his godson, and his son Sean were like brothers. Bobby was practically his son too. He sat down on the couch as Mike retold the whole story, showing Jason the package received from the county offices and all the contracts and stadium design specs. He covered the coffee table with everything he had.

Jason grabbed his duffle bag. Reaching inside, he removed a USB flash drive, plugging it into Mike's computer. He turned the computer off and rebooted into the flash drive operating system. He began typing, bringing up several tabs on the browser and started several other programs. He asked for Mike's cell phone, reading the URL link from the kidnappers' message and typing it into the computer. On certain web pages, he made sure, he had Mike's IP address, in case they were keeping tabs, and on others, he masked it with random global IP addresses. All the while, he was studying the URL routing, to see where it would end up. In another tab, he watched the video of Bobby, several times, looking for clues. He was looking for signs of others in the room, a reflection, a window, a view, anything of value. He then walked over to the coffee table. He reviewed the documents for a long while and then moved back to the computer. He sent several emails and sat there quietly waiting.

The older men were both on the couch, wordless, like two scolded boys, staring at Jason as he typed, read, and typed again.

An hour passed as Jason again pored over everything on the coffee table and went back to the computer, sending and receiving numerous emails and text messages. He finally leaned back and looked at his father and Mike.

"The bad news is that these guys are very good."

"Is there any good news?" Mike and Gordon asked simultaneously.

"Yes!" Jason said with a smile. "We're better."

Jason explained how these Iranians had worked the system in their favor, covering their tracks. He explained, in more detail, how the Thor Network and Onion domains worked to support all that, and how they work great if you are a person, a company, or a less sophisticated government. Jason explained how servers operated or owned by the U.S., or manufactured by the U.S. companies, performed most URL routing services. U.S. agencies, therefore, can get the final and actual destination of any URL. This was highly illegal and confidential, but possible.

The message source is somewhat known, he said, at the very least the city of origin, and perhaps even a section of the city. More importantly, there are other local players. In the county offices, there was at least one person who knew something about this or was part of the plan. Also, the chair re-design showed a new cavity, allowing something to be inserted. Some pieces of the puzzle were becoming clear. From nothing, Jason now had multiple leads to follow.

"Why not call the FBI?" Jason asked out of curiosity.

Mike explained he was not sure whom to trust. Besides, if this ever gets out, no Iranian-American would ever be trusted. There were millions of Iranians living in the U.S. Most had friends or loved ones back in Iran, and they had spent decades rebuilding their lives in the States.

Mike was not dismissing calls for help, but given the stark warning in the message, he wanted to be sure it was the safest route. His son's safety was paramount.

"We won't call any of the authorities," Jason said, "but we will have to call others. And, we'll need money, lots of money to pay for things, and to bribe people."

Mike got up and motioned them to follow him to the library.

The walk to the library was down a hall decorated with artfully framed LCD screens, which adjusted the imagery to the taste of the person closest, and who happened to be wearing a pre-programmed active RFID tag. Mike's watch contained his RFID tag, which randomly picked Persian miniatures as he walked by. They arrived in the library. The lights turned on and adjusted automatically. Mike's favorite music list came on. All the LCD images changed to a tropical forest theme. Mike pulled a beautiful Esfahan Persian carpet back from the middle of the room to reveal a steel door. It had an embedded digital keypad. He typed in a long sequence of numbers and pressed his thumb on the reader. The steel door dropped a foot and slid under the floor. Lights turned on, illuminating a stairway down into a lower room nearly the size of the library. They all walked down into the underground room, where Mike opened a large vault much like a bank's safe deposit area, with rows of different size drawers. Mike opened one of the drawers and took out a tray filled with diamonds, hundreds of them, from a quarter carat to two carats in size.

"What else do you need?" He asked Jason as he filled a velvet drawstring bag with diamonds.

"Cash in dollars and euros would be great," Jason said while standing next to his dad, both with their eyes wide. All of those years of coming to this house, and they had never known this room existed.

Mike opened another drawer and showed him the cash. He added that he has several accounts in Europe, should he need to access money while there. Jason took several stacks of hundred-dollar bills, leaving the euros behind.

"We will get the euros in Europe from your other accounts," he said. "The dollars are for our U.S. needs. I'll be asking for more as I need more."

"Anytime, any amount. Just let me know," Mike said.

Suddenly there was a commotion above them. It was Mike's wife Parisa, home from a day out with friends. She was staring down into the pit, as she called it, seeing Jason and Gordon. She smiled, surprised to see them.

"What are you guys doing here!?! Good to see you, Jason, it's been a while. Come on up, all of you," she called out as she walked toward the kitchen.

"You have to tell her," Gordon whispered as they were climbing out of the vault. Mike was the last out and pressed a button next to the last step. The door moved back into place. Mike pulled the rug back into place and walked toward the kitchen.

Leaving them alone, Gordon and Jason went back to Mike's office. Seconds later the other two arrived. When Parisa walked in, smiling, she gave Jason a big hug. Mike closed the door behind him as his wife was greeting the other two.

"What's going on?" she asked. "You're all acting pretty weird!"

Mike walked her over to the couch, sat her down, and started telling her as briefly as he could what had happened to Bobby. He told her everything, leaving out the video.

She fell to her knees screaming, the scream of a mother who had lost her child. Then she started yelling at Mike, blaming him for letting Bobby go to that god-forsaken country. She wanted to leave the office but Gordon stopped her. Mike gently brought her back to the couch.

"You have to stay here. We have to talk about things, in this office, and *only* in this office." Jason said firmly.

She held Mike tightly as Jason instructed them on how they should behave, and what they could or could not say and to whom, along with other specific cautionary notes.

"Honey," Mike interjected, "We have to keep acting as normal as possible, and let these guys figure out what needs to be done."

Parisa stood, straightening her skirt and blouse, opened the office door, and walked upstairs to her room, crying.

Jason went back to Mike's computer to install more software. He instructed Mike on how to use the new software for encrypted communication, and on how to initiate encrypted money transfers. Jason left the scrambler behind, telling Mike that all conversations about Bobby should occur in this room with the device on. Further, under no circumstances should he leave his computer on when not around. He put all the documents from the coffee table into his duffle and, handing the bag to his father, prepared for his run back to the fire station where Gordon would pick him up.

• • •

Parisa was upstairs, on her bed, with an album of pictures, each page having just one group picture for each of the kids' birthdays. Like Jason's wife, she made an album so she could quickly see how the kids were growing up, what they each looked like year to year.

She quickly went past the girls' pages until she got to Bobby's first picture. She worked her way through the years. They were all in the pictures, her family, Gordon and his wife, Jason and his family, friends, and neighbors. They were happy times.

As she looked through the group pictures, she noticed several without Jason. In actuality, there were many photos where Gordon's family appeared but not his son. She recalled the conversations, the roundabout chitchat about where he was or was not, the quiet conversations she had with her husband about what he was or wasn't doing, and all the rumors. Everybody knew just a little, just a hint, just enough to be worried, to be fearful.

She worked her way back downstairs. Jason and Gordon were getting ready to leave. She walked back into the office, closing the door. Her face was red and her eyes teary, yet she was calm. She looked at Jason, straight into his eyes.

"I don't know what you did in your secret life, before, whenever! It was something. Something we can use. So, if you have to kill every one of those fuckers, you do it, and you bring my son back, unharmed."

Jason took her hand, kissed it, and promised her just that, and nothing less.

• • •

After his run back down the hill, his father dropped him off at his rental car. Jason drove to his hotel, to study the documents and further develop his plans.

8 | MISSED BIRTHDAYS

It was Bobby's second birthday. Mike had offered to help, knowing he could not. He was busy with several large construction contracts. Added to the stress was the completion of his new headquarters building that the company had to move into within two weeks. The company was exploding, so there were all the interviews he had to do supporting the recruiting process. At home, his kitchen too was a busy place. Parisa was making breakfast and lunch for everyone. The girls were packing their backpacks, getting ready for school. Bobby was in his high chair smiling, playing, and eating his indispensable Cheerios. He was the youngest of all and spoiled by all the others.

Every morning, before he left for work, Mike would sit and stare at Bobby for a good ten minutes, inhaling the little boy's essence. That was enough to give him energy for the day.

"Don't worry about a thing," Parisa said, acknowledging his offer to help, tapping him on the backside as he prepared his briefcase and refilled his coffee mug.

"The girls will help," she said. "Gordon and Charlene will be here early to help too."

"I told you, the godfather thing would come in handy," Mike said, smiling as he left the house.

Mike had been living in this subdivision, near where Gordon and his family had moved after coming from Iran. It was his first home in the States, a little small, but he liked it well enough. It was close to the schools and in a good area, and the kids had their friends nearby. The low mortgage, allowed him to save a lot of money. The best part, however, was having his best friend and his family nearby, even though the children's age discrepancies were large. Gordon had his son early while Mike started his family much later in life. He felt a kinship with them, and better yet, both families felt a kinship with each other.

He was proud to have Jason as Bobby's godfather and proud to be godfather to Jason's son, Sean. The two boys were like brothers.

• • •

Just before noon, Charlene came by with a fruit platter, cupcakes, and presents for Bobby. She was always excited about birthdays. Bobby and Sean had birthdays near each other, so Charlene and Parisa had become a team getting the ball rolling for each gathering. They worked efficiently, as they joked and laughed about the kids, husbands, and neighbors. They set the tables, put out the food, and stacked the gifts, all the while tasting the snacks.

"What time are Jason and his family arriving?" Parisa asked.

"Oh, I forgot! Jason won't be here. Sorry! He had an emergency at work and had to fly to D.C."

• • •

Jason hated having to lie to everyone about his trips and his work life, but he had no choice. It was a matter of safety and national security. His colleagues fell into one of two groups. The ones with families, who were ultra-careful about each decision they made and were strategic in thinking; and those who had no family at all, and always shot from the hip. There was always competition between long-term thinkers and short-term achievers. The main difference between the two was one group, those with families, had everything to live for, while the other had little thought for the future. Truth be told, you needed both to make the best teams.

Gordon knew a little more about what Jason did and was always ready to keep the family and the questions at bay, vaguely implying that his son's work centered around the capitol in Washington.

In fact, most of Jason's orders came directly from D.C., after the morning CIA reviews in the White House Situation Room. The WHSR hatched new projects weekly, requiring action on the other side of the world.

Most actions allowed for planning, but occasionally a job was an overnight effort. Jason had attended several meetings at the WHSR, before actions and afterward. These visits always excited him, and the meetings were filled with people and discussions one could never share.

Each visit started with a series of checkpoints where IDs were carefully checked against an official appointment list. Finally, one arrived at the locked doors of the WHSR. Behind these doors was a conference room surrounded by smaller offices, each filled with workstations. On every one of Jason's visits, the meetings in the main conference room were standing room only. Each discussion was heated, the hard-fought decisions were final, and the results were often deadly.

• • •

Jason's first career did not start the way it ended. His first love was the Air Force. He had attended the Air Force Academy for two equally compelling reasons. First, the exciting and inspiring stories of his father, a Vietnam-era helicopter pilot. Second, an Iranian girl he met while finishing high school in Denver, who attended the University of Colorado, a short drive away from the academy, and whom he married half way through their university studies.

At first, Jason wanted to be a pilot. Initially, he focused on computer science but eventually succumbed to his deeper interest. He graduated with a degree in behavioral sciences & foreign area studies, with a minor in foreign languages. To satisfy his dad, he still learned how to fly, and well, but it wasn't to be his career. He excelled in both Farsi and Arabic, and was flawless and accent-free in several dialects. This was a very rare skill, helped by having lived in Iran, and visiting with Iranians since his time there, not to mention marrying into an Iranian family and dealing with the culture on a daily basis. He had the Middle Eastern nuances down to an art, from greetings to hand gestures to the humor. He was indistinguishable from a true Iranian and often fooled people who met him for the first time. He loved to experiment with people, telling them stories about where he was born and about the harrowing journey that brought him to America.

It was this ability, along with his psychological profile, that marked him as a strong CIA candidate. The agency pursued him vigorously during his junior year at the Academy. Recruiters wanted him to leave early, to be part of a special team dedicated to the Middle East, focusing on Iran, Iraq, and Afghanistan. The pressures were almost too much. Nevertheless, Jason wanted to finish his curriculum, just in case he needed to get a real job at some point. His dad wanted him to graduate, both for Jason's future and as a matter of family pride.

His CIA recruiter said by choice or by accident, Jason had been preparing himself for deep fieldwork. Upon graduation, he joined the Agency, going directly to Camp Peary in York County near Williamsburg, Virginia, for training. His expertise was so much in demand, given the wars in the Middle East and the lack of intelligence, that they annulled his service requirements instead of his education. At the farm, as the insiders called the camp, he surpassed in all areas of testing, from physical to psychological, with his language skills equal even to those of his trainers who were native speakers. It took less than two weeks before his supervisors realized he was a better language teacher than those assigned to his group. Three weeks into his training, he became a teacher's aide in the Farsi and Arabic classes.

His time at the farm became one of both learning and teaching. His inputs into the language curriculum completely changed the syllabus for both classes, and eventually the entire language program. His advantage over the language teachers who were foreign-born was that he had a dual culture mix that helped explain nuances of both language and behavior in a way that made the lessons stick. As his superiors knew, getting subtle things wrong could be dangerous in the field, even deadly. The foreign language teachers ignored hand gestures since they considered this a lower-class way of speaking. But, Jason, free of snobbism, knew gestures were part of speaking for the average person, a separate but important vocabulary. These gestures and mannerisms were critical on-the-ground skills for any clandestine effort. You had to present, act and smell like a local to blend in best. Jason was a perfect deep cover asset, but with a wife and a small child, he focused on special projects and not deep cover.

• • •

Jason kept his family in Colorado, to be near his parents, and to be far away from both coasts, especially D.C. and Virginia. He wanted to keep his family unsullied by his work. That meant a lot of flights, traveling, staying in hotels or rented apartments, or even on a couch at a friend's house. He felt that this was his duty, his part in giving back to his country, a family tradition. Knowing the Persian culture so well, he hated what had happened to that country. He hated the spread of the religious extremism that was born out of the Iranian revolution. He hated how it was spreading like a virus around the globe in two sharp prongs, Shiite and Sunni extremism. He would visit and revisit the sad start to it all every time he saw or heard of religious atrocities committed in the name of Islam.

• • •

It all began with three neighboring countries: Iraq, Iran, and Afghanistan. Each was its own version of a guard dog protecting the yard, Saddam in Iraq, the Shah of Iran, and the Khans in Afghanistan. Each dog kept the others at bay. Each jailed their resistors or killed them. Yes, all were dictators, but with visions of westernization and general civility. One day, Iran's Shah decided to break the British and U.S. grip over his country. He began dealing with Russia. The first endeavor was to build a gas pipeline from Russia, through Iran, to the Persian Gulf. This was followed by the purchases of military armaments. More business seemed sure to follow. The U.S. wanted none of that, so it supported and promoted a revolution. Since Iranians had as many opinions as there were citizens, an intellectual revolution would be impossible. The only common denominator was Islam. Therefore, the CIA dug up an elderly exiled cleric named

Khomeini, and that was that, for the pipeline and the Shah.

The Russians, having lost Iran, invaded Afghanistan, expecting Pakistan to fall in line out of fear. Their intention was to build a pipeline through the two countries. In the meantime, Saddam, seeing Iran's perceived weakness, attacked his neighbor to get some oil fields back. On both sides of Iran, the U.S. was supporting, arming and building the fighting forces of Afghanistan and Iraq. On one side, the anti-Russian fighters became the Taliban and Al Qaeda. On the other side, the U.S. and the ruling Baathists were working together, with no long-term progressive possibilities in mind. Iraq was a powder keg waiting to blow.

Yes, that was a simple and unfussy explanation. However, it was a quick and truthful explanation, which could go down with just one sip of single malt Scotch. The U.S. miscalculated at every step, resulting in the shit storm that is today's the Middle East.

"In the future, let sleeping dogs, and dictators, lie," Jason would say, concluding his history lessons. Of course, there was more to it, but with Americans, a short story went a lot further than a long detailed one.

• • •

All work-related flights for Jason were long ones, with the one on the day of that birthday taking him from Denver to Germany for a briefing and then to Kuwait. His trip from Germany would be on a DHL cargo plane to Kuwait City. From there, an overland trip across the border to the Shiite region of southern Iraq would take him to complete the recruiting of a new asset. The new prospect was a *mullah*, a cleric on whom they had been working at a distance for several months. Now, it was time for a face-to-face visit. Jason, who had an innate ability to read people, understand their wants and needs, and create trust, was chosen to close the deal.

"He could steal steak right off of the devil's plate and be thanked for it, by no less than the devil himself," his father would say.

That trip was not too dangerous. But, Jason was sad to be missing Bobby's birthday. He loved his godson like his own son. Having only one child himself, he loved that his son and Bobby were like brothers. He had a picture of them in his wallet, the two sitting next to each other smiling, holding crude wooden swords he'd made for them. He was studying the snapshot intently when the announcement came over the speaker in the cargo section that the flight was on final approach and the group leader would collect all personal belongings and run through a checklist of paperwork, ID cards, money belts, satellite phones, and anything else that might be needed.

"OK Jason, hand over the wallet," the group leader said, interrupting his revelry. "And, give me your wedding band!"

"Wait a second!" One more gaze. "OK, here you go."

"What about your wedding band?"

"I don't wear one in the summer. It leaves a tan mark, so anyone can see it missing."

Jason inventoried his paperwork, checked his satellite phone, money belt, and weapon. He reviewed quickly the folder with the asset details once more. He couldn't carry the folder with him and had to memorize it all. On foreign soil, it was always better to be a crook than a spy. Smuggling was the best crime, honorable in fact, especially if you were smuggling things like American cigarettes, cell phones, even weapons. As for the gun, that was easy. Everyone carried one, given the lack of security and the highway robberies one faced routinely. Holdups were so common you could lose half of your inventory on the road. Nothing was a better shield than having cartons of Winstons or Marlboros handy. Back home cigarettes could kill you, but here they saved your life.

They finally landed in Kuwait city. The plane's doors opened and immediately all the cool air left, replaced by dry heat. It felt like opening the oven door, six inches from your face while cooking a turkey. Everyone quickly grabbed duffels filled with sample cigarettes and digital 'contraband' and ran down the motorized stairway, then into the waiting SUV, praying it had air conditioning and that it worked. The heat was stifling, with the first hour or two being the worst. There would be a three to four-hour drive to *Basrah*, then a two to three-day stay if all went well.

The SUV was new and well equipped, with spares, gas tanks, and a large repair box strapped outside in the back, including shovels for digging out of the sand. Inside, in the rear space, was a water tank holding 20 gallons of fresh water. The car was well air-conditioned and ready for the drive through the desolate desert as far as the eye could see. There would be no fuel or service until the border. The best thing about the drive was the lack of any speed limit. However, a driver had to be vigilant constantly for sand drifted across the road. It could be life ending to hit those at a hundred miles per hour.

They reached the Kuwait-Iraq border after two hours and refueled before crossing. A thousand dollar donation and a carton of Winston's helped expedite the crossing. That was the safe part of the trip.

The rest of the drive would be through troubled parts of Iraq, though somewhat safer than Baghdad. Thirty minutes across the border and an hour after a satellite call, an escort from out of *Basrah* met them, sent by the mullah to help get them into town safely. They drove two more hours. Traffic was a major worry. The driver had to re-route several times to avoid being stuck in a jam. That was when attacks were the hardest to avoid or escape.

Eventually, they found themselves at a building near the river. They pulled into a gated, barren yard, crowded with other SUVs and armed men. This was *Grand Ayatollah Muhammad Sadiq al-Sadr's* compound for the day. The meeting was with his son, *Moqtada al-Sadr*, a twenty-something, fast rising cleric with whom the U.S. had established ties hoping to help control the southern Shiite population. He was an enigmatic, charming character with a powerful presence. At that point, he was still a medium ranked religious figure, yet he was politically and religiously influential, with a very strong and obedient following, just like his father.

Over the next two days, Jason and his group met with the young cleric several times. The most heated stages of the negotiations covered weaponry for his army, the amount of autonomy he would have over his region, and how much cash flow he should expect. The first two points were nearly non-starters, leaving Jason only the third to work with. The U.S. would not deliver any arms, ever. Nor should the potential asset expect any autonomy. In the end, Jason, negotiating with his usual persuasiveness and calculated vagueness, promised the man the autonomy he knew might eventually develop, and all the arms he knew might be acquired sometime in the future. Finally, he promised an enticing cash flow, should they achieve the negotiated milestones, cash that the U.S. had taken from Saddam's vaults after the first Gulf War, which had been hidden throughout bunkers outside of Baghdad.

In short, Jason gave him nothing of ours, knowing he would get nothing from *al-Sadr* in return. However, the time with him resulted in a great profile for future reference. Yet Jason had a feeling of foreboding about where the man was going. The meetings were positive, but deep down Jason knew this man would be yet another thorn in the side of the U.S. But, he followed orders, despite feeling strongly that they were wrong. He should have killed the man instead, which was another option discussed in the Situation Room. The yard full of armed bodyguards, however, would have made this a suicidal option.

• • •

Every trip Jason took to the Middle East was filled with equal amounts of joy and pain. He could not forget his own happy years there as a young boy and felt bad for the people whose lives had changed so dramatically in the decades since. He had many friends who had left the region to find a better and safer life elsewhere. No matter whom he spoke to, each one longed for the day they could go back home. Even Jason longed for those days as a child in Iran, which left a lifelong impression on him.

So many things were not what one expected. There were no standards. You could not find a plumbing fixture to replace a broken faucet. For that, you had to go to a specialist who would fashion something for you based on the sample item you furnished. There were no lines and no basic order. All lines looked like an arrowhead, starting with the first person, then two standing behind, then three and so on. It was a *first shove/first serve* model. Nothing was firmly established; everything was negotiable. Chaos reigned.

Yet, the warmth of the people, the simplicity of life and the social graces made up for so much of what was missing. Choices were always between a sparse set of things, but all useful. There were only two T.V. stations with very little to watch. The grocery stores had one kind of toilet paper, not dozens of different brands.

But, the food, fruits, and ingredients were fresh, safe and free of chemicals and preservatives. Life was slower, smoother, and oddly more satisfying. It was not a race to see who had the best and most recent iPhone, car, or clothing. Iran was somehow a great place to raise a child.

• • •

In the end, whatever the trip and assignment, the important thing for Jason was getting home to his family. His meeting with the asset was a job well done. Everyone got home safe.

Maybe the next birthday, he would be with his family and not try to change the course of a region.

9 | TINS OF CAVIAR

Yasmin Akbari was in a constant state of shock and anxiety. She went through the day in fear for her husband and daughter. Both were stuck somewhere in Iran. She had no idea where.

Are they in prison or some other horrible place? She constantly asked herself.

Most of her friends and all of her family lived in Iran. She didn't dare call anyone there because she knew the intelligence groups monitored all calls inside Iran. At least back in Atlanta, she had friends she could turn to, but in Copenhagen, she had no one. She was new to the city and to her job. She didn't know how things worked, nor did she trust anyone to help. Yasmin had worked for years at the Centers for Disease Control (CDC) in Atlanta when unexpectedly she got a great offer, a significant promotion and the opportunity to run the Vaccines and

Biologicals Division of the World Health Organization (WHO).

Six months ago, she took charge of the division and was the United Nations' liaison on that subject. While at the CDC, she had worked in both Africa and the U.S. She was the foremost expert on deadly level-4 biologicals (BSL-4). She had written dozens of research papers and delivered countless seminars globally. She was now at a facility where they conducted deep research on BSL-4s, and where many of the biological samples were stored.

When Yasmin first received her text message, she thought it a joke, done in poor taste. When she did not hear from her husband, and then received worried calls from her relatives asking when he and their daughter would arrive, she knew the message was no joke. Out of fear for her loved ones, she told people in Iran her husband had canceled the trip. To people back in Atlanta, she said the two were enjoying their visit to Iran.

The text message instructed her to deliver a precise quantity of a specific substance. She knew the material, a virus, was extremely dangerous, and to take it would be illegal. The only solace she had was that the delivery system for this disease required complex mechanisms to create an efficient cascade effect. And, to weaponize the material as an aerosol required sophisticated dilution techniques. A hard combination to come by, she thought. Regardless, she wanted her family safely back. She would obey.

• • •

The WHO headquarters was celebrating an important anniversary, for which caterers had supplied food and drinks to satisfy many tastes, given the cultural diversity of the facility's staff. The place was bustling with trucks bringing tables and chairs, flowers and table settings, and food and drinks. Everyone had to go through the main gate, to be checked against a database of approved vendors and visitors. The building's courtyard could accommodate over 500 people seated in a climate-controlled outdoor/indoor structure. Kitchen and service areas had been assembled on the outside, adjoining the inner courtyard structure. Stoves and refrigerators were set up. Generators were humming.

One caterer provided Persian caviar. They were a local business with close relationships with an Iranian importer out of France who specialized in Beluga, Osetra, and Sevruga caviars. The Paris-based importer had its own facilities at the port of *Anzali*, in the *Gilan* province in northern Iran, from where they processed, packaged and shipped worldwide. The caterer dropped off 20 kilos of the precious roe in a variety of 250-gram tin cans, on ice and ready to serve. Additionally, there was a small cooler containing five 500g containers of Beluga marked for delivery to Yasmin Akbari, with a congratulatory note mentioning her new role at the WHO.

• • •

There was a knock on Yasmin's office door. A man from the mailroom walked in with the package, handing it to her with a smile.

"I believe this was brought in for you. Congratulations, your very own caviar."

Yasmin knew the time had arrived for her to do as instructed. She opened the cooler to inspect the interior. The thermometer was at the perfect range and a timer had 36 hours left on it. The package looked like a normal travel cooler from the outside, but the inside had two layers of sophisticated lining. The outer lining contained a filler material sufficient to pass the highest International Safe Transit Association (ISTA) requirements. Coolant gel-filled, the inner lining could keep the temperature for between 24 and 48 hours. Finally, a small battery-powered motor created suction for final vacuum sealing. Whoever put this package together, Yasmin realized, were not amateurs. She took out the five Caviar tins, which were glass jars carefully painted to look like the traditional tins. Each had integrated rubber rings on the lid with double snap locks. Everything was airtight. Each jar could hold three petri dishes. She had to fill all, according to the mysterious instructions.

• • •

The festivities finally started. Yasmin began her walk down to the gathering. During the evening, she would commit a major crime, with potentially devastating consequences, all to save her family. Once in the WHO courtyard, she grabbed a glass of champagne and a small plate of food, pretending to be part of the celebration. She was tightly holding both, but too nervous to eat or drink. She carried on with the small talk, intermixed with some details about her groups' plans, and any other pleasantries she could manage with a growing knot in her stomach.

It's almost time, she thought.

Finally, everyone sat down for the presentations and speeches. She would commit the crime during this formal part of the event. She quietly slipped away, walking down a corridor off the main courtyard and toward the elevator to her office. In her office, she picked up the cooler and headed back to the elevator and up to the bio-storage labs on the uppermost floor. At the main lab, she slid her card through the reader and faced the biometric reader for a retinal scan. Lights turned green, and the lock clicked open. She entered a small changing room where all the safety suits were stored and where a secondary door opened onto an airtight hallway. She dressed in a safety suit, pulling it over her evening dress, and then pressed the entry code on the large keypad. The second door opened. She entered the glass hallway. Sensors constantly checked the air. All was good. The third door opened.

She walked into freezer room C-25 and carefully lifted fifteen empty petri dishes from storage. She then proceeded to freezer room K-112, where she entered and removed fifteen Hemorrhagic Smallpox dishes. She peeled and switched the Radio Frequency Identification (RFID) tags on all petri dishes, then placed the empty dishes back in the place of the smallpox samples. She worked quickly but carefully. Her heart was beating rapidly, like a timpanist on speed. She felt every pulse all the way to the tips of her fingers. She opened the travel cooler, took out the five fake caviar glass jars, and placed three smallpox petri dishes in each. She closed the jars, placing them back in the cooler. She closed the cooler lid and pressed the vacuum seal button. The cooler was now sealed, airtight, and locked. Unknown to her, an embedded explosive was automatically set as part of the sealing process. Should anyone open the box without the proper code, it would explode.

Now the package was ready for shipment. Her heart still beating wildly, Yasmin walked over to the door that led back into the glass hallway. This would be the test. The sensors were so delicate they could detect the smallest microscopic trace of a stray biological, trigger the alarms, and lock her inside. Again, she keyed in her code on the opposite keypad and the doors slid open. She entered, holding the cooler tight against her body. The doors closed and sealed tight. The air was pressurized, and the room was vacuum shut. She could feel the air circulating around her. All collected air samples would then pass through sensors that would run through all the usual tests, but also conduct a deeper test for items based on which freezers she opened. This was a much longer process than the entry test. To Yasmin, it seemed like an eternity. Finally, the lights turned green, unlocking, and opening the second door. She was almost hoping to trigger the alarm, so they would stop her. But, in the end, she was more worried about her family than the world. The quality of the cooler made her feel slightly better. It had passed all the tests, and it seemed safe for transport.

She walked back to the courtyard area, finding the caterers responsible for the caviar. She handed the container back to them.

"Thank you very much for this very generous gift. However, we may not accept gifts of any kind. Please return this to the sender with my regrets."

She walked away and back to the courtyard area. Finding her seat, she sat, picking up a glass of water with both hands shaking. She took a sip. A sip she could hardly swallow.

The package was now on its way.

10 | THE MINDERS

Bobby had been in custody for over a week. Other than the occasional treadmill walk, in the fully equipped gym, they kept him locked up. They served him three meals a day. The menu consisted of bread, cheese, and tea for breakfast. For lunch, they served him rice and some *koresht*, a Persian meat or vegetable stew, and more tea. Finally, they served a sandwich for dinner, with soda or juice. The food was limited but good. How he loved Persian food. Yet, after a few days, he craved a simple burger or a pizza and a nice cold beer.

Except for his minder, no one else visited him. He still had no idea what the reasons were for his being here, nor when he might be released. The minder, who had given his name as Hamid Parvaresh, visited daily for an hour of unthreatening conversation. Apparently, "guests" had a designated person who watched over them. They maintained the guest's sanity, with deliberate and routine human interaction.

Parvaresh was a well-informed and well-educated minder, fluent in English with a slight Boston accent, well versed in the subtleties of American life. Not the characteristics one would expect of a foreign jailer. He had his favorite football teams and easily mentioned his favorite players and their stats. He knew most of the new sitcoms, their plot lines, and actors. It seemed as though he lived in the U.S. and just arrived in Tehran that morning. Their wide-ranging conversations sometimes felt like two guys chin wagging at a bar, over some beers, after a long day at work.

Parvaresh took a liking to Bobby. His stays became longer, and he directed their talks to things Bobby and Parvaresh had in common, with fewer and fewer trivial fillers. They both loved massive multiplayer online games and shared several. None of these games could be played by normal means within Iran. Instead, all games were reachable via their Qatar or Turkey satellite offices and their servers, or via an ever-changing list of Virtual Private Networks. Iran scoffed at such childish pastimes. Most video games violated *sharia* law. However, The Center, with its need to access all things Western, had established several offices in neighboring Turkey and Qatar. Piggybacking on the fiber optics lines the countries had built between themselves, a decade earlier, allowed for the ever-connected offices. The Center's servers in Qatar filled a Persian Art Gallery's back office, while the Turkey servers filled the storerooms at the Iranian *Bank*

Mellat branch. The art gallery was a highly profitable business. However, the bank branch was only a shell of its former self, after the U.S. imposed sanctions on Iranian banks. Because of its location and super security, that branch was to remain open no matter what.

The Center tech lab had finally hacked Bobby's hard drive. It was much harder than the average traveler's machine. It had a very strong password, which logged you in and decrypted the drive. It seems the conversations between Parvaresh and Bobby came in handy. Special Artificial Intelligence software would take the recorded conversations, digitize them, and extract keywords and constructs, to create a personalized dictionary. Within days, they extracted the password. This was done with a brute force method, made possible by an intelligent dictionary. Yet another one of many programs designed and written by Iranians while working at U.S. companies and organizations. The program that opened the door to Bobby's hard drive came by way of the National Security Agency, crudely titled 'Smart DIC.'

• • •

"Good afternoon, Bobby." Parvaresh entered the room carrying Bobby's laptop.

"I've been instructed to allow usage of this laptop during our visits. Should you want to read old emails, look at pictures, or maybe work on projects you have going on."

Bobby happily reached out, taking his laptop.

"And, just so you know, we've cleared the password, fully inspected all files and programs, and have even removed certain ones."

"Is there any Wi-Fi?" Bobby asked with a smile.

"Not even a hint. Not even for us. Everything here is hard-lined. All outside windows are double paned with reflective gel fillers. They insulated all the walls with aluminum-infused material. And, every inch of the building has frequency masks," Parvaresh said proudly, but with a hint of sadness. He missed checking his private messages during the day.

"So, no Wi-Fi, no cell service, and yet you have a cell phone hanging on your belt," Bobby said as he opened his laptop.

Parvaresh took off his cell phone and confessed his love for all things Android. He had recently ordered the new Google phone from one of their U.K. based businesses, on which he flashed a custom operating system, a ROM. He placed it next to Bobby on the table. He was showing off.

Bobby found one of his favorite playlists and played the tunes on his laptop. He then took the phone and started casually looking at it. He felt the weight, the general feel, the screen and color resolution, all the basics. He had one like it at home. Handing it back to Parvaresh, he walked over to his bed and sat leaning against the back wall.

"That's a great phone. I think I'll order one if I ever get back home."

"You can have mine. If they ever let you leave." Parvaresh offered.

"You know, Mr. Parvaresh, I can help you with your phone. I've built an entire custom ROM for my last phone and still have all the code on my laptop. I have nothing better to do."

Parvaresh perked up. Custom ROMs were phone operating systems with a cult following, typically fine-tuned to a particular taste. Some people liked their phones highly customizable, some liked their phones super-fast and light, while others liked a barebones approach with just the original software. Bobby could see that Parvaresh was a believer. To some geeks, Custom ROMs are like porn.

"If you could make a wish list of features, what would you like to have on your ROM?" Bobby said, having felt the fish bite on the hook.

Bobby engaged Parvaresh in a multi-faceted conversation about Android. He wanted to listen to his tunes for longer and didn't want Parvaresh to leave. They discussed all the features that phones should have, the things they could do with them, the look and feel of modifications and customizations that make a phone personal and unique. Clearly, Bobby had found a deep passion in Parvaresh, and the reason he always carried his phone on his belt. They spoke for as long as the battery lasted on the laptop.

The tunes finally ended and Parvaresh excused himself, collecting the laptop. At the door, he stopped and agreed to a longer discussion on the subject, promising to bring the laptop charger next time.

11 | THE COUNTY OFFICE

Jason was at the Denver Marriott City Center Hotel. Out of town business travelers occupied most of the rooms, making it a great place for a local to be anonymous. Sitting in his room with a pot of coffee nearby, inspecting all the documents he had received from Mike, Jason was focusing on two critical clues in the pile of paperwork: the timing of the demands, and the cavity in the redesigned handicapped seats. The timing and the location strongly coincided with the upcoming Super Bowl, planned for the Super Dome that Mike's company had built. Then there was the armrest cavity that appeared in the new seat design. Clearly, this space could hide something. The game, the half-time live show, and global viewership all made perfect sense for a visible attack. He studied the new seat designs in detail and imagined himself as a terrorist.

What would I do?

The blue LED lights were an interesting addition to the original design, as were the self-contained battery and solar charging kits. Everything came back to the timing and the cavity. Cavities in shaped plastic pieces, Mike had told him, were more expensive to build in the injection-molding process.

He took detailed measurements of the space. It was slightly larger than a Churchill cigar. Room enough for an ounce or two of explosives. Between the limited explosive weight and hard plastic wrapping, it would be a minimal outward explosion. However, if each seat had a small amount, collectively that could be a powerful statement.

How do you make them all go off at the same time? Or, at all? He thought.

Security at the stadium was nearly perfect during the week of the game, but not good enough for this kind of plan. Bomb-sniffing dogs would run the full course and sweep every seat but were unlikely to find built-in explosives planted inside a hard casing.

He moved forward with the assumption it would be explosives, and the master plan was an attack during the Super Bowl. Now he had two major objectives, to save Bobby and to stop the attack. He called Mike and asked to have an engineer meet him near the county offices with all the plans, permits, and paperwork.

• • •

That afternoon, the head engineer for the Superdome construction project met Jason at a café several blocks from the county office. The engineer had with him the full planning, construction packet, and four compact disks. He also brought a laptop containing more of the project deliverables, a massive amount of paperwork more easily searched in digital form. He wasn't sure what Jason wanted or what he would look for, so he'd brought everything.

They sat over coffee, discussing the permitting process for a replacement project of that size. They focused on the approval process and all the differing signatories who would have to give the okay. The engineer fanned all the new permits across the table and described systematically how one goes about getting permission for every aspect of the project. They reviewed all the old permits on the laptop, matching new to old, looking for some paper trail. The search eventually narrowed down to several names, with only one of Persian origin, Mehdi Karimi. Jason felt instinctively that this was his man.

Was he a good guy or one of the bad ones? Finishing his third coffee, Jason thanked the engineer, walked to his car, and made calls.

Within the hour, Jason had a full background check sent to his phone, including credit, criminal and DMV records, and recent addresses and phone numbers. With a smartphone, and email address, and $19.99, anyone could get troves of data from public sources, all collated and delivered within the hour. Best of all, Jason had many friends and contacts in the agency more than willing to help run a report or two, in addition to what's available online. In one financial report, he even found details on

Karimi's off the book activities, namely a gambling habit that had placed a heavy burden on his credit cards, and a debt he'd recently paid in full. None of this was enough to accuse the man but enough to force a conversation. To be more precise, a special visit.

Jason began his surveillance of Karimi at work and at the man's apartment. The apartment search was detailed and complete. The man was single, with an appetite for cheap food and even cheaper liquor. For all the money he made, thanks to taxpayers, he still had cheap polyester suits, wash and wear shirts, and ties a decade old in style and width. Jason could see that this guy worked only to feed his habits, gambling, booze, and all things in between.

On the second day of surveillance, Jason made another visit to the apartment to plant video equipment. With the advent of the internet of things and the ever-connected home computer, surveillance had become much easier and cheaper. Jason spent just ten minutes in Karimi's home office. He created an open guest account on his Wi-Fi, then planted and connected several mini Wi-Fi cams, all streaming, and recording to servers accessible by his cell phone.

The time for a personal visit was soon upon them.

Having studied Karimi closely, Jason designed a meeting specifically for the man's state of mind and fixations. He made several stops in preparation. He visited a veterinary supply store, a home improvement store, and a Halloween costume and gag store. From each, he purchased several items to complete the elements he'd need for his plan. Jason truly enjoyed these special visits. He prided himself on spending the time to understand people, to get inside their psyches, to help facilitate conversations. He loved this part, the game, the mind fucking.

On Friday afternoon, Jason was homing in on Karimi. It was 3:30 p.m., the end of another workday for most county employees, lazy and overpaid as they were. In the parking lot of the county offices, a man Jason instantly recognized as Karimi was loading his car with some tubes of the kind used for carrying blueprints and a bulky briefcase. It looked like a working weekend ahead.

Could that be, a county guy working on a weekend? Jason thought, cracking his first smile in days.

Jason followed the man home for what he thought would be a night of quiet surveillance. Less than thirty minutes later, Karimi came out still in his working outfit, pulling a wobbly carry-on back to his car. With the car loaded, the man drove out of town. Jason followed him for an hour and a half, in traffic, to Black Hawk, Colorado.

Once there, Karimi pulled into a casino, parking his car at the long-term lot. Getting out, he continued pulling his carry-on towards the main entrance. Jason quickly parked and followed him, safely at a distance, hidden among the crowd.

Karimi stood in the quick check-in line and within minutes had his room key. It appeared he was a regular. With his card key in hand, he worked his way through the sea of gamblers toward the guest elevators. Jason followed a group of three rotund gamblers, reeking of cigarettes and booze, into the same elevator. He followed Karimi until he saw him enter room #218. Jason decided to conduct his visit in that room that night. Given the man's proclivities, he would have the whole weekend to work on him.

Jason returned to his car, retrieving his gear. He returned to the hotel and located a janitor's closet, which he opened with little effort. He was looking for a house cleaner's cart. He knew each house cleaner had her own key card, but because of the rush to clean rooms quickly, each cart had an emergency key card hidden, just in case a card didn't work, was damaged, or had been accidentally locked inside a room. Minutes into the search, he found a card taped to the underside of a cart's lower shelf. He pulled it free and headed back to room #218.

He knocked several times, calling out "Room service."

There was no answer. He entered with the house cleaner's key, placed his bag of goodies in the closet, then went back to the lobby for something to eat, and to keep an eye on Karimi. Jason ate his steak and potatoes, a casino special for $6.99. The casino figured diners would make up the difference in gambling losses or on alcohol. Soon after, comfortably full, he focused on Karimi again. His target was still at a blackjack table where he'd begun the evening. Two empty glasses stood next to his small stack of five-dollar chips. It looked like another losing night for the man.

Over the next several hours, Karimi kept ordering more drinks and having the pit boss fetch more chips. With his credit balance back at zero, the casino was more than happy to furnish him with all the chips he wanted. The drunker he got, the worse his playing became, as evidenced by the speed at which his chips dwindled.

Toward the end, Karimi would see the dealers' six up card and would draw on his hard 19, looking for that elusive 2. He made dozens of mistakes, probably losing an entire paycheck and more in one sitting. Free booze, dropped off by scantily dressed women, plus highly oxygenated air, could make an addict drop a load of cash. It was, by any measure, the perfect swindle.

Jason watched from a distance, avoiding direct eye contact with the cameras, especially in the elevator. Cautiously, he wore a baseball cap pulled low, and on the elevators stood behind others while looking at his feet. The night was about to end for many. You could always tell by the length of ash hanging from cigarettes glued to the lips of the slot machine players. The longer it was, the more tired they were, and the closer to quitting time. Jason took the hint and worked his way back to Karimi's room. He needed a break.

• • •

At two thirty in the morning, the lock clicked and the door swung open, the handle banging hard on the rubber bumper. The lights were off. Karimi reached for the switch by the door. It didn't work. Jason could smell the stench of cheap whiskey as the inebriated gambler walked towards the bedside lamp, all the while holding the walls.

Drunk as he was, he found the lamp and clicked it on. That too didn't work. Miffed and still holding the wall, he stood straight looking around. His eyes finally adjusted to the dark room. Before him stood a man, his face covered.

"Am I in the wrong room?" he slurred with both arms now reaching for the walls.

"No. You're where you're supposed to be." Jason punched him hard, dropping him to the ground. Walking back to the door, he hung out the Do Not Disturb sign, latched the safety lock, and turned on the TV.

• • •

It was nearly dawn when Karimi finally woke up. The TV had been playing infomercials all night. There was a stink of vomit coming from his shirt. His arms were duct taped to the desk chair. His legs, with bare feet, were taped to the chair legs. His mouth was also taped. His entire upper body was taped to the backrest. All he could move were his head and neck. His left hand was bandaged and bloody. Several fingers were missing. Looking around, he found those missing digits in a glass on the dresser by the TV. He started to scream. You could only hear a muffled sound through the tape over his mouth. Karimi was now fully awake, in a state of shock.

Jason was making himself some tea. Using the Lipton tea bags found on the bathroom counter by the coffee pot. It tasted like shit, as did all free hotel food. He knew too well, having spent years living in many lodgings. He had polished off all the pistachios, almonds, and cashews in the mini fridge. He came out stirring the tea, his face covered by a black and white Arab *kufiya* scarf. He pulled up the room's other armchair and sat across from Karimi.

He took a slow sip and in perfect Farsi, with a slight and charming *Esfahani* accent, whispered, "This tea is horrible!"

"Nothing is like tea from back home. I miss the bread and cheese from home too."

He took his time drinking his tea, calmly reminiscing. He fondly recalled one short story after another from back home.

"I remember this one teahouse right outside *Masjid Jom-Eh*. It had the best tea. They would add to each cup just the right amount of fresh rose water. They would serve two cookies with each cup, homemade cookies they were. Late in the evenings, they would also have the most aromatic tobaccos burning in the water pipes. It was a heavenly and relaxing place to be."

He took another sip.

"Have you ever been there?"

He drank every sip of tea slower than the one before, stretching out the inevitable painful outcomes for the poor tied up man. Karimi's eyes were welling up with tears. He was crying and shaking uncontrollably. He was way past the shock, and deep in a state of terror.

I think my man is ready now, Jason thought as he placed his tea down on the floor.

Jason took out the meds and syringe he had bought at the veterinary store. He prepared a proper dosage of local anesthesia, tapped the syringe for air bubbles, and squeezed a little from the top. He injected the liquid into Karimi's right foot. He then reached for the bloody branch-pruning clipper placed near the glass holding the fingers.

"You'll be very quiet now! Yes?" he stood next to Karimi, speaking coldly, in Farsi.

"We don't want your fingers to have more friends in the glass. So, I'll ask questions. You will answer. In return, I will let you keep your toes." He continued as he removed the tape from Karimi's mouth. Karimi nodded in agreement.

Holding the clippers in one hand, he reached for his tea and took another sip. He then asked Karimi whom he had told, with whom he conferred, and with whom he's shared the secrets related to the permits. Jason wanted to gauge if Karimi had any clues. Asking a straightforward question was the best way to get started. Why waste time asking for their name, their address, and other irrelevant information. This was not a polygraph test. The baseline had already been established, with the missing appendages.

Jason had only taken two more sips of tea before the terrified man spilled the beans. He spent fifteen minutes telling Jason the entire story.

"I did everything I was asked. I told no one. I know nothing." Karimi finished, shaking and begging for mercy.

"Again, tell me only the facts. What exactly did you do?" Jason asked.

"I invalidated the permits, re-submitted new orders for a change to handicapped seating, just like the directions you guys sent me," he said sobbing.

Jason kept asking the same questions in a different order. The answers were all the same.

Karimi was definitely the man. It took thirty minutes to get all the details out of him. Jason had planned on a weekend with this guy. What a shame, now for the confirmation part. Jason put the tape back on Karimi's mouth. Bending down, he poked the sharp edge of the clipper into the bottom of the bare foot.

"Can you feel this?" he asked.

Karimi shook his head, *no*.

Jason made a cutting motion and dropped a little toe into the glass next to the fingers. Karimi started his muffled screams. The chair creaked from his uncontrolled shaking. He lost all bowel control. The stench of urine, crap, and vomit were overwhelming, a common occurrence and one Jason had anticipated from other such visits.

"I don't believe you, and you pissed all over the place! Now I'm angry." Jason made another cutting motion, adding another toe to the holding cup. He then walked over to the nightstand, looking for something.

He grabbed Karimi's iPhone. He walked back, turned it on, and placed it under Karimi's working hand. He demanded that he enter the proper security code or lose more toes. Karimi, trembling with fear, pressed the keys and unlocked the phone, after three or four wrong, shaky tries.

With the phone open, Jason navigated to the messaging app, found the specific text message with web links, and read the text. He then followed the URL links. He found and read the detailed orders. It was as Karimi mentioned, and all for a reduction in gambling debts of $100,000. They paid this poor bastard just to push permits through the backdoor, no hostages, and no threats needed. They had this guy figured out as quickly as Jason had, a greedy, selfish, scared alcoholic little man, with a gambling habit.

Jason copied the URLs, deleted the messages, and wiped the phone memory. He then turned the phone off and tossed it on the bed. He collected his gear, placing the empty glass of tea in with his gear. He turned Karimi's chair around, facing the window, and covered his face with a pillowcase. He cut the tape on the arm containing the hand with five fingers intact. He then walked to the door, looking through the peephole. Seeing no one, he replaced the scarf with his baseball cap and stepped out of the room. He walked out of the hotel with his gear and the intelligence he needed.

• • •

Karimi eventually broke free, having spent an hour unwrapping the duct tape. He was stewing in his own sewage and vomit the entire time. Fear, the hangover, the weak character, all made him expel his bowels several more times. He sat there for a few more minutes, shaking, crying, and looking out the window, his one leg still numb. Eventually, he dared to look down. To his surprise, all of his toes were in place.

He stood only to fall again. He crawled over to the dresser and grabbed the glass, pouring it on the floor. He picked up a finger, realizing it was a plastic prop. He quickly unraveled the bandages on his hand to find all his fingers were in place, numb, stiff, but all there. Jason had bent them inward, bandaged them, and poured red dye all over the bindings.

With all digits accounted for, he crawled to the corner, curled up, and sobbed uncontrollably, holding the plastic fingers and toes in both hands.

12 | CELL PHONES

Bobby was back on his laptop, enjoying his music. It eased his mind. It made him feel less scared, more motivated, energized. The conversations with Parvaresh were becoming a little stale. There was only so much one could talk on the subject of cell phones before it became trivial. But, they were both guarded. They would not speak about personal things. Bobby kept thinking there had to be a way to engage him and to figure a way to get out, at least to do something to get help, even if he could not get out on his own.

"Mr. Parvaresh, do you think it's possible for me to do some programming on my laptop?"

Bobby refused to call Mr. Parvaresh by his first name. He never wanted to feel close or familiar.

"Do what you want with your laptop," Parvaresh responded. "However," he continued, "at the end of every session, I must take the laptop away for inspections by the computer people. They may delete whatever they see as unfit or may take your privileges away."

Bobby didn't care. He wanted to do something productive, intellectual busywork, anything. He agreed to the conditions. He stopped the media player and brought up his Integrated Development Environment, an IDE loaded with programs used to modify the latest Android operating system, which he used to write a ROM for his own Google phone. This was a duplicate of what Parvaresh dangled on his belt.

"Mind if I watch?" Parvaresh sat next to him on the bed.

Bobby moved over a bit, sat straight, and continued typing on the keyboard. He ran several commands, started the onboard phone simulator, and booted the Android OS. It looked gorgeous. Parvaresh was watching with eyes wide open, nearly drooling. Bobby navigated to the settings section, where all the goodies were, and ran through a gambit of possibilities. Parvaresh took out his Google phone and navigated to the settings section for comparison.

"My phone has none of those possibilities," Parvaresh said greedily as he gawked at Bobby's laptop.

I know. Bobby smiled.

Almost instantly, it hit Bobby like an explosion. *I think I have a way out.*

Parvaresh knew a little about flashing ROMs. Mostly, he thought they were for visual items, unaware of the full built-in potential of Android. Bobby continued setting and resetting more features. From CPU speed control to memory management, to full system level blocking and control for calls and text messages. These features existed in all android phones but were never exposed to the public. It was a way by which vendors such as AT&T and Verizon could more easily control their customers.

"Do you think you could flash this ROM on my phone?" Parvaresh asked eagerly.

Bobby, knowing the Google phone intimately, mentioned that he had never worked with Parvaresh's phone before, and would have to do testing and evaluations beforehand. A simple flashing might brick his phone. Render it useless.

"What exactly do you need to do on my phone?" Parvaresh asked nervously.

"Nothing serious or invasive just some setting adjustments, some test runs, simple validation of things." He, Parvaresh, could supervise the entire process.

"I'm going to have to think about it." Parvaresh got off the bed and moved to the chair, a little deflated, knowing all changes would violate internal security protocols.

Bobby nodded casually and went back to reviewing his old projects. Now he was exploring the possibilities of doing something to help himself. He just had not figured out the exact steps. For ideas, he looked over all the projects he had completed and even looked over the incomplete ones. His brain had shifted into analytic mode as he searched for a way to communicate, to get a message out of a vault completely walled off and encapsulated by tech countermeasures.

Lunch was soon over. Parvaresh got up, collecting the tray items, asking for the computer. Bobby turned the laptop off, tucked it into the computer bag, and handed it to Parvaresh. Placing the strap on his right shoulder, Parvaresh picked up the tray and walked out, locking the door behind him.

Bobby kept staring at the door. He tried to recall all the other departures in which Parvaresh carried the laptop case. It was always on his right shoulder, with the computer bag hip-high touching the cell phone. The laptop and cell phone were within inches of each other for as long as it took to carry the bag from the room to wherever it was stored. Bobby figured at least a 15 to 30-second walk. He smiled as he figured out exactly how he would communicate.

A door is opening. If only I can have his phone for several days. Bobby prayed.

As all great programmers do, he wrote code in his mind. He sketched out the entire process and all the necessary steps.

• • •

Bobby programmed this way for nearly the entire time between lunch and dinner. By then, for the first time during his captivity, he was actually starving. The door finally opened and Parvaresh carried in the dinner tray, the laptop hanging from his right shoulder, as always. He placed the tray on the table and the laptop on the floor. He sat on the bed with a magazine he had brought with him. He was still thinking about his phone and the sexy new ROM he could have. His was typical of the all-consuming passion among serious Android fans, the idea of manipulating the phone in all ways possible to take ownership, unlike the iPhone, where Apple owned you and gave no access to the inner workings, like a babysitter with a child. Apple being the babysitter.

There were forums dedicated to every popular Android phone, with subsections for changing every part of those phones. It was a religion. Bobby could see that Parvaresh was indeed a disciple. He had drunk the Kool-Aid and more than one cup's worth at that.

Dinner was quick that night. Bobby wanted to work on Parvaresh. He asked what his concerns were. Parvaresh recited rules against modifying Center phones and security protocols. Bobby explained in detail he would not touch the existing ROM. There could be a dual boot system in place. While at work, Parvaresh could run the phone as intended. On his time off, he could boot into his custom ROM. Parvaresh knew that was against the rules too, but felt it was safe enough given that no programs or apps on his phone would be touched. He figured he'd just play with it for a couple of weeks, then delete the new ROM. Parvaresh gave Bobby the OK but insisted he is involved in every step of the process. Bobby agreed.

• • •

They both sat at the table, Bobby opened the laptop and they began to work. Neither had been this excited in some time, but each for different reasons. Parvaresh might get a new toy and Bobby might get to communicate out. They placed the laptop and phone near each other. Bobby grabbed a USB cable from his bag to connect the two devices. Given that Parvaresh had already flashed a ROM, the phone *was* rooted with administrative privileges and had backup and recovery capabilities. Bobby began by creating a shared partition where they installed the new dual-boot manager. Parvaresh was gawking at the screen without blinking. Bobby then opened the notepad, leaned back in his chair, getting ready for some Q&A time.

"OK. The basics are done," he said with a satisfied smile. "Now I have to get requirements from you, and I need to check my download archives for the source code for your specific phone. Hopefully, I have it!"

He went over all the steps taken so far, making sure Parvaresh was comfortable. He then identified some of the custom configurations that Parvaresh might like. In reality, his aim was to manipulate the startup sequence, and some of the startup files. He typed and asked Parvaresh a series of benign questions about his usage when at home or on weekends. Having finished, he told Parvaresh he needed to place these custom configurations into the baseline OS before they flashed the ROM. He could always change them himself later.

"Sounds good," Parvaresh said, blinking once, and again staring at the screen.

Bobby opened up his development environment, with as many confusing tabs as he could, mainly as distractions for Parvaresh. At first, Parvaresh watched very closely but quickly his eyes glazed over. He sat back and started playing with his phone, still connected to the laptop.

"You can look, but just don't touch any buttons," Bobby said, happy that Parvaresh was looking away.

Bobby manipulated several areas of the entire startup sequence to achieve his goals. He wrote several short scripts, made changes to the order of several startup events, made sure several processes were always kept alive or restarted if they were turned off. In re-naming several processes, he used hard-coded names so that the new names couldn't be changed. An hour into it, he was done.

Watching someone program is like watching paint dry. Midway through Bobby's intense and solitary work, Parvaresh was busy reading his magazine on the bed. Bobby pressed several more keys, and the download was complete. The changes saved to the phone. Now a brand new custom ROM was in place, with hidden scripts running in auto mode. Background communications were running.

"All right, my friend, your phone is ready to go." Bobby disconnected the phone and handed it to his minder. He closed his laptop and put it in the case.

Parvaresh was brimming with excitement, like a kid in a toy store. He took the phone and, sitting close to Bobby, went through the process of booting between the two operating systems. Playing with features, he asked dozens of questions. Then he stood up and while collecting the dinner tray, profusely thanked Bobby. As usual, he placed the laptop bag on his right shoulder so that it hit against the belt clip holding the phone. Saying goodnight, he closed and locked the door.

• • •

Bobby had programmed the phone's Near Field Communications (NFC), Wi-Fi, GPS, and data network capabilities to remain on at all times. He created a simple messaging system so that the phone would ping a specific URL address every 15 minutes with a simple message, a message that included GPS coordinates and some text.

HTTP://TOWERSCONSTUCTION.COM/35.703670-51.410930-MIKESHAMS

His computer could update the text message as needed if held within six inches of Parvaresh's phone. Bobby knew no data would ever leave the electronically secure building, but he was anticipating communication once Parvaresh left the building. On the outside, there would be a ping every 15 minutes while the phone was on.

The messaging system was in place. Bobby could only hope it would work, and that those back home – network administrators at his dad's company – would notice the anomaly and do their jobs.

13 | THE START UP

Afshin Noezad was so excited to be part of a new startup in Silicon Valley. The valley was always buzzing with stories of new inventions, success stories, old technologies applied in new ways, and the overall tech vibe that was nerd nirvana. He was happy to have finished his Ph.D., and that he had the offer to work on a project based on his dissertation. It was a great finish to years of schooling and a great start to his career.

As with many startups, there were long periods of secrecy and bootstrapping. He was comfortable with the low pay, all the non-disclosure contracts, slender resources, and having to work in a stark warehouse. It was all very charming, in the classic manner of the northern California culture of tech optimism.

The startup he joined had only three people working for it. One co-founder had worked for decades for nongovernmental organizations in African believing in vaccinations as important life-saving measures. These NGOs focused on cultures that neglected vaccinations for a variety of reasons, including cultural and religious. The other co-founder was an immunologist who had also worked at NGOs in Africa and Asia. The two had a plan to build a new connected delivery system on top of an adaptive, self-correcting network. A new network, controlled by software, could present vaccines through aerosol dispersal, adjusting for recipient size, age, and weight. The system would also have microinjection features, as part of the casing, for situations where the device was to deliver vaccinations when touched, for example, the armchairs on theater seats. These systems would be portable and easily placed inside village community centers.

One section of the warehouse had the design and manufacturing rooms with several high-end computers running a powerful suite of Autodesk design software. Nearby was the most expensive device in the building, a Selective laser sintering 3D printer that could print anything in metal, plastic, or ceramic. It was Noezad's dream lab. He could design prototypes and print the final products, all from his desk. On the other side of the warehouse, closed off to him, were the bio labs where testing was to be done on the delivery system with live animals. The only time he saw anything of the labs was when he passed by as the door was shutting, just as he had come into the building. All he saw was a glass room, bio suits, and a dozen cages filled with mice and rabbits. That was not his area and so he did not care much.

Noezad had a tight deadline on his shoulders. He had to re-design his dissertation prototype to new specs, build 120 of the devices connected and controlled via a ZigBee networking protocol, and have them all working within three months. Fortunately, the dissertation had most of the work documented, and ready for use.

Life was good, but he had his work cut out for him.

As for the other two, in reality, they no longer cared about NGOs or vaccinations. They were just two top-notch biochemists, assigned to do a job.

14 | THE LOG FILES

Mike was sitting in his office looking over plans and project schedules, trying his best to keep busy and divert himself with work. An unexpected call from the IT department startled him. An internal caller was trying to reach him directly. A junior network manager wanted to schedule a meeting to discuss some security issues that had recently cropped up. This was not normally something with which to bother the CEO, but in this case, the manager felt that certain oddities were worth mentioning directly to him. So Mike scheduled the meeting for later that day.

It was the evening of a long day. His secretary had left by the time Mike heard a knock on his office door. The IT manager opened the door, peeking in shyly.

"Is this still a good time?" she asked.

Mike waved her in as he sent the final email for the day. She walked in carrying a three-ring binder. He cleared his desk. She sat right in front of the clearing.

"So! How can I help you, given I know absolutely nothing about network security?"

She placed the binder filled with printed network log files on his desk. She went into details about transaction logs, how they recorded all attempts to reach the company servers. She described how hackers always tried to break into company systems by automating the process of testing all entry points. She described how they ping all ports, and when they find an open port, they begin penetration tests.

Mike stopped her before she went further into more obscure details. He told her he really did not have the time for this.

"Please let me finish. This is important!" She nervously interrupted him, her voice quivering, and her hands shaking as she opened the binder.

She explained that pinging is a very simple form of trying doorknobs to see if the door was open, just one simple turn per door. Here, the pinging had a message and a bunch of numbers attached. It was as if, beyond testing the doorknob, someone was yelling aloud, asking if anyone was there. It made little sense, she said. Mike stood up, irritated, telling her he was not the appropriate person for this. He helped her out of her chair and steered her toward the door. Grabbing her binder clumsily, she walked, still talking and pointing at a page.

"Sir, the messages have your name in it, and they're coming from Iran, according to the trace reports." She tapped a yellow highlighted line on an open page and then showing more pings against their servers, all including his name and a series of different numbers.

He halted, snatched the binder from her, and walked back to his desk with it. She followed, sitting down again, quietly facing him. She had finally made her point.

"Where did they come from and do we know who sent them?" he asked urgently, and then bombarded her with dozens of questions, to which she had very few answers.

He asked for all the data in digital form and told her to keep an eye out for any other similar anomalies. Hel also ordered her to report to him ASAP. She pulled out a DVD from the binder sleeve, with the weeks' logs. With the disk in hand, Mike stared at the pages once more, confused.

She walked out, knowing her first meeting with the CEO was a good one.

• • •

Mike was driving home with the DVD on the passenger seat next to him. He could not wait to dig deeper into the data, looking for clues. Reaching home, he walked to his office, turned on his PC and logged into the secure email software Jason had installed. He wrote a quick message explaining what he had heard and attached one of the smaller log files containing the anomalies. He pressed the send button and waited for Jason's reply. An hour later, he received a short, mystifying email back.

YOUR SON IS A GENIUS. I'LL SEE YOU TOMORROW.

• • •

The next morning, an hour before his drive to work, Mike was cooking breakfast in the kitchen, when he heard tapping on the window. Jason was standing outside, sweating from his run over the hills. Mike opened the door. Jason walked right to the sink, took a cup, and drank two fillings of tap water. He then filled the same cup with coffee. Mike went back to the stove and served himself the scrambled eggs he had just cooked. Without asking, Jason took the plate from him and wordlessly ate the breakfast in several quick mouthfuls as he walked toward Mike's office.

Mike placed the frying pan in the sink, grabbed a banana and his coffee, and followed.

Jason had already entered the office. He turned on the scrambler and sat at the computer.

"Is the DVD in here?"

"Yes," Mike said.

He opened several log files, staring for a while. He then highlighted one of the line items, pointing to the numbers. They were not random numbers, but rather GPS coordinates. He copied one, separated the latitude and longitude with a comma, placed the decimal points in the right place, and then copied the string of characters into Google search. Google Maps came up, with a location right in the middle of Tehran.

"I need time to work out a pattern. Why don't you go on to work? I'll stick around and work on this."

Jason spent the next hour writing a script and parsing the entire DVD. He extracted and mapped all the relevant data points. Every ping was fifteen minutes apart and came after Iranian work hours. Clearly, this was not Bobby wandering around town at night or early in the morning. But it was someone who knew something about him roaming the streets. The best part was the spoke and wheel configuration of the mapped points, centering on the source of many of the pings with smaller clusters away from the central location, marking the general area where this person lived and visited.

Jason wrote a quick secure email to Mike with the news, asking Mike's office to deliver any additional and new data to Mike's home PC. He then wrote simple instructions on how to run the automated script, and how to map the data. Emailing the instructions to Mike, he shut down the PC and walked back into the kitchen where Mikes' wife was drinking her coffee. He walked up to her, whispering in her ear.

"I know where Bobby is. I'm going to get him back. Tell Mike to check his email as soon as he gets home."

She smiled a brief but warm smile.

He stepped out of the kitchen door for the run back to his car.

15 | THE EXPORTER

Paris' Charles de Gaulle Airport, a major hub for exports and imports, was busy, loud, and hectic. A newly arrived shipment had brought in the manager from Shah International Foods for a quick inspection and re-routing to San Francisco and other cities. He arrived early in the morning with enough fresh baguettes to feed a dozen men, with the tops of several loaves missing. No one could resist eating the crusty ends. The aroma of fresh-baked bread filled the manager's car. The customs officer's moods were better early in the morning, especially when bribed with fresh bread.

The social part of the meeting was long, as usual, filled with lies about lovers, and lies about money. After indulging in bread and coffee and gossip, the inspectors and the manager went over the crates due for inspection and those for re-routing. Twenty cases of California red wine and 200 kilos of caviar from Iran required import inspections. Crates of salted herring and ten cases of Australian Syrah wine were scheduled for rerouting, with minimal inspection required. The customs officers did not care about rerouted items since they'd be leaving France. With little interest, they walked the dogs around them checking for explosives and only rarely took an x-ray. If nothing got the attention of the dogs, the shipments were given the *INSPECTÉ* stamp. Then every one ended with another half-hour lying a little more about love affairs over another cup of coffee and more bread. By mid-morning, several crates were on their way to California, via Air France Flight #84.

• • •

The two crates arrived in San Francisco twelve hours later. Seven hours after that, a scan for nuclear materials, and a dog walk around for drugs, all showed no threats. Customs released the crates, with notification emails going out to the addressees for pickup. Within the hour, a delivery van arrived at the airport to pick up the crates, followed by a visit to the sprawling wholesale flower market in South San Francisco. The van with the two newly arrived crates of herring packed in dry ice parked in the vast parking lot among hundreds of other vans, trucks, and cars. All the vehicles were being loaded with seasonal flowers. The van's driver went into the building to pick up the daily allotment for his restaurant table settings.

A short time later, he was back at his van ready to load his flowers. Opening the back door, he noticed that one of the herring crates had toppled over, dumping ice packs all over the floor. He was surprised since the drive from the airport was on a smooth freeway and he hadn't stopped short in the parking lot. But he shrugged and quickly cleaned up, placing the vacuum-sealed fish and ice packs back into the crates. He then closed the crate lid and continued loading the van with flowers. Within the hour, he would be at a San Francisco restaurant, to deliver fresh flowers and his imported fish.

• • •

Going in the opposite direction, down Highway 101, the California-based minder was carrying toward Silicon Valley the newly freed, and somewhat fishy-smelling travel cooler that contained the last and most important material for which the startup founders had been waiting. He had to get the package to the warehouse and away from himself. He knew what was in the cooler and, although sealed and not yet weaponized, he wanted to be a safe distance away. Given the high death rate associated with the contents of the cooler, it was better to be safe than sorry.

After dropping off the package, he had to get back to his real job as a sales rep for one of the world's largest software companies. Based in Redwood City, he worked with clients up and down the freeway from San Jose to San Francisco. He had full control of his schedule, making side projects easy to squeeze in. Working with The Center for over ten years, most of his tasks were relatively simple; intelligence gathering, some bribery and strong-arming, and several extortion projects. This new assignment was the most exciting, and most consequential. He had dreamed of such a project for a long time.

To attend training and conferences for his software sales work, he had traveled to Europe frequently. With each trip, he took time off for traveling. In one case, he spent his work sabbatical in Ireland at a secret training facility, learning about explosives and weaponry, from assembly to usage and disposal. These were skills he needed and had always wanted to gain, and for which he had to wait a long time to build trust before he could attend the coveted training program.

This current project was the riskiest, given the biologicals. He was not too fond of weapons of mass destruction. But, he was getting a great paycheck for this operation. And, he felt a patriotic duty to help in any way he could. He changed the station on his radio, upped the volume, looking forward to a fruitful day, happily enjoying a perfect white rose he'd picked up at the flower mart and which he stuck into the air vent on his dash.

16 | STATUS REPORTS

Back in Tehran, The Center was bustling with activity, another day of planning, evaluating projects, and watching for opportunities. Parvaresh was busy with his analytics work and his minder duties and happy with his new phone. His conversations with Bobby were going well. He was learning quite a bit about American culture and places, some of which he had visited, but most of which he had only read about. To top it off, he was getting his fill of all that was Android.

In another cubicle, an analyst was reviewing TOR network traffic, the dark web, the underground of web activity, for ongoing vectors and projects. He recognized an anomaly triggering an alert. The cause was a URL visit, from an IP address an hour outside an authorized area. He couldn't be sure if it was a breach or an off-the-books visit. In either case, he scheduled a videoconference with the project head, Ali Najafi along with the Denver minder responsible for all Colorado assets, including Mike Shams and the county clerk.

• • •

The meeting started with a check of security protocols. All video conferences occurred over a 128 kb encrypted system developed by The Center using the SIP Communicator Software as its base. It was a kind of Skype for people with lots of secrets. Attendees had all logged in. The meeting began with a review of the URL navigation status reports and then continued with a detailed Q&A session. Najafi grilled the Denver minder about his assets, asking about their whereabouts and movements, and their visitors.

The minder reported on all assets and their activities. Mike Shams had been behaving normally and within expected boundaries, with no unusual visitors. And as far as he could tell, all manufacturing efforts were on schedule. As for the county clerk, he had delivered the permits and collected the payments. The minder was unsure why the clerk would revisit the URL. More perplexing was the location from which he visited, a casino in Black Hawk, an hour or so outside of Denver. No matter, Najafi ordered the minder to re-evaluate the county clerk for any new risk factors.

• • •

The IP address was for a casino resort, with the visit occurring in the early hours of Saturday, Colorado time. There was nothing odd about the casino. Karimi, the county clerk, was a gambler after all, and the place was one of his haunts. The timing of the visit might be odd, but not too upsetting. Yet Najafi had to know for sure. The minder would begin a more in-depth surveillance of Karimi, following him for several days, between work and home and all the stops in between. There were to be regular check-ins between the minder and the Center's analytics group.

After a period, no anomalies cropped up. The clerk's behavior and socializing were all within normal parameters. Another secure video conference was called to review the findings.

To Najafi, those findings were not entirely reassuring, so the minder was instructed to question Karimi directly and in person. No ambivalence could be accepted.

• • •

At ten in the morning on Saturday, Karimi got up with a nasty hangover, after another night gambling at a local underground card house. He strolled to his kitchen to make himself some tea. When the microwave beeped, fraying his raw nerves, the tea, nearly boiling over, was ready. He pulled the cup out, adding three cubes of sugar, and stirred as he walked to the living room. He sat on the sofa, blew on his hot tea and took a sip while turning on his television. As was his habit, he went straight to CNN to watch a minute or two of news regurgitated from days earlier, sandwiched between ten minutes of advertising. An overall waste of time, but it went down well with tea and a hangover, a quick respite before getting on his computer to check on the Friday night lotto drawing.

Everything would change if I could win once. All the things I could do. All the places I could visit, with my best friends along with me. I would be the king of the hill once again. This was the weekly dream for the clerk.

There was a knock on his door. A knock with which Karimi was familiar. It was the fat woman across the hall coming to say hello. How he regretted that drunken sleepover with her months earlier. She was a lonely woman, big but with a beautiful face. She thought of him as a chubby chaser, available for an occasional night of sex. He now regretted having been in bed with her, her weight bearing down as she rode him, gasping and slobbering as they kissed. He felt sick remembering it.

She was cute in the face, though, he thought, smiling to himself.

He walked over to the door, his mild arousal forming a tent in his pajama bottoms. He opened the door, torn between being dismissive or inviting. His neighbor was not there. Instead, a man was pointing a gun at him.

"Not again!" Karimi whimpered.

The man gently stepped through the doorway, firmly pushing the silencer-equipped gun almost into Karimi's right eye socket, ordering him to step back. The door closed behind them. Still walking backward, Karimi moved into the living room. The minder turned up the TV volume and directed Karimi to sit on the floor.

"Not again?" the unwanted guest repeated in Farsi, this time as a question.

"Have we met before?" he asked, sitting on the couch and pointing the gun at Karimi on the floor.

"No! I thought you were the neighbor. I mean a mugger. I've been mugged and robbed before!"

The minder paid no attention to the nervous reaction. The gun was obviously making Karimi babble. The minder went straight to work and began his inquiry.

"You've received your payment. We told you to delete all messages. So, why did you visit the website from the casino?"

Karimi pleaded. He had done exactly as told, he whimpered. His first excuse was that his cell phone had been stolen at the casino. He thought he had deleted the message but he must have forgotten. Over the next fifteen minutes, he went through several variations of his story, none of which made any sense. Clearly, he was scared and hiding something.

The minder got up and walked over to Karimi. He reached for the robe's belt as Karimi cowered, fearing a punch in the face. From behind, the minder pushed Karimi onto his stomach and tied his hands behind him with the robe belt, pulling it painfully tight. He then rolled him back over, propped him up against the couch, stuffing a smelly dishtowel into his mouth. He then looked around the place, searching the kitchen counter, the dining room table, and took a quick look inside the bedroom where he found Karimi's iPhone. He walked back, holding it out.

"Is this the stolen phone?" The minder stood there watching the clerk's eyes widening with fear and confusion.

"I'm going to ask you one more time before I kill you," the minder said. Almost instantly, he punctuated his threat with a silenced gunshot.

Karimi's left ankle exploded, bone fragments hanging by a piece of skin, blood gushing all over the cheap carpet. Karimi fell back and rolled up into a ball of blinding pain. This was real. An actual shot, not a prop, nothing fake. The minder methodically made a tourniquet with another dishtowel to stop the bleeding. He did not want Karimi to die before he could speak. Bending down to show the writhing man the cell phone, he promised to call for an ambulance if he was satisfied with answers to all his questions.

Karimi spent the next thirty minutes recounting the casino visit. Writhing in pain, crying and begging, he told the entire story. He included the fake torture session and the perfect Farsi spoken by his captor. He mentioned how he thought it was them, testing him, making sure he was keeping quiet. The minder listened carefully for any clues, asking repeatedly a series of questions. He had the story recounted several times just to be sure. Fully satisfied with all the facts, he got up.

"No. It definitely wasn't us. We don't fake torture."

He leaned over Karimi, helping him onto the couch. He gave him the phone so he could dial for help.

"Before you call, let me see you reset the phone and clean the internal memory."

He waited patiently, watching, while the clerk resets the iPhone to factory defaults. He then began his walk to the door, turned back, and shot Karimi twice in the head.

• • •

The minder messaged in his report:

SOMEONE KNOWS, AND HE IS NOT AN AMATEUR.

17 | THE LAB

The drive south from San Francisco to Silicon Valley was always busy, with almost everyone on a cell phone. The activity and pressure along this tech business corridor were so intense it was evident on every face. Each minute had to be productive. In fact, for someone not on a call, the best part of the drive was looking at the drivers' expressions. They ranged from calm to furious, intermixed with smiles and laughter. Each expression corresponded to the loss or gain of a deal, an opportunity, a raise, or a new job — in short, money and power.

Adding color, and some danger, to the commuting mix, was the new-money drivers of Ferraris and Porsches as they stalled their cars in the most inopportune places. These young drivers had never driven or mastered the stick shift. After every stall, you could hear the grinding of gears. If you listened carefully, you could even hear the car itself cry.

Driving down from a client visit and having recently delivered the cooler with the biologicals, the California minder was hesitant to visit the lab. Part of his job, however, was to check in and report. Once at the lab, it was a quick park and walk to the warehouse. Using his key, he unlocked the main door and poked his head in, looking around. He was wondering nervously if this visit could be the death of him.

• • •

Biological weapons typically summon mental images of smart scientists working their trade in sophisticated, secure labs. The reality, however, is much more mundane. The creation of weaponized viruses and bacteria typically happens in makeshift labs with people who know just enough to be dangerous. During the 1763 French and Indian War, it took the mere distribution of smallpox-infected blankets to win a war against the Native American tribes. In some ways, biowarfare is just as simple.

The World Health Organization spearheaded an effort, in 1967, to eradicate smallpox through mass vaccinations. By 1977, the world saw the last naturally occurring case of smallpox. Science had effectively eliminated smallpox from the natural world. But, laboratory copies still existed.

Although a vaccine against the disease was available, only medical and military personnel underwent vaccination. This Variola virus caused a potent strain of smallpox, with a fifty to seventy percent mortality rate. Signs included high fevers, body aches, and a rash that spread from fluid-filled bumps. The disease primarily spread through direct contact with an infected person's skin or bodily fluids. It could also spread through the air in close, confined environments. Circumstances typically found in the care of handicapped people.

The Center had chosen their target, specifically, to inflict maximum exposure. A super bowl game brings people from all around the U.S., all flying on airlines within a very short period. Infecting the handicapped brings about an increase in incubation and spread probability. Often, initial symptoms can be mistakenly seen as being part of their existing conditions. So, there was the possibility, after the Super Bowl, of 120 or more patient zeroes spread all over the country.

The ZigBee-based system allowed for full control of the delivery vessels. Each handicap seat in the network could communicate with every other seat. The network would be self-healing, so if a seat malfunctioned, other seats could take over the communication role. The seats had their own power source, with solar chargers. They also had a built-in antenna for communicating at a distance. It was to be an instantaneous domino effect. They needed to trigger only one seat for the domino effect to take place. What remained was to finalize the aerosol mix, and to finish and install the delivery tubes.

• • •

"Is it safe?" the minder yelled, half-joking, as he leaned into the lab.

"Yes! Come in," the immunologist shouted from the office. "There's an email for you." The email had followed a be-on-the-lookout notice received several days earlier, in which The Center identified new risk factors.

The minder walked to the office to check on his email, quickly glancing at the recently hired young engineer as he was fiddling with the prototypes. The young man seemed happily engaged in his work. The minder nodded a quick greeting as he made his way to the office, wondering why he'd received an email off schedule.

The email was identifying a new threat. The analysts back at The Center had spent hours sifting through each of the files for each of the players in the vector. They had devoted hundreds of computer hours correlating all facts related to each player. The red flags all pointed to the same person, Jason Caius. They had created a profile of him, which they enclosed in the email.

• • •

The profile was quite short:

JASON CAIUS IS THE SON OF GORDON CAIUS. HE AND HIS FATHER, A VIETNAM VETERAN WHO JOINED BELL HELICOPTER, MOVED TO IRAN IN THE SEVENTIES. GORDON, A PILOT, AND SPECIALIST WAS A TRAINER FOR THE IRANIAN MILITARY PILOTS. HIS FAMILY, INCLUDING HIS ONLY CHILD JASON, LIVED IN IRAN FOR OVER THREE YEARS. THE CAIUS FAMILY MOVED BACK TO DENVER, A CHANGE BROUGHT ABOUT BY THE REVOLUTION IN IRAN. MIKE

Once all unnecessary and misinformation was filtered out, the profile ended up resembling a glossy one-page brochure. No other details were available. It seemed impossible to find so little on someone that old, in our information age. Either Jason had hundreds of pages about him hidden, or he was a complete nonentity. But, to the Center, the unusual lack of data could only point to clandestine work.

Orders went out to all vector minders to eliminate Jason Caius.

• • •

The minder and co-founders sat down in the office for one more walk through of their parts. A fresh pot of coffee was brewing. They summoned the new engineer to make a lunch run, handing him a hundred-dollar bill.

"So, what do you guys want to eat?" he asked.

"Get a couple of salami and a couple of roast beefs sandwiches, with everything, on French rolls. And a six of diet Coke. Get whatever you want for yourself. Go to the deli on El Camino, near Matadero Ave. They have the best bread," the minder said as he closed the office door. The engineer headed out for the deli right away. He didn't recognize the minder and thought he might be one of the investors. So, he wanted to impress.

The co-founders and minder shared plans and timelines across the desk. They poured some coffee, and one founder lit a cigarette. Leaning back, he took a puff, followed by a sip of his black coffee.

"I think we have everything in order," he said, exhaling a stream of smoke.

"Put that shit out. You know I hate second-hand smoke." The minder snapped.

Unperturbed, the cigarette smoker responded with a snide remark, taking another puff, leaning further back in his chair. The minder poured himself a cup of coffee and turned around with a look best described as a cold-hearted killer's gaze. Seeing the look, the other co-founder slapped the cigarette out of his partner's mouth and apologized for the snide remark. They were both now sitting straight and attentive as the minder walked back to the desk, cup in hand. There was only one boss in this room.

They reviewed the plans, schematics, and timelines, discussing remaining issues and financing needs. The minder wrote a check for some additional equipment and the payroll, making some small changes to the plan, keeping the deadlines in mind. By the time they'd finished, the engineer had returned with the lunch and drinks.

"You can smoke now," the minder, said smiling, as he took two of the sandwiches and a drink.

He walked towards the door and out to his car. He called off the remaining meetings he had for the week. After a brief stop at his house, he began his trip to Monterey.

Everything was on track.

18 | THE HOUSE

The news was everywhere. If it bled, it led. A man found shot dead in his apartment. The reports portrayed it as a vicious attack on a long-time resident in a very safe suburban neighborhood; clearly, a home invasion went awry or was it a murder. Residents were out looking for their fifteen minutes of fame, claiming the man was quiet, very polite, and hardworking. He had lived there for well over a decade, longer than most of his neighbors had.

"He was the best neighbor anyone could have, kind, caring. He was a nice guy," sobbed an overweight woman while being interviewed. She lived across the hall from the dead man and was the saddest of the interviewed bunch.

Jason was at Mike's home office. His dad and Mike were watching the news. Jason was working on the computer. He had logged on to his servers to review the surveillance videos, which captured the killing in its entirety. He had watched it all, the night it happened; now wanted a closer look. He tried to capture a good front-facing image for facial recognition. He was paying special attention to the dialogue and accent. He watched the videos several times looking for clues, trying to get some new information, some insight into the master plan. Now there were other concerns. Someone was now onto him. He wasn't overly concerned about the local police, but the minder was another story. Jason finally captured a perfect face shot. After staring at it for a while, he sent it off for evaluation.

"OK folks, here is what's going on," Jason said to the two other men. He then recapped what he'd seen on the surveillance tapes.

He was sure Mike's family would be safe. Any changes there would draw a great deal of attention and would derail their plans. However, he felt sure that he and his family were at risk, given their close ties to Mike's family. He knew that they would link him back to Monterey and Mike in no time. In one way or another, Jason would be a person of interest to them. His son would be safe in Iraq – safe from the plotters, at least — but he had to go back for his wife.

He instructed his dad to be wary and to keep a close eye on Mike and his family and gave him some contact numbers in case he needed help. Numbers of people they could trust. Jason got up, hugged his dad, and before leaving, looked at both men with stern eyes.

"The game is on. Be careful."

Earlier, having seen the killing on video for the first time, he had called a friend, Henry, back in California. He told him that Amitis might be in danger and asked him to keep an eye on her, to stay far enough back not to be seen, but close enough to help if needed. He wanted her safe but also wanted to see whom if anyone would come after him and his family.

That afternoon he was on a plane headed home, worried sick about his wife, given the way the poor county clerk had been so callously killed. The torture and the final double taps to the head were brutal. Only a professional killer can be so unfeeling, and so ruthlessly efficient.

• • •

After two flights including a stopover in Los Angeles, Jason was back in Monterey. He got in a cab, and as he neared his house, he passed a familiar car with one of his friends, Henry, behind the wheel. By the look on his friend's face, and his extended middle finger, Jason knew all was well. He was finally home. He paid the cabbie and ran to the front door, entering to a warm embrace from his wife.

"What is going on? I've been sick with worry," Amitis said, holding him close.

He quickly closed the door and held her for another minute or two, breathing in her familiar smell. He then took her to the office, turned on his office scrambler and began to explain what had transpired. She was holding his hands in a tight grip, frozen in place by the story, a story that started strangely and kept getting stranger by the minute.

• • •

The whole while Henry was outside patiently waiting for some time to pass for the two to have their last bit of privacy.

Henry, his father, all of his uncles and both of his grandfathers were all in the army. They were a generational group of warriors, as Henry would say, and true patriots at a minimum. Jason first met Henry in Afghanistan. It was Jason's first on the ground assignment as a translator and analyst. Henry was one of several escorting Jason to the Northern Alliance HQ in the Afghan mountains. Henry didn't like Jason much at the start. To him, Jason was a typical spook, with little value or skills to survive in the war-torn area. He thought him better suited to be a translator at the United Nations or something like that. It wasn't until the fourth night of a seven-day march that they all came under fire. At first, they thought it was the Russians, but as it turned out it was the Northern Alliance thinking they were the Taliban. It was during the firefight and the last minutes of yelling back and forth, in Farsi, that Henry saw who Jason really was, highly skilled in warfare and negotiations. Jason often mentions Henry's first set of kind words directed at him.

"Jason, my brother, you are definitely not a pussy!"

From then, a long lasting friendship developed taking them both to many similar places and events. They became a trusted friend and brother to each other.

• • •

A loud knock on the back door jolted them both. Jason jumped at the sound and peeked through the shades to see his friend. He let him in. They shook hands and gave each other a quick half-shoulder bump, the he-man's hug, then walked to the office.

His friend sat in Jason's desk chair. "It's been a while, bud. What the fuck is going on? And where's my beer?"

"Good to see you too, Henry," Amitis said sarcastically as she went to get him a beer.

She had never really liked this friend. His many tattoos, crude language, and all-around crassness grated on her. But, she could not overlook the fact that the two men had been friends for over twenty years. She brought the beer into the office and handed it to him.

"Thanks, babe." Seeing her peeved look, he slapped her on the rear as she walked by.

He opened the beer using his car keys even though the cap was a twist off, yet another bad habit. He turned to Jason.

"So, I've been watching the house. No issues. But, my man watching your office had a different story. He has seen the same dude several times. He visited your secretary three times. The man was definitely not interested in your secretary, or in your classes, but he was very interested in you."

He continued, "My guy could tell he was a professional by his mannerisms, the way he drove, his changes of clothes, his walk, his street craft."

The news confirmed Jason's worst fears. They were onto him and quickly. They would soon find their way to his house. He called his secretary to tell her he was back and checked on his calendar. She mentioned the man's visits. She was not overly concerned. The man was merely asking questions about curriculum, different teachers, their strengths and weaknesses, all normal conversations.

If only she knew, Jason thought.

Instead of waiting for the minder, Jason decided to speed the game up, driving it to its conclusion on his schedule. He and Henry discussed what to do next. Henry would keep watch on the house and Amitis. Jason would set himself up as bait to draw the man out.

Would this be an interrogation or assassination, or both? Jason worried.

• • •

The best way to bait the minder was to act as normal as possible. Jason started his morning with his daily routine, a morning run, followed by a drive back home on the same road he always used. He then drove to work on his normal route. He parked his car in his office parking lot, sensing that the minder was close. He was happy to have the minder on him and away from his wife, and happy Henry had her under observation. The plan was to have one of Henry's men watch the minder watching Jason. Everyone watched by someone. He wanted to play the minder's game but stay several steps ahead. The game involved people he cared about and he needed details. He needed things to move forward on their end undisturbed. Yet, he had to have something more to go on.

Two days into Jason's return, Henry's man reported that the minder followed him everywhere — at his house, at his work, even on his runs. The minder quickly figured out that Jason was careful, and not an easy target. Though generally predictable, Jason had become random in the details. He drove the same road but not at the same exact time, sometimes early, sometimes very early, and at times right on his normal schedule. He never drove the same speed. He changed lanes and watched who followed. When running errands, he always parked where people would be nearby or where it was particularly safe, in front of the police station for instance. He even looped his jogging runs at different distances, so he would pass by his car several times or none at all. Jason, the habitual professional, changed things just enough so that a plan could not be developed.

This was not going to be an easy snatch and grab. The minder had to think bigger, smarter.

•••

Henry and his crew had dozens of photographs. They had the minder's fingerprints, not from his motel or car, but from the microwave at a gas station convenience store, where he bought and heated a burrito. They sent all the data to Langley for a full background check. The man was a legal U.S. citizen, highly educated, and well-travelled, with combined years in Europe and Australia. Nothing stuck out causing any red flags. The man had no criminal record, not even a parking or speeding ticket. This was the second minder Jason had come across. They also had fully profiled the Denver minder, with nothing out of the ordinary showing up.

Who are these people? Where were they trained? Whom do they work for? Jason was getting irritated.

Both minders were of Iranian origin. Neither had any relationship to any Middle Eastern groups, cultural centers, or mosques. None had any fanatical friends or affiliations. They were definitely not the stereotype terrorists were thought to be — the dark-haired, bearded, olive skinned, badly dressed man you see in every FOX newscast, the ones you envision driving cabs in Manhattan or running a 7-11 around the corner. These two were the kind of people you might want as friends or employees. They blended in perfectly.

Jason knew the only physical constants in his life were his office and his house. No one would attack him at the office. It was on an old military base, one still busy with military people training in varying languages, and one still with the barbed fences and controlled entrances. He did not fear a simple kidnapping. He was too careful for that, and Henry's men would never allow it to happen. The house was the real risk. The house had to be the final target. They were unsure what would happen, but they decided to set the stage. They would open up the house, letting in the minder for whatever was to be. This would be their arena.

• • •

The next evening, Jason decided to take his wife for a relaxing dinner at a local restaurant. They took a leisurely drive to the restaurant. Once there, Jason handed the valet the keys and a twenty, asking to have the car parked in front. The boy, with the twenty in hand, smiled and nodded. They went into the restaurant for what was to be a two-hour romantic meal.

The minder had followed them and watched through a window until they began ordering. He then rushed back to Jason's house. He had studied the house many times and already had his entrance planned. He started by turning off the power to the house, and then disconnected the cable and phone lines, cutting off any communications. Finally, he cut the wires to the outside alarm speakers. He expertly picked the lock of a back door, and once inside, he set down a duffle bag filled with explosives and began opening the alarm system cover. The very first step was to reset and reboot the alarm. Having done that, he planted explosives all around the house, turned on the attached short distance receivers, and quickly worked his way back to all the cut and disconnected wires and cables for a fast, almost invisible repair. Then he went back to his car, parked some distance away, and waited.

The minder was not planning on a conversation, and he had concluded a snatch and grab would be impossible. Any conversation would be fruitless. Direct contact with

Jason would be more trouble than it was worth and might even be dangerous. As ordered, he was to eliminate the threat. So eliminate it was.

Jason, however, was hoping for a conversation. He needed to have a conversation.

• • •

The dinner was wonderful. Jason and his wife finally felt a little love coming back into their life, removed for the moment from all that was going on. They ate and drank slowly, chatting at length about their boy Sean, about Bobby and his family, and their lives together. Being with his wife gave Jason so much energy. They were great friends and a great couple. Shortly before dessert, Jason got a text from Henry. He looked down, raised an eyebrow, and put the phone back in his pocket. Finally, the freshly made cake arrived, with the heady scent of hot melted chocolate filling the air around their table. The coffee too arrived, a nice cup of strong coffee for Jason and a decaf for Amitis.

Nearly two hours had gone by. They were done with dinner and were driving back home. Jason was deep in thought. He was getting ready in his mind. He wanted to be ahead of the minder in this game. His wife's life depended on it.

Given Henry's text, Jason knew things were not going to go exactly as he wished.

• • •

They arrived back at their home. Jason parked the car in the garage and closed the garage door before leaving the car. The minder was sitting in his car, several homes away and across the street, waiting. He was waiting for a light to turn on in the house. He saw the light in the kitchen turn on. He paused for several seconds and pressed a button on his transmitter. Nothing happened. He pressed repeatedly. Nothing happened. He got out of his car. Walked several feet towards the house and raised his arm. Pointing at the house, he pressed the button. Success.

The concussion from the explosion pushed him back hard against his own car. For blocks around, car alarms were going off. He quickly got his bearings, jumped back in the car and drove off, followed in the distance by Henry's men.

Just as the Denver minder had, he texted in his report.

I ELIMINATED THE PROBLEM. WE ARE BACK ON TRACK.

• • •

On the road behind Jason's house, Henry sat in his car. While the minder waited in the car out front, Henry entered through the back door and quickly removed the short distance receivers. He then located the explosives and took several bricks to the front door. He fashioned a homemade detonator with a blasting cap and some wires that he stretched to the back of the house. He filled a bathtub with water and put the remaining explosives in it. He hoped to save some of the house's contents, at least try to do so, without losing the effect. He finally connected his detonator to an egg timer and a car battery from Jason's garage.

As soon as Jason and Amitis were in the house, he and Henry rushed her through the back door. Henry set the timer to thirty seconds, turned on the kitchen light, and ran to the back fence. Climbing over he ran down the small hill to his car where the other two waited. Jason and Amitis crouched low in the back seat as Henry drove.

"The things you can do in the dark, with pliers and household goods, are incredible. So, now you're dead. What next?" Henry said as he sped and away from the house.

"Now, I will hunt them down, and scorch them and the earth they stand on." Jason was holding his wife close.

Then he sent Mike a text, telling him they were well, safe, and on the move.

He also contacted Warren Spencer, the CIA Deputy Director, and Jason's handler of old, asking for a major favor.

Henry drove them to his home in Salinas.

19 | THE SHORT GAME

The local police had the entire block cordoned off from the public and media. All the surrounding homes had been evacuated. Two fire engines were at the scene. The fire was nearly out, with a few hot spots left. FBI agents were on site. The media had been reporting the explosion and fire as an accidental gas leak. However, the police initiated investigations in all other areas, as a matter of procedure. Later in the morning, several black vans and an SUV moved in, well past the police line, driving right up to the half-burnt house, with one van backing into the garage area.

The police and FBI agents spent another hour sifting through the rubble and smoldering rooms, finally letting the news crews approach. They had to stage the closing parts of the on-site investigation just right. This took many phone calls until approved under national security protocols. The news media rushed as close as allowed and filmed from every angle. So many bright television lights were on that it could have been high noon. Suddenly all cameras focused on the removal of two body bags, each carried to the black van by two men. All news channels aired every bit, live and with all wanted details in place. Briefed by the FBI, reporters announced the death of a decorated civil servant and his wife. The cause of death was under investigation.

• • •

Gordon was sitting in Mike's office with the entire family, watching the late news on FOX. They truly enjoyed the animated commentary on that network. FOX loved talking about terrorism, conspiracy, and anything that could help boost their ratings. Fear-provoking coverage fitted perfectly with Rupert Murdoch's agenda, shaping the political culture of the countries in which he operated. Fox was the most effective outlet for reporting Jason's death. That was exactly what they wanted.

"So when's the funeral and do we have to go?" Mike's daughter asked with a smile.

"Jason always wanted to be cremated," Gordon laughingly explained.

"Seriously," he continued, "the bodies would be at the morgue for at least four to six weeks while going through the autopsy and investigation. We've bought ourselves some time before we have to figure out actual funeral plans, as fake as they have to be."

• • •

Half of the initialed agencies in Washington were sniffing around for details on this new threat assessment. They all wanted to know what was going on, with more than a dozen communiqués among several agencies, going in every direction. Jason received one email from Warren Spencer, asking one simple question.

EVERYTHING WENT AS PLANNED. WHAT'S NEXT?

Jason sent a quick response, with more information and a request for continued help for him to stay dead in public, and finally, for some time. Spencer responded.

I'VE GOT YOU TWO WEEKS TO GET ME SOME ANSWERS.

• • •

Jason left his wife behind with Henry's family. He and Henry then began their trip up to the San Francisco Bay Area. They would be there within a couple of hours. Henry's friends were well on the tail, following trackers placed on the minder's car and luggage. With Jason seemingly out of the way, it would be easier to collect detailed intelligence and to put better plans in place.

These people were not, in any way, amateurish or hesitant to kill people. If they could execute someone on U.S. soil, they could do much more back in Iran. They could definitely cause major havoc right here in the U.S. Jason needed more than his own abilities. He desperately needed help.

Having dropped off Amatis, Henry and Jason eventually caught up with the men who had followed the minder. They met at a local food truck for a burrito in the late afternoon. They were several blocks away from the warehouse building housing the startup and the minder's first stop. An hour later, Henry got a text from his other man with an address in Palo Alto where it seemed the minder lived, and his second stop.

The entire group met back at a nearby motel. They chose to be closer to the warehouse than the minder's house. They were not sure either location was important or even played a part in anything. The warehouse seemed a more likely site, away from public scrutiny. They waited until well after dark to split up and head out. Henry and Jason went to the warehouse. The other two men went to the minder's house. The surveillance had been reversed.

• • •

At three in the morning, the warehouse district was almost empty. Not empty enough to allow a break in, however. Many of the warehouses were used by startups, with the usual odd working hours. Most, if not all, had tight security. All the startups were afraid of having their intellectual property stolen. In Silicon Valley, the smart money – and a lot of it — was in IP.

"Don't these fuckers ever go home? Get real jobs, fuckers!" Henry was getting sleepy and irritated.

Henry had to vent. Ranting was his vice. He hated everything that came out of Silicon Valley. He shouted that Twitter and Facebook were bullshit. Who had time to waste all day on Facebook? And, who gave a shit enough to read other people's daily trivia, or see pictures of their lunches? What a sad bunch!

"But you know," he said, taking a breath, "I found one of my exes on Facebook. Happy I didn't marry her. What a dog!" He smiled.

"*You* have Facebook?" Jason asked, incredulous.

"*No*, my wife is on it all the time. I just check to see what she's doing!" he replied.

Jason shook his head, smiling. He didn't care for the Facebook addiction either, but he wanted to get back to the subject back to the warehouses. These days many of the warehouses rent to startups, he said. Part of the lease payment was always stock options. A lot of them move out quickly to bigger places, but the property owner keeps the stock options, and leases to a new group, at an even higher price. He could have options for dozens of companies. Some become rich leasing to these guys, which was not a bad gamble. However, anyone wanting a small space had little chance of getting a deal. The valley was great if you were in tech and sucked for almost everyone else.

Henry was ready enough to vent about tech millionaires. "The bastards ought to …" then he stopped. "Wait, the lights just sent out. It looks like the guy who's leaving the building was the last one there. About time, fuckers." Henry was eager and ready.

"OK, let's go," Jason said, stepping out of the car and moving off with Henry right behind.

They rushed to the building, easily picked the lock and got inside. Henry had already done a walk-around and had suspected the building security wasn't connected.

He had called in for repairs to be sure. The building had no contracts with any security company. Before they moved another foot, they scanned for other devices and found small localized, directed explosives embedded in the doorjamb, all mechanically triggered. It was enough to kill but not destroy anything. Henry disabled the device, and they both entered.

Henry planted surveillance devices while Jason went after hard data. Jason made his way to the office and looked through the desk and drawers. The drawers were empty. This was definitely a shell company. He could not find a single invoice, contract, bill, receipt, or any other indication that real business was transacted at this spot.

Having taken pictures of everything in the office, he walked over to an open area where a series of computers were still on. There was a 3D printer in the corner, and a large conference table with electronics, brass tubes, and blueprints. He lifted one of the electronic boards, took several dozen pictures, front, and back. He placed a quarter next to the tubes for scale and took several more pictures from every angle. He then went to the 3D printer to check on the filler materials, taking samples.

"How's it going, Henry?" he whispered loudly.

"Don't rush me, fucker! I need another thirty minutes."

Jason walked to the opposite side of the warehouse, coming to a walled off section with a door. He reached for the door, finding it locked. He scanned the door for electronics and explosives. There was nothing, so he picked the lock. Halfway through the doorframe, it hit him. They were not working on explosives, but something much more dangerous. He counted two DuPont Level 4 hazmat suits, cages filled with mice and rabbits, and an airtight and gloved testing chamber. Without taking a step closer, still standing in the doorframe, he took several high definition pictures panning the room. He then quickly stepped back out, gently closing the door.

"Henry, we have to leave right now!" he said firmly as he reached for his friend, pulling on his shirt. "This is a biohazard zone and we have to get out ASAP."

Henry heard the urgency in Jason's voice, and they left without a trace of having been there and drove back to the motel.

"What the fuck was that about? Henry asked nervously.

"Biological weapons," Jason said, "But what exactly, I don't know."

"How do you know it was biologicals?"

"They were refrigerated. You don't do that to chemicals."

"Well, shit man that raises the price on everything." Henry jokingly said as he lit a cigarette.

"Oh yeah, I forgot. You and your team's money is in the duffle bag in the trunk. I hope cash is OK?"

"Dollars only my brother," Henry said, inhaling another lung full of smoke.

***

Once in the room, Henry and Jason took off their clothes and threw them into a black trash bag, duct taping the bag shut. Henry jumped in the shower, washing vigorously, demanding Jason do the same.

"Come on in, I'm not going to fuck you," Henry burbled through the shower of water.

Jason was not too worried about the biohazards. If it was something airborne, it was too late for him, anyway. Otherwise, he never got close or touched anything. Nonetheless, he washed down as quickly as he could too. He jumped in the shower, shoving Henry to the side. The other two were deep in sleep when woken up by Henry's yelling. It was early but not so early. One of them got up, got dressed. Shaking his head as he saw the two grown men in the shower together, he left to get coffee and donuts.

Within thirty minutes, they were dressed and waiting for the food. They had a great deal to discuss and analyze. The more time passed, the hungrier they all got. It was an adrenaline-induced hunger. The food finally arrived.

• • •

An hour into it, nothing but crumbs was left of what had been four dozen donuts and bear claws. They were now on motel coffee, the kind you could use to shine your boots. They loaded the pictures Jason had taken onto a laptop and analyzed the details. Jason also brought up the blueprint photos for Mike's new handicapped seats. The puzzle pieces began to fit together. The dimensions of the chair cavity, the size of the brass tubing, the attached spray nozzles, and the biologicals all pointed to a mass attack, a bio-attack at the Super Bowl. The only puzzling part was the tiny electronic board, who would trigger the bio release, and how. Henry studied the photos for a while before he smiled.

"I know what these are," Henry said, as he squished all the remaining donut crumbs into a small ball of calories, and then stood up and explained.

The electronics were Arduino Boards, but much smaller, tiny controller boards used for almost anything you can imagine. They were cheap and easy to program. They came with built-in Wi-Fi and ZigBee communication chips, for a much smarter networking capability.

"These fuckers will connect all the tubes into a smart network. Man, these guys are good." Henry sat down again, smiling and still hungry, but very satisfied with his expertise.

The other three men were looking at each other, as though Henry had just sung the most difficult opera aria like a dazzling pro, then burst into deep laughter.

"Not bad Henry, for a redneck. Who would have thought you knew this shit," one of Henry's friends blurted out.

"I read fuckers. You should try it too!" Henry glared back at his friend.

They continued to analyze every single picture from the lab. They counted the petri dishes visible through the glass door of the freezer. They identified as many pieces of the visible equipment and any other useful items. From the office search, they found only one name, Yasmin Akbari. The name was on a congratulatory note dropped back into the travel cooler by Yasmin in her rush to get the package back to the sender. The note was on the desk and appeared in one of the pictures.

A quick background check on Yasmin yielded the source of the biologicals and its location. The puzzle pieces were coming together. They needed to figure out what and how much Yasmin gave away and why, and to whom else other than these guys in California.

What part did she have in all of this? Who else in and outside America was part of this plan? Jason had to find out.

This was the most sophisticated plan since 9/11. All the people involved were highly placed, professional, well educated, and socially accepted. Not the typical poor, angry, uneducated recluses' one associated with lone wolf acts of terror. Not the Islamists you heard about who visited strip joints in Florida, or who had a DUI or two on their records, all jobless, hanging around some local mosque.

Jason finally told Henry about Bobby, held in Tehran, asking Henry and his friends to keep a very close eye on those in the group they knew about so far. Should these people make any efforts to move anything, Henry and his men should do whatever it took to stop them. In the meantime, Jason needed time. He needed to get Bobby out of Iran. Henry promised to keep all this quiet and to give Jason all the time he needed.

Jason called his wife for a brief talk and then booked a flight from San Francisco to Copenhagen.

• • •

Before getting on his flight, Jason sent secured emails to Mike, with a simple update, and one for Warren, detailing all of his findings. He told Warren he was on his way to Europe to follow leads and asked for more background checks. He wanted details on Yasmin Akbari and the whereabouts of some assets with whom he had worked in the past. He had the U.S. covered, but needed people in Europe and beyond.

• • •

The overnight flight to Europe gave Jason plenty of time to put together a plan. He needed to assemble some missing pieces, finalize the timing, other locations, and to pin down the magnitude of the attack. He then pored over the names he had gotten from Warren. Trying to think which people might be best equipped to help in any part of the plan. He recognized several old friends whom he had not seen in quite some time. But people he knew he could trust to help. While on the plane, he drafted several emails and some text messages. He wanted them sent off as soon as he landed.

When SAS Flight #935 arrived in Copenhagen, Jason moved through customs quickly and received his three-month short-stay visa stamped into the passport.

"Welcome to Denmark, Mr. Jones," the customs agent said, closing the passport, handing it back.

He was off the grid, yet knew Warren would try to follow him and his actions. He did not want them to encroach, at least not yet. He stopped at a Tele-Denmark Communications store and bought a local SIM card and cell plan. He loaded it up and then connected to his secure VPN service. The emails and text messages all went off immediately. He then walked over to the rental car kiosk, inserted his credit card, and got his car model and space number. A short bus ride later, he was in the car and checking out at the security gate. A guard scrutinized his passport and credit card, then finally scanned the barcode on the windshield and raised the bar.

"Thank you, Mr. O'Brien. Have a nice stay," the guard politely offered.

Jason was on his way to the World Health Organization (WHO), housed in the newly built UN City.

• • •

Given that every asset had a local minder, he visited Yasmin at her work, where she wouldn't be closely surveilled. He was not sure if Yasmin was a player, a pawn like Mike, or a patsy like the county clerk. The detailed dossier he received indicated nothing out of the ordinary about her. But then again, the minders too had spotless profiles. He would not take any chances. He was even prepared to kill Yasmin, a step he was comfortable with if it was necessary.

On the way to the WHO, he stopped at a local men's store to purchase a suite and tie. He then made some calls in advance of his visit. He needed to set the stage since, without a proper invite, he could never get an appointment. He was sitting in a café, by now looking very much business like, when he got an email indicating he had an appointment, thirty minutes only, as a representative of a U.S. pharmaceutical company. He was only twenty minutes away.

On *Kalkbrænderihavnsgade* Street, a star-shaped building housed the main European offices for the WHO. He eventually got to the main gate where he showed his passport and received parking directions. He parked, straightened his tie, put on his suit jacket, and walked to the building where he was to meet Yasmin. In the lobby he heard so many languages, he felt as if he were at the United Nations headquarters. He waited only ten minutes when a young woman approached.

"Mr. Jones. *Yah?* Would you follow me please?"

• • •

He walked up to an elevator for a ride to the second floor. Then it was a short walk to a very large office overlooking the deep blue waters of the *Øresund*.

"Hello, Mr. Jones." Yasmin walked from behind the desk to shake his hand. "I'm Yasmin Akbari. Please have a seat." She directed him to a conference table, closing the office door and sitting across from him.

"I was told by my superiors you were here on a short visit and needed to meet urgently. How may I be of help?" she said, looking at her watch.

Jason started on his cover story, telling her about the invented project for which he was responsible, what his company was interested in proposing, and their impending deadlines. She was very professional, Jason thought. She seemed relatively calm, neither nervous nor scared, but definitely preoccupied, looking away from Jason and out through the windows several times for a brief but revealing gazes. She was hiding something. And, was anxious or gnawed at by guilt. She was clearly preoccupied with something other than work.

Jason went all in. He got up, moved around the table, and sat next to her. He wanted to hit her with some facts. To see how she reacted. He wanted to be close enough to eliminate her if needed. Once seated, he leaned closer and spoke to her in Farsi, a shock to her in and of itself, since he'd seemed to be an American pharmaceutical executive just a second earlier.

"They've kidnapped my godson and are holding him in Iran. What do they have on you?"

She immediately broke down and cried as if a floodgate had opened. She got up abruptly and walked over to her desk to grab a fist full of tissues to blow her nose and wipe her face dry. Jason followed. She then stood in front of her office window, looking out, wiping her tears. Jason kept a close eye on her and stood close enough to react. That moment was a critical decision-making time for her, fight or flight. She could not stop the tears. She sat back at the conference table, trying to compose herself.

"They have kidnapped my daughter and husband, and I've done a terrible thing," she said. She told Jason everything.

She didn't care anymore about what might happen to her. She wanted her family back, and the biologicals destroyed. I would pay for this by going to jail forever she offered. Thirty minutes were almost up when her secretary opened the door.

"Madam Akbari, your next appointment is waiting."

Wiping her tears away, she instructed the secretary to cancel all her remaining appointments.

"Is something wrong?" the secretary asked.

Jason stood up, telling the secretary that Ms. Akbari received a call just a few minutes ago about a death in the family and was trying to compose herself. He then gently led the secretary out, closing the door.

He asked Yasmin for more details, sharing nothing with her. She gave him all the details about the biologicals, the quantity, and genetic strands she gave them and discussed theoretical means to weaponize and disperse the biologicals. She gave him details about her husband and daughter, and their family in Iran. She spent an additional hour writing everything she knew. She didn't care who Jason was. She wanted it over with.

"What will happen to my family? What's going to happen to me? What am I going to do Mr. Jones?"

Jason told her a little more about the minders. Any move that strayed from what they expected could put her and her family at risk. He told her to stay put, act normal, and he would get back to her when he found out more. She was to talk to no one.

"By the way, do you have any nicknames for your family that only you would know?" Jason asked. To which she curiously responded with two names.

Jason thanked her and left.

He had to get to Germany where he was to meet an old friend for help.

20 | THE PUNISHMENT

Parvaresh and Bobby were eating lunch. The lunchtime conversation on that day was about video game designs and improvements made over time. Suddenly the door opened and two massive men entered, lifted Bobby right off his chair, placed a hood over his head, and dragged him out. Parvaresh sat there, mouth open, staring. Clearly, he was not in the loop. He tried to follow but was repelled by a strong hand hitting his chest, with orders to back off.

• • •

Bobby, with his head still covered, sat in a room tied to a chair. Bright lights were shining on him. He could feel the heat. A long time passed before others walked into the room. They removed his head-cover. He had been in that room before. Two brick-solid men were on each side. Several nicely dressed men were standing in front, speaking in English to each other. There was a video camera aimed at him, with the red record light glowing brightly. One man spoke behind the camera, to Bobby's father, while the massive men on each side beat Bobby.

"Mr. Shams. Let this be a lesson. Do not interfere with our plans and do as you're told. Should you talk to anyone, ever again, your boy will be killed, slowly."

The beating then continued for another ten minutes. They recorded the entire beating, every punch, every kick, and every sound.

• • •

Later that day, Bobby lay in a bed with bandages covering his face. His upper torso was wrapped tightly. He tried to turn. His whole body was in pain. He tried to call out but every breath hurt. Breathing slowly and shallowly was the only way to endure the pain of broken ribs. He had an IV tube in one arm, monitors beeping and flashing numbers above his head. At least he was alive. He gently lifted his head, seeing several other beds in the room. In the far end of the room lay another man, in what seemed to be a similar physical state. He was motionless, looking straight at the ceiling.

• • •

Back in Denver, Mike was following his daily routine. Work was a great distraction during rough times. He was halfway through the day when he got a text message, from an unknown local number. The text contained a new link to follow. The link took him to a video of his son being severely beaten. Behind the scene, you could hear a voice warning Mike to do as instructed. Mike was shattered beyond words.

• • •

Yasmin was back home after a quick, diverting workout at the gym, feeling a little stronger and better for having shared her secret with someone who might help. She took a long shower, got into her cozy home clothes, and was about to serve herself some tea. While she waited for the water to boil, she looked at a framed picture of her family. She missed them so much. She poured some hot water over her teabag when her cell phone beeped with a text message. She placed the tea on the table and checked her message. She too had a link to follow. Her video showed her husband being beaten.

At the end, she could hear a voice saying: "We are always watching. Do as you were instructed. Or your daughter will be next."

She was not sure if it was the visit by Jason or that something else had happened. She would not speak to anyone. She would obey. Fear and depression conquered her once more.

What have I done? She thought hopelessly.

• • •

The Center was taking a strong stand, across all relevant assets, making their presence and power felt and well understood.

21 | THE SMUGGLER

Hamburg was a four and a half hour drive and one ferry ride, from Copenhagen. Jason called the car rental agency, extending his time and drop off point. He needed to meet some Turks he knew who were now living in Germany, people he'd worked with before. Rather than take a quick flight, he chose a longer drive. Time was critical, but a drive from Copenhagen would allow him to study his tail, to catch any who followed, be they minders or Warren's men. The drive was indeed long, with the ferry ride the riskiest. No one was following him or if they had, they were no more. No one knew where he was or where he was going. He felt safe enough to focus on planning and sending emails out to others in Europe. He wanted to have backup plans should the Turks not be able to help.

• • •

The Turks and Germans had a long history, going back to the Ottoman Empire. And now, Germany was the number one destination for those migrating out of Turkey. Nearly two million Turks lived and worked in Germany legally and illegally. The distance from Turkey to Germany made them very adept at smuggling people, contraband, and pretty much anything and everything else, with heroin the biggest moneymaker, coming from Afghanistan through Iran to Europe and finally to the U.S.

Turkey's Muslim majority tried hard to be westernized, making the country a major importer of everything that other Muslim countries banned but loved to have, contrabands such as liquor, foreign cigarettes, and movies.

From Turkey, all those goods would go into Iran, Iraq, Syria, and spread to every corner of the Middle East, by car or caravan. History and circumstances made the Turks some of the best smugglers around the region.

• • •

Jason arrived in Hamburg, hungry for some good Turkish kebabs and homemade bread. He found his way to the *Meram* restaurant where he was to meet Baba, his friend from days working projects in Iran and in the Kurdish region of Iraq. Baba, his name, meant father, befitting a man with seven sons and two daughters. Jason parked his car and walked into the restaurant. The place was full of local Turks and a few Germans. Jason saw Baba at the end of a large table, near the back wall of the restaurant, surrounded by a family of all ages. He had gotten quite heavy. Retirement had been good to him.

Baba saw Jason, stood up with his napkin still tucked in his shirt collar, waving him over with one hand while holding a piece of bread with the other.

"Jason! Over here." His voice boomed across the restaurant.

Baba dropped his bread on his plate, grabbing and pulling away the napkin from his shirt. He wiped his hands clean and put the napkin on the table. He gave Jason a giant bear hug, kissing him on each cheek. He dragged Jason to his side of the table, preparing a place for him to sit. Jason felt like a rag doll in the man's grip and warm embrace. Baba had aged quite a lot too, but he was as strong as ever.

"It's so good to see you, my brother. You are still looking young and in shape. Don't you ever age? How is your family?" Baba bombarded Jason with questions.

Baba introduced his family to Jason. Several boys Jason knew, but the rest were new additions. Then there were the grandchildren. Baba went on a tangent with every child. He divulged every proud fact he could recall. He was a happily retired man who was enjoying the fruits of years of smuggling everything in every direction. The introductions took twenty minutes.

"So my friend, what brings you to my humble town? Are you visiting or working? No worries, let us all eat, and we'll talk later."

They spent the next two hours sharing mixed meat grill plates, salads, fresh bread, and yogurt drinks. In the large and jovial family, amid talking and laughing, hands moved in every direction, grabbing food, passing plates. Jason and Baba caught up on family related stories. Every now and again, an elder son would get a text, after which they would whisper in their dad's ear, followed by sending a text message back. Baba was retired but still in charge.

Dinner was finally over, with most of the family departing for their homes. Baba, three of his eldest sons and Jason, stayed behind for after-dinner drinks. Baba never drank alcohol in front of the young children. It set a bad example. Still, he loved his whiskey. The restaurant had no liquor license, so all drinks came discreetly in paper cups, and only for their best customers. But, on that night, Baba had to take Jason somewhere more posh.

"Let's leave this place and go someplace else to talk." Baba got up, leaving a wad of cash on the table. He grabbed Jason's arm and started for the door. Jason had thought the night was over, but now there was more to come. He was exhausted.

They left Jason's car behind and drove a brand new Mercedes Benz a short distance to the entrance of a narrow alleyway. They drove straight down to the end of the alley. Their car was the only one in the alley. A young man quickly ran out, opening the car door, greeting Baba as though he was a king. Baba handed him a twenty-euro note and started walking, two sons in front and one in the back with Jason.

The *Hookah* bar was smoke filled and dark. Small groups gathered around water pipes, smoking a variety of tobacco blends, some peppered with hashish. They went to a corner table. The table and chairs were all low to the ground, yet quite comfortable. A waiter arrived with a bottle of Johnny Walker Blue Label, glasses, some ice, and a big bowl of salted pistachios.

"I get these from Iran. Not as good as those from California, but better markups," Baba said cracking a couple of pistachios. "And I sell them all over Germany."

His son poured the drinks, handing one to his father and one to Jason.

"Your boys don't drink, Baba?" Jason asked, feeling bloated from over two hours of eating.

"No. They can drink when they retire." He smiled, taking a large sip, and then whirling the ice cubes, cooling off the next sip. "They do not like to drink when they're with their father," he continued. "Respect for elders, religion, and all of that."

He knew they drank but loved the respect thing, and they knew it. He stroked the nearest son on the head, handing the young man some pistachios as though he were still a young boy. Baba took another big sip and a puff of his water pipe.

"So Jason, my brother, tell me what's going on."

Jason spent the next hour describing all that had happened, from Bobby's kidnapping to the attempt on his and his wife's lives. He told him about the biologicals and minders, who were resource-rich, well trained, and blended in like no other group he had ever seen or studied. He had never met such a sophisticated Iranian terror group, dangerous at the global level.

To Jason, what mattered most was getting his godson out. Baba's boys were both leaning in, focused on every word. It had not been this exciting in quite some time. They had heard many great stories from the old days, the adventures of Baba and Uncle Jason. They always referred to him as Uncle Jason from America, the family's own version of James Bond. They loved the adventures where their father was an integral part of the story. Knowing their dad was a great storyteller, they knew his part was probably not as colorful as Baba recounted it. But, it didn't matter, since listening to the stories was such fun.

Baba leaned back, settling into his comfortable seat, moving the water pipe closer. He took a couple of puffs from his pipe and signaled his boy to pour another glass. He mulled the story over for a while, staring at his boys, all the while cracking more pistachios. Giving each boy a handful and even handing Jason a couple now and again. He took one more large puff of his water pipe, blowing the cloud of rose water scented smoke into the air.

"I will help you with everything I have." Family meant everything to Baba.

"But not for the Americans. For your godson and the insult to your wife."

The conversation continued for hours.

• • •

The next day started much later than normal for Jason. Battered by the smoke filled air, heavy foods late in the day, and whiskey until three in the morning, he finally worked his way to the bathroom, shaved, brushed the taste out of his mouth, and put on his jogging gear. He walked downstairs to find everyone up and dressed, around a table loaded with food, energetically eating breakfast.

"Have something to eat, Jason," Baba said invitingly.

"Not yet. I have to run and get some of the tobacco out of my lungs." He walked to the door and was about to step out.

"Wait. I can't let you go alone. My son Erdal will come with you. Just wait a minute."

Jason had his own running pace and really hated to have an unknown partner. He obliged. He was a guest and had to be polite. The two men started running at a slower pace than Jason was used to, each testing the other. Jason wanted to be careful not to tire the younger man.

"You can run a little faster if you want, Uncle Jason."

Jason picked up his pace. Erdal followed in stride. Jason kept increasing the pace. The young man kept up. He started to run up any hill he could find. Erdal was right with him. Jason finally reached his turning point and started back. In the last half-mile, he started to sprint. On the final stretch before the house, Erdal darted past him. Several seconds later, Jason arrived at the door to find his companion calmly waiting for him, breathing easily as if he had never run. Meanwhile, Jason was breathing hard, sweating from every pore. He desperately needed water. After all the food, drink, and smoke, he was a desert inside. Stepping into the house, he moved quickly into the kitchen to get some water.

"Did I mention that Erdal is a national decathlete champion? I must have forgotten." Baba laughed, handing Jason a glass of water.

After a quick shower, already slightly full from swallowing his pride, Jason sat down for breakfast.

• • •

The house finally cleared of all Baba's family not involved. Jason laid out his requirements. He needed to get to Tehran and then back to Europe, bringing with him either one person, alive or dead. He was not sure of Bobby's status. In either case, he was going to bring him back. While in Iran, he needed access to a safe house and other resources. However, he was not sure how long he would have to stay in Iran before making a rapid exit.

Baba could not go himself. Instead, he offered his sons and anything else Jason might need. He told Jason about his storage facilities in Tehran where they could wait for him. Also, since the family smuggled Caspian Sea fish and caviar, cold storage was possible in case they had to transport a body.

Jason handed Baba a small black velvet pouch filled with a quarter of the diamonds as payment, which Baba refused to take, leaving it on the table untouched. Jason knew, as in Iran, it was impolite to take payment so overtly. After he left, he was sure the pouch would find its way to Baba.

"Let's go. We have planning and bribing to do," Baba said.

They spent the next day planning logistics and arranging for a meeting place in Ankara, the staging spot inside Turkey, and one of many trucking yards belonging to Baba and his business.

22 | ANKARA

Jason and Erdal sat in a small tearoom in Ankara, playing backgammon, drinking tea, and waiting. It had been two days since they left Hamburg. They had flown, while the other two brothers were driving their trucks from Istanbul, where they owned several large warehouses, and where they stored many of their products for transport. In both Germany and Turkey, Baba stored his goods according to what was legal locally or what required bribes. Baba's smuggling operation could make any logistic expert weep with envy.

"Uncle Jason, you're a good player," Erdal said. "Better than my dad. Where did you learn?"

"From an Iranian friend I used to play with a lot. It's his son we're going after."

"If the man is better than you, I should like to play him some day. I love this game."

The games were fast and the tea sweet. They played and chatted about the trip, things to do, and things about which to worry. Both had made that same trip frequently, Erdal for smuggling and Jason for other reasons. They practiced their Farsi, cracked Persian jokes, and got into their roles. On this trip, Jason would be the second driver, the loader, an all-around helper. Erdal would be the boss.

When Erdal's brothers arrived, they had a package for Jason. In it was all Jason needed for travel in Iran. He had appropriate, typical clothing, an Iranian driver's license, and his *Cart-eh-Meli*, a national ID card, a must have for every Iranian. Iran's systems were now as sophisticated as any western country. Everyone was numbered and tracked. However, most local police, small border crossings, and roadside revolutionary guards were not equipped with technology to verify credentials. Well-forged false documents were the best way to get around; add to that an adequate supply of bribing material, from cigarettes to dope to cash, and you were good to go.

They walked to the trucks, made final inspections, and began the twelve hundred kilometer drive to the Iranian border. With a fifteen-hour drive across Turkey, the first step of the plan was unfolding.

• • •

The two-truck convoy moved with Erdal and Jason in front, the other two brothers behind them. The farther eastward they drove in Turkey, the less populated the countryside became, but the entire drive was spectacular, combining beautiful plains and rolling hills and mountains. Parts of the route were flat, straight highways and parts were winding roads with dramatic mountains rising on all sides. They drove straight to *Dogubayazit*, the last city in Turkey before the border crossing, a well-deserved rest stop. The drive, done in three-hour shifts, was long and exhausting, demanding a good warm meal and a night's sleep to recover.

• • •

The next morning, having had their fill of bread, goat cheese, and tea, they began the first hurdle, a series of checkpoints. It was a relatively short drive to the first checkpoint, on the Turkish side of the border, at *Gurbulak Gumruk Kapisi*. The large customs area contained a massive truck stop, inspection areas, and truck repair facilities. The funny thing about borders was that no one cared what you have when leaving a country. They only cared when you came in. So, at the first checkpoint, the trucks were inspected quickly, inside and out, and stamped for departure. The trip back would be entirely different. They drove to the border gates and waved across into Iran. Stop number two was next.

The Iranian side of the border was quite another story, with a much larger setup, farther away from the actual border, spread out and more disorganized. The confusion allowed for easier bribing and circumvention of the process, but it was time-consuming. Iran's border agents do little, knowing the revolutionary guards conduct stricter random inspections along the road and at final destinations and doled out much harsher punishments. The crossing took several hours due to lines, but they finally made it to *Bazargan,* the first Iranian city. They stopped to make one final inspection, checking the trucks, the goods, and all of their paperwork. From there on, the road trip would be serious and potentially very dangerous.

• • •

The drive to Tehran was shorter, at around nine hundred kilometers, again through spectacular scenery. It was a chilly time of the year, with the mountains showing off colors and shapes with majestic grandeur. The highways were more modern than in Eastern Turkey, making for a faster drive. Apart from several stops along the way for gas and local guard inspections, there was little trouble. Erdal and the others were expecting a clear path all the way to Tehran, where anyone could get lost in the megalopolis. They thought the nighttime crew of police and revolutionary guards would be as lazy as usual and make for an uneventful trip. Luck was not on their side, though. Sixty miles outside Tehran, in *Karaj,* trouble began.

The crews kept the trucks close enough to help each other if the need arose, but far enough apart to be inconspicuous. A jeep filled with revolutionary guards pulled over Erdal and Jason. The brothers drove by, barely nodding. One guard jumped out while the jeep was still in motion. Walking around to Jason's side, opening the door, he ordered them out of the truck, demanding their paperwork.

The guard inspected the papers, briefly, looking over the truck, and talking to the others. Finally, all the guards piled out of the jeep. The first guard went over with the papers, giving every other guard a chance to look and comment. That was how it worked in a country with a different opinion for each person. Eventually, two of the guards walked back to the truck and ordered Erdal to follow the jeep back to the local station for a full inspection.

Following behind the jeep, they could see two in the back seat facing them with machine guns pointed straight at the truck cab. They passed the two brothers who had pulled over on the highway, and who then followed them at a distance. Baba's boys had gone through this cat-and-mouse game before. They were prepared for anything.

Before long, Jason and Erdal found themselves in a local police station parking lot. In the lot were more revolutionary guard jeeps, several police cars, and a dozen men milling around outside the station, smoking and chatting in groups. One guard in the jeep told them to get out and stand in front of their truck. The driver of the jeep turned the vehicle around, pointing the headlights at the two standing men.

Once the lead jeep came to a full stop, all the guards piled out, this time with more conviction. They were showing off their astuteness, vigor, and love for the job. Several moved quickly to the back of Erdal's truck, trying to open the door. They tried several times before it dawned on them to ask for the keys. They shouted, demanding that it be unlocked. Erdal handed one guard the keys, pointing to the one for the lock. The remaining guards again demanded their paperwork and IDs, forgetting they had everything in the jeep. After some confusion, several guards went inside with the paperwork in hand.

Erdal desperately wanted a manual check and not a computer check. Everything was fake. Roadside stops were one thing, but station stops so near a large city were very different. Erdal knew his brothers were close. As at other times, the brothers waited close by with several grenades in hand. Two guys with guns would not be sufficient for an escape. However, a loud explosion was good enough to scare most of the local police away, while the four men killed the rest if need be. Sometimes the confusion and concussion grenades alone were sufficient. Finally, two guards got the truck's rear door open and climbed in. The others gathered around, each with an opinion as to what might be inside.

"I wonder what they're smuggling," one said, triggering a chorus of answers.

The two inside opened crates and moving boxes around, handing several to the men standing outside. They opened the boxes only to find tin cans with Turkish writing on them. They asked what it was, to which Erdal in fluent Farsi replied.

"I don't read their language, but I think it could be compote. Open one and see."

One guard took out his knife, struggling to open the can. The others laughed at his incompetence. Another guard showed up with a can-opener, grabbing another can from the box. He opened it, finding cherry compote. The guard opened several more and passed them around.

"Do you have any other flavors?" he asked, slurping straight from the can.

They moved more crates around, removing more boxes. They brought over a mirror on a long handle to look under the truck's body. Finally, they started clumsily reloading the boxes and at last re-locked the rear door. They handed the keys to Erdal, telling him and Jason to follow them to the office.

They walked into a smoke-filled room, lit by flickering fluorescent lights. A policeman or soldier filled nearly every seat. All were smoking and drinking tea. Jason and Erdal sat in whatever open seat they could find. A young boy quickly ran up to them offering tea and cookies. They politely accepted. The woman who sat behind the desk, covered with a tight scarf covering her head and shoulders, turned out to be the officer in charge. She was staring up at a monitor, rapidly typing information into online forms. Between every other keystroke, she stared at Erdal and Jason in disgust. Every time she turned to stare, the monitor glow exposed her thick eyebrows and mustache fuzz.

"I don't see any information for you. Where did you get your ID card?" She barked.

Jason pleaded, in his best *Esfahani* accent, "I applied and picked up my card in Esfahan, and I am up to date on all my paperwork."

"Well," she yelled over all the chitchat echoing in the room, "those Esfahanis may think they're funny and savvy businessmen, but they're lazy and useless with technology. They did not enter the data into the national database yet."

One of them probably screwed her over, Jason thought, with a smile.

She stood up and walked over to the copy machine, taking with her the ID cards. She took a photocopy for faxing to Esfahan for verification. The copy machine took a quick scan and shot out the photocopy. Jason and Erdal looked around at all the armed guards. They were all high on caffeine and bored out of their minds. Both men planned for an exit.

She grabbed the warm photocopy paper and walked to the fax machine, shaking her head at Jason. She typed in the phone number and fed the paper in. The number was busy. She put it on auto-dial and walked back to her desk. Fifteen minutes went by, and nothing. She checked the machine again and saw that the number was still busy.

"Those idiots are using the fax machine number to make phone calls," she snarled. Beads of sweat were pooling around her lips and eyebrows.

She tried to call them directly. That number too was busy.

"IDIOTS," she screamed, handing all the paperwork back to Erdal.

"Go on. Get out. Get lost, the two of you."

• • •

In no time, they were back on the road, laughing hysterically. Erdal was laughing the hardest, repeating the scene with the man trying to open the can, and the bitchy woman, her mustache, and the fax machine.

"IDIOTS," he laughed. "See, I told you, Uncle Jason, it's going to be a fun trip."

It was a narrow escape. She could have just as easily called the head office in Tehran and asked for verification. That call would have gotten an immediate response, an accurate response.

They drove for another two hours to their Tehran warehouse. Baba had purchased the whole building thirty years before and had kept it as a storage facility and safe house for his boys and himself. No one knew about this spot, apart from his family. They drove in through massive gates, happy to reunite with the other brothers. They both hopped out with Erdal still chuckling. He quickly told the others the story, giving his brothers a good laugh.

Jason went to the back of the truck, staring for a while, before asking what they actually brought into the country. The brothers opened the rear door and removed the boxes of compote. Erdal explained that no one measured the trucks and even if they did, they wouldn't have a clue what size or weight it should be, and what might be suspicious. He pointed out the difference between the inside panels and the outside panels. Once the brothers removed all the boxes, Erdal showed Jason the sophisticated, removable inner paneling and the hidden haul of cigarettes and whiskey.

"Getting people out is much more difficult, Uncle Jason, but we will be here and ready for you when you show up."

They gave him their local cell number, a satellite phone, and a ride to a location of his choosing. Jason had chosen that location, a square, where there'd been the most pings from Parvaresh's phone.

23 | THE HOTEL

Jason had been to Tehran on many occasions, both before and after the 1979 revolution. The city seemed to grow nonstop, mostly upwards. High-rise apartments were sprouting like weeds over the landscape, seemingly out of control. The citizenry was moving from smaller towns into the capital in search of work and a better life.

All around town, there were short-stay and longer-term hotels catering to the weary traveler or the new resident. No one questioned anyone. No one cared. Jason found a hotel near the main square and rented a room. All he had to show was his ID card, which was briefly looked at. He had to pay the weekly rate in advance, in cash. No one took credit cards. Even though they existed, they weren't trusted. Almost all businesses would scoff at a credit card. They gave you a look as though you were pulling a gun out and were about to rob them. Cash was and would always be king in Iran.

The hotel Jason chose was near the largest cluster of pings received by Mike's company websites, sent by someone, somehow. Whoever sent them knew about Bobby and his whereabouts. The largest cluster pointed to several ten-story apartment buildings. From this central point were a series of other smaller clusters. Jason scouted them all. Restaurants, a dry cleaner, a gas station, and a barbershop. The largest secondary cluster included a small restaurant open for all meals, in which sat about twenty people. This would be the best and easiest place to start. A great point to launch his search for the central source of the pings. *Golestan Kebab* restaurant was to be his new hangout.

He next had to find places from which to communicate with people outside Iran. He had his satellite phone but needed options for email. He knew the government monitored all internet traffic, focusing on internet cafes. He had to find open Wi-Fi connections nearby. He started War Walking, looking for open Wi-Fi connections using his phone in search mode. Within several blocks, he found a two-story carpet store and a grocery store, with great signal strength, right next to a small coffee and pastry shop. He had found his wireless messaging outlet. He walked back to the hotel to rest and prepare for the hunt. Hard days were ahead.

• • •

He was up late crafting three detailed encrypted emails for Henry, Baba, and Warren Spencer at Langley. The Langley letter included more details about the startup and information about his whereabouts in Iran. He detailed his plans, asking for help and local contact information. Henry's letter included updates and instructions for Mike to send all pings from the *Golestan Kebab* coordinates to Jason as they happened. The letter to Baba included a request for a favor.

The next morning and after a good night's rest, he started toward the coffee shop. Once there, he went onto the open Wi-Fi, found a Turkish Virtual Private Network to which he connected, logged into his email account and shot off the three emails. Finishing his coffee, he bought a local paper and walked to the restaurant for his first meal of the day.

The *Golestan Kebab* restaurant was almost full for breakfast. Although most of the pings had come from there at dinnertime, Jason wanted to establish a presence and memorize faces. He would eat every meal there until he identified the source. He sat at a corner table, read his paper, waiting for the waiter.

"Good morning. I haven't seen you before! What can I get you?" a waiter asked.

Jason ordered tea, bread, and cheese.

"Oh! You're from Esfahan! What are you doing here?" The prying waiter continued while taking the order.

The *Esfahani* accent was charming, typically associated with a sub-culture of great wit and humor, and with savvy business people possessing superb negotiating skills who negotiated everything. Others in Iran prided themselves for correctly identifying this accent as though they were the only people skilled in the art. They then followed by trying to be funny or making smart-ass remarks about the prices being fixed and non-negotiable. In truth, they were just nervous, afraid of a fleecing, or worse, becoming the butt of a joke.

Jason endured some traditional ribbing because he needed to befriend the waiter. An eavesdropping waiter can be the best source of information. Jason mentioned he was in Tehran looking for work. He gave the waiter a quick skills pitch and asked if any of the customers could help. Jason had his back-story prepared and was ready to spend time at this place, days perhaps if needed. Soon enough he had his breakfast, after which he chatted up the table next to him, studying all the faces.

On the way back to the hotel, he made one more stop at the coffee shop to check his emails. He ordered tea and some sweets. While sipping away at his drink, he downloaded several zip files, the newest updates of data. Finishing his tea, he bought a small bag of sweets and returned to the hotel. There, he unzipped the files and checked the time stamps on the most recent pings. On average, the source spent about forty minutes at meals. Two to four pings came during that time, usually starting around seven.

• • •

It took four days of three meals a day before he had identified two probable choices. On the fifth night, he asked one of these if he could recommend a dry cleaner. The man mentioned a local shop that had been in business for ten years, an informative answer, but not what Jason was looking for. While paying his bill, he asked the other possible source the same question and received a short but more detailed reply with the cleaner's address. That address was near another cluster of pings, making that man the better of two choices and the likely source. The next step was to follow the young man, see where he lived and where he worked, while still maintaining his presence at the restaurant, in case he was wrong about that choice.

Jason waited for the man to leave the restaurant and moments later began the tail. It took several blocks of following to figure out that the man was not lost and confused but skilled in street-craft. The way he walked, changing his gait at random, crossing the street and crossing back, all were telltale signs of training in counter-surveillance. He did it so naturally. Jason followed the man for twenty minutes but eventually got to his apartment building, one building in the main cluster of pings. Jason knew he had his man.

Finally, he could eat somewhere else, free of the humorless, annoying waiter. Jason was happy. He came so close to punching the waiter on numerous occasions. Being an *Esfahani* had its price.

• • •

Old school was the only way to go about watching his man. Jason had no support or equipment. He started by purchasing a motorcycle at a used cycle shop. He needed something small but fast in order to traverse the heavy traffic and it blended with the hundreds of other bikes and scooters always on the road.

After several days of following him, Jason had identified most of the man's stops, his home, his work address, and his hours. He took full advantage of those work hours to break into the apartment to do a full recon. He had to be careful. The apartment had triggers placed all around to leave traces of an intrusion. Fortunately, there were no alarm systems. An alarm in Iran was useless since no one would ever come to check, and most neighbors would cut the alarm wiring if it went off more than once or twice.

This man was nothing like the county clerk, Jason thought.

Jason found the man's name, Parvaresh, and as much as he could about his personal life. He was educated and very westernized, as shown by his taste in music, videos, food, and artwork. He also knew English and German and had a large collection of books in those languages on his bookshelves. He worked at a cultural center of some sort, about which Jason could find very little. He checked neighborhood guide shops and spoke to locals, but found nothing concrete. What little was uncovered were more rumors and stories about what might go on inside the building. The more Jason dug around the more convinced he was that the cultural center was the place he was looking for. What added to the mystery was that no pings ever emanated from within or near the building. Either they had a no phone policy, highly unlikely in a cultural center, or the building had frequency and radio wave dampening measures. Ending the uncertainty, Jason did a walkabout. The Center windows were double paned and gel filled to prevent laser listening devices, with signal masking devices attached to the base of each window. He had only seen those windows at high-end security buildings. This was no cultural center.

I've hit on somewhere important. These people clearly have secrets to hide and protect.

On his way back to the hotel, he stopped at the coffee shop for another email roundup. To his joy, he received contacts from which he might get help, people with more resources. He called one number provided and set up a breakfast meeting downtown.

• • •

Early the next day he got up for his routine jog, shave and shower. One of which he should not do and one he could not do, so instead he just showered. Having an ever-present beard, at any stage of growth, caused less suspicion for the revolutionary guards, and allowed for a more anonymous passage through the crowds. As for the jogging, nothing was more suspicious than exercising in public, a very Western trait. It might even look as if you were running away from something, forcing a takedown by a curious and bored crowd.

Clean and feeling fresh, he got on his bike and rode into downtown, well away from where he was staying. He wanted help but would not trust anyone. Langley had sent a good list of vetted Mossad agents, but they were not Americans, and Jason would not take chances with his godson's life.

Roads were busy as always. People drove with minimum regard for rules of the road. Each trip would guarantee at least a dozen small accidents resulting in a mini-revolution as crowds would gather to express their views, leading to arguments and a harmless scuffle. Red lights were mostly decorative. Lanes provided only a suggestion of where to be. The basic approach was to squeeze in or by if you could. Finally, please use your horn for everything, from hailing a friend to pointing out an infraction to flirting with someone. Or, as an accompaniment to cursing.

Jason pulled up to a café, parked his motorbike on the sidewalk, and chained it to a tree. He stepped in, not sure whom he would find. He sat at a table and ordered breakfast for two as directed by the man he'd called the day before. He started on his breakfast, waiting. Soon after, a stranger stood in front of him.

"May I sit here?"

"Of course, please sit." He said, gauging the man, noticing the slight bulge of a handgun in a shoulder holster. The man sat and asked if the untouched tea had sugar.

"No," Jason said.

"Good, I hate sugar."

The coded introduction was over.

The man enjoyed his cold tea and started on his breakfast. They both chatted about Tehran, weather, and traffic while finishing their breakfast.

"It's time to go," the man said. "Leave your bike. We'll take my car." They paid and stepped outside, waiting at the curb.

A car pulled up with two others inside, one driver and the other in the back. The man put Jason in the back seat and followed after. With Jason in the middle, they drove off. The other man placed a dark, dusty hood over Jason's head as they continued their drive. Jason counted in his mind, tallying left and right turns and any auditory clues he thought important. He memorized the entire trip.

• • •

The drive ended in an underground apartment garage. The men guided Jason up a staircase and into an apartment. Once inside they removed his hood, and he saw several other armed men, some communications equipment, and a small portable satellite antenna system. He heard them chatting in Farsi and Hebrew, intermixed with some Arabic words.

"Welcome to our home. My name is Gideon, and this is my crew." He introduced the men, offering a little about each team member's background and skill set. A small, fully capable attack group, Jason thought.

"So tell me, Jason Caius — yes, we know a little about you — what are you doing here?"

Jason told them as little as he could, focusing on his mission to save his godson. He told them about Mike's accumulated wealth and that the kidnapping was for ransom, that the parents were sick with worry and wanted

Jason to bring Bobby home alive. He needed to keep everything else hidden until he knew more about these people.

"What's your story?" Jason asked, in return.

Gideon too was cautious. The U.S. and Israel were staunch allies and shared a great deal of intelligence, yet remained very untrusting of each other. Not all the countries' belief systems and agenda were alike. Even though the U.S. Jewish lobby was powerful, the Christian right was more powerful and had never much liked Israel. Gideon described his group as residing inside Iran simply to collect intelligence, just typical Jews with Iranian heritage, trained in counter-espionage, who could live under cover for a long time. His group was responsible only for gathering information related to Iran's nuclear program, he said, and for finding more assets inside Iran.

The way these guys were equipped, the way they carried themselves, they were a far cry from being typical Jews. The way they had brought him here, along with dozens of other clues, hinted to more than just information gathering. Jason became even more cautious.

"So, how can we help?" Gideon asked.

"I'm interested in intelligence, for now, and am looking for hands-on people in case I need manpower," Jason replied.

Jason spent more time with Gideon's group, to continue his surveillance before committing to any more activities with this crowd. He had to find out more about them. They hooded Jason again and dropped him off back at his motorbike. Arrangements were made for further visits, at random places and times.

Back at his hotel, he wrote another email to Warren Spencer, asking for everything about Gideon.

• • •

Three days of meetings and exchanging inconsequential intelligence later, Jason had received a full dossier on Gideon. He met him alone; a meeting at which he hoped Gideon would come clean.

They met at a teahouse in the northern hills of Tehran, with outdoor seating, a respite from the heat and above the smog. Jason narrated what he now knew about Gideon's background. Amazed and angry, Gideon quizzed Jason how he got this information, which very few people knew. Gideon felt vulnerable and in the underdog position. Clearly, Jason was more in the loop, with high-level relationships. To ease the discomfort, Jason shared most of what he knew. He also added some new intelligence. He told most of what he had learned from the text messages and pings. He could see Gideon's relief and assumed that certain aspects of Jason's story were things that had eluded Gideon and his crew for years.

Gideon then followed with their complete story. His group's main objectives had been to interfere in Iran's nuclear program. To date, they had been responsible for eliminating nearly a dozen nuclear scientists. Most famously, they had delivered the Stuxnet virus to a nuclear power plant, setting Iran's centrifuge development efforts back years, they thought.

Unfortunately, as hard as Gideon's group tried, the Iranians were always ahead of the curve with access to technology and manufacturing processes. The group kept coming across organizations, companies, people, and resources outside the country that fed technology and money back into Iran's various programs. The U.S.-sponsored sanctions had done nothing to hold them back. He laid out detailed accounts of these points of interest, but could not find how and where they linked back to Iran.

"There is a group somewhere in Iran that is planning all of this shit, and we can't find them," Gideon said bitterly.

"I believe I have an answer for you, Gideon, at least one worth checking out if you're willing to help!"

Jason went deeper into the story, adding more details about the biologicals, the looming attack on U.S. soil, Parvaresh and the pinging locations, and finally The Cultural Center. He kept the center's exact location to himself, however. He needed to maintain some advantage.

"This definitely interconnects with what we believe to be an intelligence group within Iran dedicated to intellectual property," Gideon said. "This could be a key final point in our long search. Where is the place?"

"Hold on," Jason replied calmly. "I will tell you, but I need your help to get my godson out if he's in there. You can do whatever you want with the place after we get out. Do we have a deal?"

"Yes. I believe we can help," Gideon replied. "Let's work together to make this happen. It's a win-win."

To which Jason offered more details.

24 | RECOVERY

Bobby was feeling a little better though his ribs still ached with every breath. He finally got to the other man, two beds over, to meet and talk. The Center thugs had beaten the other man as well. Haltingly, they paced the room together, trying to get their strength back. The thugs had filmed his beating, with a warning to his wife. Neither Bobby nor the other man had any idea why any of this was happening.

The two shared their backgrounds and family details, without finding clear correlations. The only thing they had in common was the kidnapping from the airport and delivery to their jail cells. The man was most concerned about his daughter, his eyes tearing up with fear and sadness. Bobby kept reassuring him. His daughter would be fine. He really had no clue, but what else could he tell a father?

Parvaresh and the other man's minder alternated visits. Despite the beatings, they tried to make sure all was well, to continue with their relationship building. As much as Bobby hated these people, the visits brought him access to his laptop and a way by which he could message out. He could only hope that his plan was working as designed.

• • •

Later than usual one evening, Parvaresh dropped by with some Persian sweets and Bobby's laptop.

"Good evening, Bobby. I brought you both some dessert."

He laid out the sweets, taking some to the other bed. Dropping off Bobby's laptop, for a thirty-minute break, he left to make tea. Taking advantage and knowing the room was most probably bugged, Bobby whispered an innocent but critical question directed at the man.

"Just curious, but do you and your daughter have nicknames?"

"Why do you ask?" the man nervously responded, with half a cookie in his mouth.

"I'm putting it in my notes for my journal, quickly, please tell me!"

The man whispered back the names. Bobby quickly typed them into the computer. Saving the file, he launched his media player.

Parvaresh opened the door bringing in tea for everyone. "Here you go guys, some tea to go with your desserts."

They all sat around Bobby's laptop listening to tunes, enjoying Persian sweets and tea. They chatted about music, their favorites, laughing about some oldies but goodies.

"Time is up," Parvaresh said, exactly on schedule.

He placed the laptop in the bag, shouldering it as he stacked the plates and cups on a tray, and left for the evening.

"Seriously, why did you want the names?" the other man asked, once they were alone again.

"I may someday write about this ordeal and want the details." Bobby turned his head around and buried it in his pillow. He was in pain, but feeling stronger. The urge to escape conquered many discomforts. He could only hope that all new details were making their way out.

25 | CHAIR DELIVERY

Mike's company delivered the first set of redesigned chairs to a local San Francisco storage warehouse. The shipment came from Denver. From there, it would be forwarded to *Khartoum* and then to *Laqawa*, a small village in southern Sudan. In this village's town hall, the experimental delivery system would be tested and evaluated. *Laqawa* was a Muslim village with a severe distrust of anything foreign. All attempts to vaccinate the children against polio had failed because to the villagers it was another western-based trying to hurt the Muslim population. This was the story the company founders repeatedly told the Stanford graduate hire as a justification for building the delivery mechanism.

The startup crew picked up the chairs within the hour and took them to the warehouse in Palo Alto, where they relabeled all the crates and prepared the forwarding documents, for show, in case someone evaluated the paperwork, whether an insider or an outsider whilst in transport. The back-story had to match. Once inside, the crates were unloaded. Inside each crate were the parts for three blue stadium chairs made of hard plastic with folding arms and seats. Each seat bottom had a built-in lithium battery, charged by solar cells embedded in the armrest.

After assembling one seat and completing the wiring, the Stanford graduate excitedly ran to his work area and took a completed cylinder prototype to check the fittings. He brought it over to the chair, lifted the right armrest, and found the snap-in lid. He popped it out, inspecting the wires, the holding brackets, and the female vapor nozzle and micro-needle placement slots. He gently placed the brass cigar-sized cylinder into the holding bracket. They clicked into place perfectly. He connected the wires on the back and placed the airtight lid back on.

He began his tests, starting with connectivity. He went to his computer, clicking on some icons that started the application and diagnostics software. He sent a command. The blue LED lights on the top backrest turned on and then off. Good. That worked, now for the other tests. He had a neutral, pressurized green gas in the cylinder, ready to be tested. He sent another command. A small amount of gas gently floated up as per the command. Following that came the timed and other release tests. Next, the microneedle injection test. All were perfect. Great, he assembled and tested the other chairs, separately and together, controlling the chairs using an app on a cell phone. The chairs as tested were perfect for both usages, humanitarian and as tools of terror.

Both the founders were watching with excitement, tapping the young man on the back with great fervor and joy.

"Great job young man, you will be famous for this humanitarian work of yours," one commented as he started back to the office, to send some emails and to make phone calls. He had to pull the trigger, so to speak, for the manufacturing of all the remaining seats.

• • •

Henry and his people were keeping a close watch on the group, every person, every location. They had the successful test on their video feed. Henry kept an eye on all activities inside the startup while his men followed the startup employees. Emails to the FBI, including video clips, were assembled and ready. The prompt would be a call from Jason or a move by the startup. Henry wrote a special email for Jason insisting on haste and providing him an update on what they had witnessed. He wrote another email to update Gordon. He sent them both off and then called his wife to check on the home front.

Henry loved calling his wife with updates. To him, his wife was the big boss. He hated being away from her. He shared everything with her. This was a surprise to Amatis, still staying with Henry's family. Jason did not talk about work at all. Amitis was pleased to be getting the full scoop from Henry's wife.

Amitis and Henry's wife exchanged many timelines and stories about where and when the two men had worked together. Although Henry's wife was forthcoming, she knew to keep her mouth shut on certain aspects of what she had heard. But, she thought it only fair that Amitis should know a little more about the good that her husband had done despite the means used.

"Tell me, what's with the middle finger Henry waves around at Jason all the time?" Amitis asked with a smile.

"Oh, that. I keep telling him to stop. It's rude. But to Henry, it's like pulling teeth. When they first met, Henry would always salute those he didn't respect with the middle finger, especially Jason's type - educated, smart, uppity and with no battle experience. Now, though, it's just to get under his skin. He loves and respects Jason so much, like a brother."

"They're a funny pair, the two of them," Amitis said pouring wine into both their glasses.

They joked, laughed, and shared mores stories. Amitis was grateful to know more, but it added to her fears and worries.

26 | SECOND PING TEST

Having sent the sample chairs to California, Mike felt depressed and worried. He knew there was a plan, with disastrous outcomes, over which he had no control. He was exhausted from lack of sleep and felt dead to the world. Gordon visited daily, as both a distraction and a rock for the family, even though he too was worried about his son. They asked each other questions, actually, the same question asked both verbally and through facial expressions.

Is everything going to be okay?

On that evening, they were sitting in Mike's office playing backgammon, drinking red wine, their lit cigars balancing on a nearby ashtray. The room was quiet except for the sound of dice rolling across a handmade wooden backgammon set.

Mike had brought an original hand carved set from Iran decades ago. All the pieces were original, with the square dice smoothed at each corner from years of play, making each roll spin for a long time, adding to the charm. This made each game longer and disputes about which number it landed on the more colorful.

They were on their sixth game of the night when the computer beeped. Mike hurried over to his desk, moving the mouse to wake up the screen. It was a message on the secured email software. He had the app up and running every chance he got, hoping for news.

The email was from Henry.

"Come over here." He called Gordon over, to read the email with him. They both leaned in.

JASON IS WELL AND SAFE. HE THINKS HE'S FOUND BOBBY'S LOCATION. HE HAS FOUND HELP AND SUPPORT. AMITIS IS HERE AND DOING FINE. PLEASE TELL GORDON, I'M SENDING HIM ANOTHER EMAIL WITH MORE DETAILS.

They moved back to the game, not playing, just sitting, and staring at each other.

"So Gordon, you think he can get Bobby back? Is this going to end soon?"

"I don't know, Mike, but he's gotten close, and he's in good company." He got up to end the evening. "I need to go back home to see what the other email says and I'm tired."

He could not wait to get home, worried there might be bad news. He had to know.

He bid Mike good night and left.

• • •

Back at home, Gordon walked lightly past his wife sleeping on the couch. Giving her a quick kiss on the forehead, he went to his office. He booted up his special OS and logged into the secured email application. He opened Henry's email.

JASON IS IN TEHRAN. HE FOUND THE BUILDING WHERE HE THINKS BOBBY IS LOCATED. HE HAS SOME TURKS, OLD FRIENDS, TO HELP GET HIM IN AND OUT. HE HAS ALSO CONNECTED WITH SOME ISRAELIS TO HELP IN TEHRAN. JASON WILL CONTACT US WITH FINAL EXTRACTION PLANS, AT WHICH POINT YOU WILL HAVE TO TAKE CARE OF THE DENVER MINDER. I WILL SEND YOU THE TIMING, AS BEST AS I UNDERSTAND, AND LOCATION. I WILL SEND HELP. BE ON THE LOOKOUT. BE READY.

Gordon turned off his computer. Went back to the couch and gently lifted his wife up to take her to their room. He placed her softly on the bed and covered her. He then went to his safe, in the garage, taking out his old service revolver. He began a complete field strip, cleaning, and reassembly. He was not sure, if he was preparing to kill someone or if Henry's man would do the deed. In either case, he was getting ready.

• • •

Mike was busy at work the next morning after the long night of playing backgammon and worrying when the young networking manager responsible for tracking the pings came rushing through the door. She was excited, holding a cup of coffee and a stack of printed-paper.

"I have a bunch of pings, but a different message." She sat and laid the paper in front of Mike.

"Show me," Mike said, sitting straight in his chair.

"The numbers are still as before." She highlighted a line with the new data and handed the paper back to Mike. It read.

PINCHY;KHOOCHIKAM;MOUSHEE;35.7626;51.4190

Mike read it, immediately feeling excited and energized. He called Gordon and asked to meet him at the house as soon as he could. After several business calls, he left with the stack of printed pings in his briefcase and a new CD loaded with data.

• • •

Mike arrived home to find Gordon already waiting inside. He rushed in, grasping his wife's hand and pushing Gordon towards the office, nearly dragging his wife. He closed the doors, turned on the dampener, and announced, "He's alive. Our boy is alive!"

He slapped one sheet of paper from his briefcase on the desk, pointing at one word in a page full of lines.

"See. There it is. Look at it. It's him."

Gordon and his wife both looked. Gordon was confused. Mike's wife grabbed the paper and sank into the couch with a big smile on her face.

"Gordon," she said, "we used to call Bobby 'Pinchy' when he was a little boy. We haven't used that name for well over ten, no, fifteen, years."

"Wow, that boy is one smart cookie. We must send a message to Jason ASAP." Gordon smiled.

"It's already done," Mike interrupted, "Remember, we automated the whole process. Jason gets any new data stream as soon as we do. They're sent to his email account hourly."

27 | THE APARTMENT

Back at the safe house, Gideon was evaluating maps and notes from his crew's analysis of the Cultural Center and its surroundings. The maps detailed all entry and exit routes, local businesses with their work schedules, the nearest fire, and police department, the revolutionary guard stations, the nearest mosques, and the electric grid substation. Included in the report were the neighborhood phone junction boxes and much more. His men had found, marked, and identified anything and everything that could be a point of failure or of value during an urban assault. To be sure, Jason had done his own analysis separately. With all the notes on the table, they sat down to review their collective findings.

"Your guys are very thorough," Jason commented.

He kept reading, took more notes, and queried the crew on other entry point possibilities. Seated around the table, they discussed and argued points and counter-points.

"I wish we had an inside man," Gideon said, with a sense of urgency.

I know a guy, Jason thought.

Jason pondered for a while and eventually decided it would be best to share information about Parvaresh, even though it was giving up another advantage, possibly his last.

"I know an inside man that might be of use to us."

He described how he came to find him, from the pings and GPS coordinates to his home and name.

"So, you're saying that this guy is pinging his location to you guys every fifteen minutes?" Gideon said with a surprised laugh. "Who's the smart guy behind that?"

Jason had more news to share, having stopped by the café earlier to check on his emails, and to send other emails.

"It is definitely my godson, and he is alive." He showed them a line from the new ping package he had received that explained Bobby's nickname and the other nicknames that presumably belonged to the husband and daughter, and who he wanted to save.

Gideon stood up irritated. "Jason, we can't save everybody. We're there for any intelligence or data. You're responsible for the people. We'll help as much as we can, but you're on your own."

"I have it covered," Jason said. All he needed, he said, was support getting into the building, and then out again.

"Good," Gideon said, nodding in agreement. "Now tell me about the inside man."

Jason offered everything he knew and thought about Parvaresh, including his work schedule, details gleaned from his apartment, his likes, and hobbies. He and Gideon decided that Parvaresh would be the man to squeeze for details on floor plans, headcount, security, and anything else they needed. The upcoming Thursday would be the day to execute their plans. Thursday night, the beginning of the weekend was the laziest night of the week in Iran.

One of Gideon's men was assigned to shadow Parvaresh. With Thursday just around the corner, they continued intensely planning.

• • •

Thursday afternoon. Parvaresh dropped off his dry-cleaning and picked up a takeout order from his favorite kebab joint. He was on his way home to enjoy some rest, a hot meal, and maybe some satellite television to keep his language skills fresh. He drove into his underground garage, parked, and gathered his food and belongings for the elevator ride to his floor. Walking down his hallway, he could hear the radio in one apartment, a couple arguing in another and the neighbor child crying next to his apartment. Sounds were low and you could hear them only as you walked by the doors. He was happy to be at the end of the hall. He liked to listen to his music a bit loud.

Quickly scanning the doorjamb and frame, he placed his key in the door, unlocked it, and stepped inside. He placed his briefcase by the door. Walking into the kitchen, he put the takeout food on the counter. He wanted to change out of his work clothes for dinner. He walked to his room, to the closet, and opened the door to find a man in a gas mask standing in front of him. He froze, just briefly. Before he could make a move, a spray of knockout gas hit him. He fell to the ground after just one breath.

Gideon dragged Parvaresh to the kitchen and propped him up in a chair. Taking off his gas mask, he bound the unconscious man's hands and feet. He then opened the front door for the others who were by then waiting in the hall. Jason and another of Gideon's men walked in, closing the door behind them. Gideon's man placed a worn, well-used leather doctor's bag on the table, from which he pulled a necklace bomb and several other items. He placed the necklace around Parvaresh's neck, closing the clasp and moving the three combination dials randomly into a locked position. He then snapped open an ampule of smelling salts and stuck it under Parvaresh's nose. Parvaresh's eyes flew open. He was confused but alert. He took a deep breath. Tied to the chair, he calmly and quickly gauged his surroundings, measuring everyone, scanning for weapons, looking for solutions.

"Wake up!" Gideon yelled in Farsi, smacking the man's face.

"How are you feeling?" He grabbed the necklace, pulling it forward so the man could feel it.

"Should you get farther than five meters from us, this necklace bomb will go off. The explosion is small but large enough to take your head off. Now we have several questions."

Parvaresh took several minutes while he feigned gaining his composure. He was still analyzing. Moving his head and neck around, he felt an object tight around his neck. He turned his head to see his reflection in the window, to get a visual on whatever it was. As the intruder had said, it was a bomb. He recognized the design and origin.

"You are Israeli, yes?" he asked in Farsi. He asked again, in English.

Gideon replied in English.

"Just speak English. Don't bother with Farsi," Parvaresh continued in English.

"Either way, the questions are the same," Gideon responded.

"So what now? Are you going to torture me?" Parvaresh asked calmly.

"No. We're going to ask you some questions, and then we shall ask more, and maybe more after that. If you're truthful, we will leave you be. Let's start with where you work."

Parvaresh gave a long, earnest, well-rehearsed speech about his work at a cultural center. He gave tours to people around Tehran. His many foreign books were for learning about the tourists. He loved his job, and he loved interacting with foreigners.

"You are too calm, with a bomb around your neck, to be a tour guide," Gideon said, moving his chair closer.

Gideon stuck an ice pick into the man's thigh to let him know they wouldn't be patronized. Parvaresh, with his lips quivering, nearly screamed with pain, but bit down hard instead, keeping completely quiet.

"See, I knew you weren't a tour guide. A tour guide would have pissed his pants right about now." Gideon pulled out the ice pick. He asked him again, the same question. Parvaresh spewed out more details about his career, his favorite tours, tour locations, and his love of English.

"I would love to take you on a tour of the old Shah's palace someday," Parvaresh said with practiced sincerity.

Gideon dragged the chair with Parvaresh in it over against the wall. Removing a painting on the wall above the chair. He pulled a small, full IV from the doctor's bag and hung it on the nail that had held the painting. He rolled up Parvaresh's shirtsleeve and tapped on his forearm, looking for a vein. Finding one, he efficiently inserted the IV needle. He then stabbed him in the other thigh with the ice pick.

"That's for wasting my time. And, to raise your adrenaline so the meds could go through your body faster."

Gideon went to the kitchen for a drink, to allow the drugs to do their thing. He opened the fridge and found a nice cold beer. He sat at the dining room table telling Jason about this new experimental drug they've been using and how it worked. It created this warming sensation, feeling hotter and hotter as though acid was flowing through the body. It literally boils your blood inside your body. It will not kill you but can cause severe brain damage if too much is given or for too long. He nodded to a second IV on the table and identified it as the coolant, the only cure.

They were all staring at Parvaresh. He was sweating. His skin tone was changing to shades of pink and red. He kept biting down on his lips, clenching his fists, trying his best to endure the pain. He lasted almost ten minutes before begging to have it stopped. He answered the first question truthfully. Gideon stopped the IV flow and added the second IV as a coolant. Jason asked him several control questions, about Bobby, the other prisoners, and the biologicals.

"You are lying," Jason yelled.

Gideon switched the IV flows for five more minutes until the Iranian shook and begged for relief. The process started and stopped several more times until the truth poured out in sentences and paragraphs.

They asked questions about the building. Starting with the outside, with which they were already familiar, followed by detailed questions about which they knew little. Parvaresh seemed to cooperate. All control questions matched the answers. They would validate all other questions in short order. They spent over three hours with Parvaresh getting what they needed and learning about one major snag: The employee entry system required a swipe card in combination with a biometric iris scan.

"Well, we'll just gouge out both eyes and off we go," Gideon said with a grim smile.

"A dead eye won't work," Parvaresh groaned. "The scanner checks for unique patterns in a person's retina blood vessels and concurrent dilation."

So the assault team would have to drag him along alive. They quickly increased the coolant and added a saline solution to help dilute the chemicals, to make sure he did not die before opening The Center doors.

Gideon sent his man ahead to pass the intelligence to the others waiting at the site, to help complete the entry points. There would be three entering via the roof, as planned, and three others going in through the main employee door, in the parking lot behind the building, Parvaresh being one.

• • •

Within the hour, the group was prepped and ready for the assault.

28 | THE CENTER

Past midnight on Thursday, Jason, and Gideon cleaned Parvaresh up, preparing him for a drive to The Center. They tied his hands behind his back, then placed a roomy jacket over him and zipped it all the way up. They added a scarf and a ski hat. He looked wrapped and goofy but was ready to go. Jason left the apartment and walked the hall several times and checked the staircase. There was no activity. He waved down the hall to Gideon, signaling the move.

Gideon grabbed Parvaresh by the belt and walked down the hall. Parvaresh was still feeling the heat throughout every blood vessel. His thighs ached and bleeding from the ice pick. He needed help walking and leaned heavily on Gideon. Jason caught up with them, moving to the other side of Parvaresh, taking him by the arm to steady him. They ambled down two flights of stairs, to the garage. They got into Parvaresh's car, Jason with the Iranian in the back and Gideon behind the wheel. Gideon's men were already on site.

• • •

They went by the café for a quick email stop. Jason lifted his cell phone up towards the car window, moving left to right, searching for a strong Wi-Fi signal. He let several emails piggyback the Wi-Fi out of the country. On receiving verification, he tapped Gideon on the back, and they headed toward The Center. Jason read while Gideon drove.

They drove up to the gate of the employee parking lot. A license plate reader scanned the car. Gideon opened the window, sliding Parvaresh's magnetic card through the card reader. The heavy gate opened. The car went through, with one of Gideon's men following on foot, placing a small device on the gate hinges, then running to the car, holding up ten fingers. He then quickly ran out before the gate closed, to the waiting car.

"We have to hang on for ten minutes," Gideon whispered in Jason's direction.

• • •

Ten minutes later, at the local mosque several blocks away, there was a large explosion. The mosque was getting ready for Friday prayers. People were working to clean the place, laying out the carpets and preparing for the thousand of worshipers. The police, ambulances, and fire engines rolled in from all directions, converging on the mosque. Gideon and Jason kept a close eye on their building looking for any movement, an open door, an office light coming on or off, but there was nothing. They stepped out of the car, got Parvaresh on his feet and walked towards the employee entrance. At the door, Jason lifted the Iranian's arm near the RFID reader, with Gideon placing Parvaresh's face near the biometric reader. Parvaresh stared into the opening. First, there was a low-level red flash, followed by a retina scan, up and down and then side to side. Parvaresh blinked twice and moved his head back. The door opened.

• • •

At The Center's main guardroom, on level B2, the alarm jolted the guard on duty. He sat straight, scanning all the monitors. He quickly found the monitor covering the employee entrance where the alarm originated. The scanner had read the two winks as a coded message, one employee with two extra and unwanted visitors. The guard sounded the internal silent alarm. Guards, armed with automatic weapons, came quickly out of their dorm rooms and moved toward the main guard duty room to get their orders and place themselves in the best position for a counter move. On the security camera screens, they watched as Jason and Gideon slowly moved Parvaresh down the corridor in the direction of the staircase. Several of the guards ran out to ready themselves. Those who stayed behind kept watching for other intruders. They watched as Jason, Gideon, and Parvaresh walked past B1 and toward B2.

Having seen no others on any other monitor, the remaining men moved out to support the first group of guards.

• • •

Gideon's three other Mossad agents had chosen a roof entrance on the Center's blueprints and had accessed it using a zip line launched from a commercial building behind The Center. The roof entrance was tricky, but necessary since that they had to disable the satellite and microwave communications links. These were the last of the communication systems. Earlier, they had placed explosive devices inside the neighborhood telephone junction boxes. Communications could be cut in an instant should that be required. They bypassed the alarm system triggers on the roof door and made their way down to B2.

Jason and Gideon were near level B2.

• • •

The armed guards waited patiently for the B2 stairwell door to open. They were given second by second updates from the main control room. The guard was focused on just the one monitor and no other. Gideon was the first to step out, followed by Parvaresh and Jason behind him. Within seconds, lights blinded them from several directions, with the guards yelling in Farsi, ordering them to get down. Moments later, the ceiling lights went on and all was visible. Guards had surrounded them.

Meanwhile, the duty guard from the surveillance booth went back to watching the commotion at the mosque utilizing the outdoor cameras and so missed the other three Mossad agents coming down the stairs, closing in.

Two guards of the group around Gideon, Jason, and their hostage moved onto each man on the ground, zip tying their hands and legs. When reaching for Parvaresh they saw his tied hands, so they merely zipped his legs. Parvaresh yelled at the guards. He was a prisoner of these two Israelis. The last guard came out of the control room with a portable biometric reader. Rolling Parvaresh over, he scanned his iris, confirming his identity.

"Well, you are who you say you are," the ranking guard said, "but you'll still be tied. However, you may sit." Two guards lifted Parvaresh and moved him towards the guardroom.

Gideon started counting, looking at Jason. "One meter … two meters … three meters … four meters … five meters."

There was a sudden explosion around the corner. Half of Parvaresh's neck was missing. His jaw was hanging on his face by some strips of skin and muscle, blood was squirting everywhere. Suddenly the blood flow stopped, and he fell to the ground, dead. The guards escorting him were in shock, gawking at the nearly decapitated body, Parvaresh's blood splattered all over their faces. The other guards ran towards them. They were circling the body wondering what just happened, talking excitedly while the two cleaned their faces and cleared their eyes with their shirtsleeves. Everyone except Jason and Gideon was now far away from the stairwell.

At that moment, the stairwell door to level B2 quietly opened.

Once over their shock, the guards went back to collect the other two intruders, though they now moved cautiously. They walked back and around the corner, right into three men pointing guns at them. A quick barrage of silenced gunfire followed. All the guards were killed instantly.

One agent stayed behind to release Jason and Gideon as the others ran around the corner to be sure no other guards remained. In the control room, they killed three more guards. Checking the guard's dorm room they found more guards, they too were killed in a barrage of silenced gunfire.

Having cleared the room and general area, one of the assault team sat down to operate the security monitors, to keep an eye out for more guards and to monitor the premises.

Jason shot Paraveresh's arms off at the elbow carrying them around not knowing if both had RFID chips. Gideon did the same to one guard as he too needed the RFID chip for access throughout the premises.

With Jason and Gideon free, the plan was once again on track. Gideon took one of his men to B1, the data center. While Jason and another of Gideon's crew stayed on B2 to look for prisoners.

29 | PRISONERS

Jason walked the halls on B2, checking room after room, an automatic pistol at the ready. Looking for where Parvaresh had said the guests stayed. By the second door, he was only carrying one severed arm. He opened yet another door, revealing a new corridor to inspect. The lights automatically came on. He walked past an open room with lockers, a small kitchen, and a small circular table with chairs, obviously for staff. He went to the next room. Looking through its small window, he could see it was empty, as were the next two. The fourth room had a person in the bed. He waved the detached arm by the reader and unlocked the door. Opening the door slowly. Pointing his gun at the bed, he turned on the light. He saw a young a girl, sound asleep. Without waking her, he turned around, closed the door and moved to the other rooms. They were all empty.

At the end of the hall were bi-directional swinging doors. He pushed through them into what looked like a small hospital emergency facility. Surrounding the nurses' station was a series of rooms. He started on the right, checking each room. Someone was in the third room. He walked in and, under the dim night lights, counted six hospital beds. He turned on the overhead lights, again pointing his gun as he moved forward. He heard a young man grunting.

"It's too late for a visit, Mr. Parvaresh!" Bobby yelled, burying his head back into the pillow.

Jason immediately recognized the voice. He walked over to Bobby and whispered, "Hey Pinchy, wake up, it's time to go home."

Bobby rolled over groggily. Perhaps it was just another happy dream.

"Turn off the lights Mr. Parvaresh!" he said. Then suddenly and painfully, he sat up, looking around.

"Who said Pinchy?"

He found himself face to face with an unshaven, dusty looking man wearing local garb, and staring back at him.

"Uncle Jason!" He cried, reaching out.

"Ouch! My ribs!"

Jason wanted to hug Bobby for a long while, but time was short. Leaving Bobby, he walked over to another bed and asked the man lying there for his nickname.

"Why does everyone want to know my nickname?" the man said, followed by a softly whispered answer.

Ordering them both to get up, Jason explained what was happening, and what the next steps were. He pushed them to get dressed and put on shoes. He had found his people. It was time to get out, and quickly.

"Why are you holding a dead man's arm?" Bobby asked nervously as they started walking.

"I needed an extra hand," Jason responded with a smile.

30 | LEVEL B1

Jason took Bobby and the other prisoner down the hall to pick up the young girl while Gideon's man made one last check of the remaining rooms. Bobby was in the locker room looking for his belongings. The father and daughter also looked. They found all of their belongings in those lockers. Bobby grabbed his backpack and laptop.

"These are mine, bitches!" he said smiling.

They found the other carry-on and brought them out. It was too much. Jason told the father to pack as little as he could in the smallest bag. The father took some clothes for his daughter and her favorite doll. He left all the rest behind. He stuffed the items in his daughter's Mermaid Backpack and followed Jason. He needed to focus on carrying his daughter if need be, and no luggage. After a short visit at the surveillance booth, they left the floor, moving up to B1.

• • •

They walked up the stairwell to level B1, opening the door to what seemed like a scene out of a sci-fi movie, with sophisticated technology wall-to-wall. Gideon and his people were busy working. Gideon was placing explosives while another man was working on a computer.

"What are you guys doing? Let's blow the place and get out," Jason yelled towards Gideon.

"We have plenty of time. The floors above are practically empty of most workers, the guards are dead except for the ones on rotation above, and we're keeping an eye on them from the control room. Besides, we need to get as much intelligence as we can," Gideon shouted back from the other side of the floor.

Bobby, now fully awake, stood behind the man on the computer and watched for a couple of minutes. He could see that the man was clearly out of his league.

"Uncle Jason do we really have time?" Bobby asked.

"Yah, we have around fifteen to thirty minutes and perhaps a little more. Getting in and out of a secured building is the most dangerous. Once in, you can do all manner of shit," Jason replied.

"Ok, do you mind if I have a go at the systems?" Without waiting, Bobby walked around, passing all the data processing servers, looking for the data vaults.

He found an HP x510 data vault, and next to it two dozen more. He knew they must all be connected and knew it was easier getting in from the back door versus the front door. He picked the first one and connected his computer to it. He started typing, running scripts, staring at his laptop screen. Another 20 minutes went by, with everyone nervously waiting. The father and daughter were inside the conference room, looking through the glass wall, clinging to each other. Jason was standing near Bobby looking at his watch. The rest of Gideon's men were sending status reports via earpieces every ten minutes. Gideon planted all of his explosives and was now hovering over his guy at the terminal.

"What's the holdup?" he said nervously.

"This is all encrypted data, and massive. We can't take it and we can't send it anywhere!" Gideon's tech guy replied in frustration.

"What are *you* doing?" Gideon sarcastically asked Bobby, walking in his direction.

"This is all encrypted data, and massive. We can't take it and we can't send it anywhere!" Bobby repeated, with equal sarcasm.

"But," he said, "I've solved the problem." And closed his computer.

"Let's go, Uncle Jason. I'm done."

"We have our people and we're taking off," Jason told Gideon. He thanked him and told him he too should leave as quickly as he could.

"You guys take off. We have work to do before we leave. Be safe," Gideon replied.

Jason shoved Bobby towards the conference room, waving for the father and daughter to join them. They all walked towards the staircase. Bobby slung his backpack over his shoulder and gingerly picked up the little girl, smiling at the father, even though he was in severe pain from broken ribs.

"I'll carry her for a while. You can do the next shift."

The father kissed his daughter with an approving smile and they all followed Jason.

They quickly worked their way toward the employee entrance. Jason stepped out to look around. Smoke filled the sky from the still burning mosque. He looked around. Seeing no one, they all ran to the gate. Jason swiped Parvaresh's magnetic gate card to open the gate. Looking across the street, he saw the idling delivery truck. Erdal flashed a light three times. Jason looked around once more.

"Our ride is here." Grabbing and shoving, he moved the group to the idling truck.

"We have Bobby, plus two more," Jason said pointing to the father and the little girl while shoving them into the truck.

"What happened? Were they having a sale?" Erdal smiled as he shifted gears and drove off, with all five crammed into the front cab.

Within seconds, they were blocks away and well on their way to the warehouse. Unknown to them, a pizza delivery scooter followed close behind and a car with four men was behind that.

• • •

Gideon and his crew placed their explosives and were on the way out. The data breach was unsuccessful, so the next best thing was to destroy what they couldn't steal. When they reached the employee entrance and parking lot, they detonated the small explosives on the gate hinges, dropping the door with a massive crash. They then ran out of the parking lot and around the corner to their car.

They drove less than a block before stopping. They first blew all the communication systems, on and off premises, and then triggered all internal explosives. The building charges were powerful enough to bring the five thousand gallon external gas tank crashing into level B1, gushing flammables all over the data center floor, an unexpected side effect. Fully satisfied, Gideon tapped the driver on the shoulder and they peeled away.

A group was following Gideon and his group as well.

• • •

The explosives set inside the data warehouse was intended to destroy the computer systems only. They had not considered the possibility of weak flooring and the gasoline tank above. The subsequent gas explosion brought down a large part of the building and setting the rest on fire.

The original silent alarm had notified off premise guards to be at the ready. The internal Center guards were tasked with taking care of internal issues and should it be required to signal the outside agents for support, but no signal or request was sent. In lieu of any on-premise requests, the guards were to remain outside and to follow the intruders hoping to find their operational centers or hideouts.

No one was expecting this cascade of explosions and the near destruction of the entire Center. The Center had planned for mass attacks on one end of the scale and for small intrusions on the other end of the scale. But they had not imagined a small group combined with unknown structural flaws to result in such destruction.

Fortunately, it was the first night of the weekend. All admin staff were off. The senior staff and all minders were at their own homes. The only people on site were the analysts, on the graveyard shift, and the security forces, most of whom were killed in the first hour with the remainder who were on rotation in the upper floors, dying during the final building collapse and fire.

31 | THE CAPTURE

The explosions brought more fire trucks and emergency units to the neighborhood. It seemed to be a bad night all around. Fire engines, the police, and a cadre of Center agents arriving from their homes surrounded the burning building. Added to the mix were the revolutionary guards, the military, and hundreds of onlookers. Bystanders tried to help, reminiscent of days when Saddam would volley surface-to-surface missiles towards Tehran, during the long ten-year Iran-Iraq war. This time around, the military and revolution guards were busy keeping everyone away from the building, given its sensitive nature. They told the people it was a gas tank explosion. The heat and fire would allow no one to get close or go inside what was left of the building.

The only calm people in the group surrounding the burning building were The Center agents. They were fully prepared for such an event and knew exactly what the next steps were. They were angry but kept their cool. They did not expect such destruction, but they were prepared for this Black Swan event.

Their training kept them professional and on task. With their equipment and systems in ruin, The Center agents had to re-establish communications. They needed to contact all assets, both locally and those on assignment, to notify them of the attack and implement emergency protocols. Most protocol changes were triggered automatically when communications were broken. However, sometimes, a direct and immediate contact was necessary. The first step was to deploy all mobile command centers and to redeploy agents to those units.

• • •

Jason and the delivery truck were deep in the city's industrial zone, followed by three cars and a collection of motorcycles and delivery scooters, all with practiced street craft. Although the followers switched places, drove past, and turned off, they neglected to change their license plates. Jason was memorizing each plate as he saw them, and before long he had those all tagged in his mind.

"We're being followed." Jason had warned Erdal soon after leaving the neighborhood of The Center.

"How many? For how long?" Erdal asked, looking into his side mirrors.

"From the start, and they're too many for us to handle. I think they want to see where we end up."

Erdal made several turns and got back on a main stretch of road back to a different part of the industrial zone.

"I have a plan," he said, after calling his brothers.

"We're going to an abandoned store we own with a gated and locked driveway. We will park inside, close the gate, and quickly move to a tunnel that will take us to the opposite block. Man the tunnel entrance and slow them down just a little." Erdal handed Jason some keys, telling him which to use for the gate.

Within twenty minutes, they were at the abandoned storefront. Jason jumped out, unlocking and opening the gate, while the others got ready to get out of the truck. Erdal pulled in and parked. They all got out. Erdal took an AK-47 assault rifle out of the back of the truck and handed it to Jason, giving him some final instructions. They both closed and locked the gate.

Leaving Jason at the gate, Erdal directed the rest through a broken side door, and to a room with a tunnel entrance under a carpet. Once the trap door was open, he whistled to Jason, a signal that started a five-minute countdown. Jason kept a close eye on the road through the gate bars, seeing only two cars and a motorcycle visible in the distance. They were stopped, idling, and waiting. By the time five minutes were up, several more cars had arrived, with none moving any closer to the store.

Jason shored up the gate by backing up the truck against it. He then ran into the store. He placed the carpet over the tunnel door so that when it was closed it would be covered. Any slowdown was a good thing. He climbed down the ladder and into the tunnel. It was dark and musty, the air thick with dust, but solidly built. Whatever the tunnel's original purpose, Jason knew this was surely the last time Baba's family would ever use it. Jason ran down the tunnel, guiding himself by feeling the sidewalls. A good hundred yards away, the end of the tunnel became visible, lit by the opposite opening. As he got closer, he yelled, as instructed.

"Hello, Dolly! Hello, Dolly!" It was that or be shot by Erdal, who apparently loved Broadway musicals. Soon enough, he was at the far end.

"Welcome," Erdal greeted him as he pulled him out of a manhole at the end of a short dead-end side street. They were now on the opposite side, behind a long block of buildings. Erdal quickly replaced the cover and led them to a waiting car half a block away.

"I didn't hear any shots. Did they not try to come in?" Erdal asked.

"No, they were just waiting at the end of the road."

"Good. I suppose they wanted to gather their tactical group and assault the place properly. We have lots of time now." He smiled as they both jumped into the back of a waiting taxi, driven by Erdal's brother. The father and daughter were in the front seat, the other three were in the back.

"How many cars a day do you guys steal?" Jason joked.

"As many as we need," Erdal and his brother replied in unison.

The father whispered to his daughter that the men are not stealing but just borrowing, and will return the car later.

"So! Why 'Hello Dolly'?" Jason asked Erdal, as the taxi moved towards safety.

"Oh, no reason, I thought it would be funny to hear you yell that as you ran," Erdal replied with a big smile on his face, as his brother shook his head, laughing.

• • •

Halfway across town, Center agents surrounded Gideon's safe house. The assault teams were in place. They found the building manager and the building blueprints and the roster of tenants. They discussed the list with the manager, breaking down the possibilities into two apartments, 408 and 209. The assault team split into groups. The orders were to capture them alive.

Back at the abandoned store, that assault team too was ready to move in. All three places were on a synchronized, timed assault. Watches were studied. Thirty seconds left to go.

An hour had passed since both locations had been found and assault teams put in place, ready for the takedown. Fifteen seconds left. The store and two apartments were seconds away from a full assault, with concussion grenades and entry battering rams in hand. Three. Two. One.

• • •

A truck pulled the store gate off its hinges. A Center agent tossed concussion grenades through the already broken windows. Seconds later, seven fully masked and body-armored assault members rushed in, rifles up. The place was empty. They searched for back doors, windows, and all exits. Finding none, they began a more detailed search.

The doors to apartment 209 and 408 were battered open, concussion grenades tossed in, followed by similar teams rushing through the door. They cleared apartment 209 after a thirty-minute search and interrogation. The place housed three brothers, local men, who worked at nearby shops.

Apartment 408 turned out to be a gold mine. Gideon and his three colleagues were taken in, with one shot, but not fatally. The other two were just slightly injured. The assault team prepared them for a move to the Revolutionary Guard facilities in the heart of Tehran, while another group of agents remained behind to collect all the evidence left in the apartment.

• • •

Leaving the apartment, agents in several cars drove to the Revolutionary Guard headquarters with their prisoners, while Jason and the others, in the stolen taxicab, drove to safety.

32 | BREAKFAST

The atmosphere in the cramped taxi was thick with anticipation. Driving away from the abandoned store they were all thinking, *Will we get away? Are they going to catch us?* There was a nervous quiet among them. Everyone except Erdal and Jason looked down as if by doing so, invisibility would set in.

If I can't see them, maybe they can't see me, the little girl was thinking.

Jason took the satellite phone and made a call to his father. Several tries and many rings into the process, Gordon finally picked up the phone.

"Gordon here!"

"It's me!" Jason said, followed by short sentences, "I have him. He's healthy. Be very careful because we've kicked the hornet's nest. I'll call later."

Hanging up the phone, he asked the man with the daughter if he could make a call on his behalf. To which he received a nod and a phone number. Again, after multiple tries, he finally reached a voicemail. He quickly handed the phone to the father.

"It's voicemail, leave a quick message!"

The father grabbed the phone, hearing the end of his wife's message. He talked in a shaky voice.

"*Azizam* ... it's me ... us ... me and *Khoochikam*. We're safe for now. We've been rescued from the jail. I don't know what's going to happen, but we're going to get home somehow. Pray for us. I love you." Hanging up, he handed the phone back to Jason. He then hugged his girl who was nodding sleepily in his lap.

Soon Jason hoped they could all rest.

• • •

Safely back at the warehouse, early the next morning, in the room at the far end of the building they were sitting on several sofas sipping tea. In the distance, they could hear the call to prayer. From the couch, they could see trucks through the glass window, parked throughout the warehouse area. Some were empty, and some partially loaded. All had different company logos. All had mud and dirt at least half way up the side. The taxi with which they had arrived was gone. It was disposed of by one brother.

Erdal took out a country map, laying it out on the rickety table in the tearoom. He showed all the possible exit routes. "This is the main road, and the most traveled for us haulers." He reached for his tea, took a sip, and popped a cube of sugar into his mouth.

"We're safest at this crossing, although," he said pointing at a spot on the map. "Almost all trucks are checked and inspected. But they never check for long because there are hundreds of trucks that go through every day."

Filling his cup again, he came back to the table and pointed to another crossing.

"This one is rarely used by big trucks. It's right off of highway 16 and rarely checked, but when they check, they look over every inch, hoping for some bribery money. And, on the other side, in Turkey, the roads are filled with bandits, so this crossing is usually too much trouble."

He sat back down on the couch. "As you can see there are dozens of crossings into Iraq. So, you guys pick."

Jason asked Erdal for his car keys, telling him he needed to do some thinking before he could decide. He asked for the satellite phone again.

"Didn't I already give you a sat phone?" Erdal asked, handing Jason another.

"Yes, but I left it at Gideon's place."

Jason took the keys, the phone, and walked out.

• • •

By mid-morning, Jason was back in the coffee shop where he first met Gideon. It was not very busy since it was Friday, the beginning of the weekend. He wanted to work his way back to Gideon's place. He needed to know what had happened to them. He tried to remember the countdown from that spot, through every turn, to Gideon's apartment. He began his drive, focusing on sounds, and timing. Fifteen minutes later after several wrong turns and miscalculations, he was in the general neighborhood. He parked his car on a busy street and looked for buildings he recalled seeing from inside the apartment. He walked around the block several times and finally pinned down the building he believed to be the one where Gideon had taken him.

People followed Gideon as well, he was certain of that. He had to be careful. Center agents probably had peppered the surrounding area and building. He had to be sure of Gideon's predicament. He walked around the building and eventually found his way in through the underground garage. Listening to a couple of gossiping women in the basement laundry room, he learned that there had been major action in the building. Indeed, they arrested the residents of 408, by force, and one was injured.

As much as he could have used the equipment in the apartment, he left as stealthily as he had arrived.

• • •

Jason drove back toward the warehouse and along the way found a large, somewhat active shopping mall. Parking his car away from all others, he began a satellite call to his friend Warren Spencer at the agency. The call went through.

"Hello. This is Ames Electronics. How may I direct your call?"

"Good day. I'm checking on order number 275," Jason replied.

"Please hold."

Minutes went by, with several clicking sounds, and finally, Warren answered. "Good to hear from you. Where are you?"

"Good to hear your voice too. I have my package. I also picked up an extra pair. As a bonus, I've picked up a trove of incredible intelligence. Two packages will ship through Turkey, taking our spot. My package and I will go to *Piranshahr*, then across Iraq to the Erbil embassy. We'll need air support. Can you provide?"

"Yes. Do you have the intelligence on you?"

"No, we've moved it offshore," Jason said cautiously.

"Where?" Warren asked.

"We'll tell you when we see you," Jason replied. He knew his value was inextricably tied to the intelligence.

"Make sure you can provide quick air support. I'll contact you one last time before the crossing. Thanks." Jason hung up, knowing there will be support nearby. All he had to do was get across the border.

He got out and walked to the bakery at the edge of the mall to buy breakfast for everyone.

• • •

At the warehouse, Bobby was sitting on a couch next to the little girl. They were playing games on his laptop. The father was across the room staring lovingly at her, holding her small pink backpack. His tea was next to him, on the side table, untouched. He was afraid for her, for himself.

Erdal and his brother were loading trucks, packing the right pallets in the right order, leaving gaps for the special deliveries. Erdal was working on the truck designed for smuggling people. It was a refrigerated Mitsubishi Fuso FE160 truck, with a hidden and cooled two-man sitting or four-man standing compartment right behind the main cab, integrated into the storage area. There was an opening at the base, for bathroom breaks, and food and water storage for 5 days. He filled the water compartment, and then put dry bread, nuts, and dried fruits in the food compartment. Finally, he checked the hidden door hinges, the door lock, and did a little spray painting to cover some scratches on the floor and ceiling. The partition was ready.

Jason showed up just in time for breakfast with a bag full of fresh flat bread, pomegranate juice, cheese, and water soaked walnuts. He covered the table with the food. The little girl and Bobby were the first to jump to their feet. They were craving something other than tea. The rest stood back as the youngest in the crowd took their food first and then took turns helping themselves. Erdal's brothers took their food out and ate near the trucks.

"Bobby, wouldn't it be cool eating inside one of those trucks?" Jason said, nodding toward the little girl and then at one of the trucks. Bobby got the hint and asked the girl to go have breakfast with him. She happily got up and walked to one of the open trucks with him.

Jason moved the rest of the food over and laid the map back on the table.

"What do you think, Jason?" Erdal asked, with bread and cheese in hand.

"Well, we can't all fit in your truck for four days with the little girl. She will have to sit." He filled his cup with more juice. Freshly squeezed pomegranate juice was his favorite and something you did not get as easily in the U.S.

"So, the dad and girl will go with you in our place. Bobby and I will find our way out another way."

"Which way will you go?" Erdal asked.

"I don't know yet." He didn't want to share his plans just in case Erdal was caught.

"But I know what I need." He wrote down a shopping list.

After breakfast, Jason gave Erdal a list of items for his journey. Primary on his list was a car, with clean Iranian plates, a car that would stay clean for several days or more. He also needed an Iranian national ID card for Bobby. The ID card did not have to be perfect, just good enough to wave around if need be. There wasn't enough time to forge a good one. The checkpoints on the back roads they would take most likely would not validate the

ID online. Besides the major items, there were other necessities he needed.

Erdal took the list and, after reading it, told Jason that it would take several days for his list to be complete. His brother would help and stay until it was done. Erdal, on the other hand, would have to leave that night with the father and daughter.

Jason agreed.

• • •

Jason walked over to the father who was still holding the pink backpack and told him about the plans for his family, what he should expect, and where he would be going. The father felt more relieved as he saw an end to this painful trip.

33 | FAMILY THERAPY

The *Sepāh-e Pāsdārān-e Enqelāb-e Eslāmi*, or *Sepāh* for short, also referred to as the Revolutionary Guards, are a branch of Iran's military. Founded after the Iranian revolution and headquartered in Tehran, their main purpose is to protect the country's Islamic system, to prevent foreign interference and to stop internal upheavals. With roughly 125,000 military personnel spread around the country, their numbers include the feared *Quds Force*, their version of Special Forces.

They grew into a multibillion-dollar business, taking a more assertive role in virtually every aspect of Iranian society. They inflict, on the citizenry, the cruelest treatments ever rumored to exist, with most occurring at their headquarters, where *VAJA*, the Ministry of Intelligence, occupies several floors.

Gideon and his men were in a room known as the family therapy suite. The euphemism 'family therapy' ironically described one of the most successful methods of interrogation the Iranians had developed, a scientific and systematic form of group torture, used mainly for breaking teams of dedicated people who had trained together, worked together, or who were actually a family. The room was white, bright, and pleasant, with ten modern-looking gurneys. The gurneys were five feet apart and were all interconnected digitally. So, activities in one bed might affect activities or actions on another gurney.

All of Gideon's men were there, including the stitched and patched up member of the team. Each was on a gurney, with his arms, chest, and legs strapped tight to restrict movement. The interrogators had attached electrodes to each captor's inner thighs, upper arms, and neck. From under the gurney, a gooseneck microphone and high definition camera curved around and over the head, with the cameras focused on each face. Both were recording constantly, each sound, each micro expression, and each word.

With the prisoners prepared, a uniformed man walked in, ready to work them over. "Now gentlemen …" The first words directed at them since their arrest. "We are not a cruel people, and we leave your destiny entirely in your hands. Let me tell you about this room and how things work." He detailed the inner workings of the room.

Electrodes randomly pulsed electric currents, with the following rules. If everyone kept their head off their gurney headrest, the pulse remained at five milliamps, annoying but not painful. The first person who placed his head down would raise the current to 10 milliamps for everyone else while his current remained at five. Each additionally lowered head would increase the current by one milliamp for the others while bringing their own back down to five milliamps. If all heads were down at the same time, the current would go up to 10 milliamps for everyone. If someone talked and divulged valuable information, the others got a full break, while the speaker's current went down to five while he spoke. If two or more people spoke simultaneously, the current went up to 10 milliamps for everyone.

"Simple," the man said, grinning from ear to ear.

Actually, neither simple nor easy to remember, once you got a dose or two of the shock treatment.

The shock was relatively more severe as the amperage rose. At levels around 7.5 milliamps, breathing became labored and at times ceased completely. For currents above 10 milliamps, muscular contractions were so strong that the victim would freeze in place. This elaborate technique had been created to break the strong bonds.

"Finally, for your information," the man said, walking out of the room, "The record before someone spilled the beans is 17 hours. So, let's start!"

• • •

Back in the control room, the intelligence group was monitoring health, speech, and content. They recorded everything from words to microexpressions, which were further parsed by the computer, with correlative analytics applied on the fly. They had archived data stores for every interrogation, and news events, police reports, crime scene reports, autopsy reports, and any other related intelligence, all centralized for quick cross-referencing. They would compare, on the fly, a person's story to what the forensic science said, or what others had said. If a story or fact checked out, they would see relief. A lot of science, technology, and experience had gone into this approach, and it had proven to be much more effective than the old school methods.

The CIA had brought the talent for torture to modern Iran, for use by the Shah to crush radicalism and to put the fear of God into anyone who dared speak or act against the monarchy. The original and basic techniques consisted of electroshock, floggings, extreme physical injury, and depravities of all kinds. As it was later revealed, the Shah was nowhere near as brutal as the Islamic state.

In general, however, inflicting physical pain resulted in unsound results. The tortured fell into two categories, those who knew little and spoke quickly, and those who knew a great deal and spoke only after tremendous pain, who only gave up enough to get themselves to their deaths with some level of final comfort.

After years of practice, the intelligence group realized that physical torture, inflicted on one person, missed the mark. The missing element was group dynamics, group cohesion, and the bond that groups had between their members, a sense of comradeship that was worth more to some than to others. Not to mention the guilt people feel inflicting pain upon a friend or a loved one. It soon became a practice to avoid capturing just one person, but instead to wait to capture a group of people. Thus began the process of collective torture. It took several years to refine the process, to figure out the way guilt, love, and caring worked in a setting such as this. Questions such as whom to free from suffering for speaking, the speaker or others, had to be tested. Eventually, and through much practice, they had perfected the family therapy room.

• • •

At first, Gideon and his men were keen to keep their heads up. They easily suffered the low current and dealt with the annoyance of keeping their heads up. An hour into it, with bodies fully rigid and tightly attached to the gurney, their necks became stiff and hard to hold up. They took turns laying their heads down for a break. Each took a fifteen-second break every fifteen minutes or so, suffering the higher amps. Three hours into the ordeal, they took longer breaks more often, and out of turn. Their bodies felt the pain of both the amps and the muscle strain. The neck pain was moving down towards their shoulders and up through to the head. Contractions were occurring regularly, without the currents. Their bodies were feeling very weak. It was at that low point that the process actually worked. They felt guilty. The need to sacrifice for friends and weighed each down.

Who will go first? Gideon thought.

Seven hours into it, and well under the record, the wounded Mossad agent talked. His first round was 20 minutes of gibberish, useless data. No one felt any reduction in amperage. Mere chitchat would do nothing. They had to give up real intelligence that could be corroborated. The wounded man's second round started almost immediately and encompassed Jason and the rescue mission. He spilled all he knew about Jason. He figured telling them something other than their own missions for Mossad would be a safe start. For that, everyone got a thirty-minute breather.

After fourteen hours, Gideon told everything. His sense of duty toward his men, the pain they all endured, especially the wounded man, proved intolerable. He gave up details on over five missions, including the assassination of nuclear physicists and the sabotaging of nuclear power plants, and names of assets they had turned. He gave up times, dates, bullet calibers, explosive switch design, and much more, details that only they would know. Everything automatically crosschecked with the database. Gideon was being forthcoming. It was a great intelligence bounty for the Iranians.

They had finally caught a major and consequential group of terrorists who had been living among them for quite some time. Much work remained to look for the other named assets. Further, much work remained to change processes and techniques that Mossad now knew. As for Jason and crew, the revolutionary guards could not care less. However, the hovering Center agents relayed what they had found back to their superiors as quickly as they could. To the revolutionary guards, Jason's story was of a man trying to get his family out of prison. They knew little about The Center and its missions.

The revolutionary guards, the ministry of intelligence, and the Center, each had their distinct roles. This was just an overlap. However, to the Center, the hunt was now on for Jason and the escaped prisoners.

34 | THE FIRST LEG

Jason and Bobby would be stuck in the warehouse for several days waiting for Bobby's documents and a clean car. Though he was impatient to get going, Jason figured he and Bobby could use the time to get to know each other better. They could share stories about each other's family, life in Iran as a child, and more.

Meanwhile, Erdal's brother was at the airport, for the car, and later went to a local university, for a *Cart-eh-Meli*, for Bobby. The car was the simplest thing to get, but the national ID card was harder. ID cards for girls were easy. It was easy because all were essentially identical photos, taken with the headscarf on, making every girl look like every other girl. For the men, the pictures had to match more closely. Usually, they would have an ID made, but time was not on their side. They had to steal one, and the best place for that was a university where all students had to carry their cards every day. If one was lost, the owner would take several days to report it, because the odds were it had been left somewhere on campus, at a friend's, or god forbid at their girlfriend's. Just image a religious and pious father finding a man's ID in their daughter's bedroom. In an Islamic country that could be a death sentence for either or both kids.

Jason had his chores as well. He picked up the satellite phone, looking Bobby over for some measurements. He stepped out of the warehouse for a shopping spree. He drove past several malls, stopping at one with a multi-level outdoor parking structure. He parked on the roof, with a clear sky above, for a satellite call to Henry.

Henry answered, "What do you want?"

Jason could almost smell the Budweiser on Henry's breath.

"It's me, Jason."

"What the fuck, man. Where are you? I heard from your dad. Good to know you fucking guys made it. I already gave the good news to Gordon and your honey."

"We're alive Henry. We can't use our escape route and had to give it up for the father and daughter we rescued. We're going to get out through Iraq, through …." and before he could finish, Henry piped in.

"What the fuck are you going that way for? Just have Baba find another ride, through Turkey."

"Turkey will be well watched and they're going to be looking for a group of four. We just can't take a chance.

Besides, I've done this road trip from Iran to Iraq a bunch of times. I even have a great lunch place to eat along the way. Bobby will like it. I'm not calling about this. I need you to do something."

"What the fuck do you want this time? And what are you going to pay? Just kidding, man, what is it?"

"You need to tell the FBI about the startup location. Please time it just right. First, take the minders out, both of them, then have the FBI hit the startup. Can you do that for me?" Jason asked in all seriousness.

"I already have a guy with your dad in Denver. Do you want them clean? And when?" Henry asked eagerly.

"The one in Denver should be super clean. The one in Palo Alto blew up my house, so I leave that up to you. Given the damage we caused here, I'm thinking twenty-four hours from now, give or take a little, will be just right."

"I have my end covered. What about Copenhagen?" Henry asked.

"I'm calling Baba after this and asking him to get that loose end tied up for us. Wish us luck and hope to see you soon." On that note, he hung up and went into the shopping center for some clothing and other items.

Bobby needed to get into some Iranian style clothing to blend in better with his surroundings. Jason visited a men's clothier, a pharmacy, a cell store, and ended the shopping spree at a toy store. With shopping bags full, he went back to the car, calling Baba before he drove off the parking garage roof and back to the warehouse.

. . .

By late evening, everyone was back at the warehouse. Bobby was now looking as Iranian as anyone his age. The two teddy bears that Jason purchased became portable storage units, one with a satellite phone and car charger, and the other with a gun and extra ammo.

"Bobby, you're going to have to leave the laptop behind or give it to Erdal to take back with him to Germany. And, stop shaving for the rest of the trip. I need you scruffy. Oh, by the way, if your Farsi is not up to par, I'll have to wrap your head and jaw with bandages," he said pointing at the first aid kit he bought.

"I'll give my laptop to Erdal. He could bring it," Bobby said, placing it near Erdal's truck.

"And, as for my Farsi, check this out." He recited some *Hafez* poetry in a perfect accent.

Hafez was his father's favorite Persian poet. Raising Bobby, Mike had read poems to him in Farsi, discussing, parsing, and dissecting them.

"Yeah, my dad killed us with that poet," Bobby followed, smiling.

"Sure Bobby, that all sounds good at a party in Tehran. In the villages and outskirts, if you can't recite the Quran, you are toast. So give me some samples in that department." Jason demanded.

To that, Bobby recited several *Surahs* from the Quran, this time with a perfect Arabic accent, as if he had been praying daily for years.

"See, I was trained well for this trip!"

"Yes, but do you know what you're actually saying?" Jason asked sarcastically.

Erdal jumped in. "Do any of the peasants know what they're actually saying? I mean, really!"

"So true!" Jason and the little girl's father both said, laughing. The girl too laughed, for the first time. Seeing her father smile and laugh made her happy.

• • •

Erdal's truck was now ready for final loading. They went over the details with the father once more and then led him to the back compartment, past a series of pallets, tightly squeezing against the inner wall as they walked by.

"OK, here are the two seats, facing each other. This hole at the bottom can be opened like this, should you need to do your business. Here are your water and food compartments, enough for the whole trip and more, so eat when you're hungry," Erdal said. He ended by pointing out the airflow inlets and light switches.

"Let's get your girl in here and give you some time to adjust. We're leaving in thirty minutes."

The father and the girl had their fill of water. They used the restroom one last time. The father then carried his little girl to the truck and through the tight side passage into the hidden compartment. He placed her in the built-in seat and told her that they had to be there for the next two days after which she will be so much closer to mommy. He handed her the backpack and stepped out of the truck. He walked over to Jason and Bobby, giving them each a big hug, thanking them both for all they did. Bobby handed him his laptop.

"Take this with you. Maybe she can play games along the way."

The father carried the laptop back to the compartment, followed by Erdal who locked them in. They then shifted the crates, covering all the gaps. Several more crates were loaded in, and the outside back doors locked. The father and daughter had a tight two to three-day trip ahead of them.

Jason and Bobby were standing by the truck as Erdal and one of his brothers got in. They were outside the cab, by the window.

"Thank you so much for all your help, and we'll see you on the other side." Jason tapped on the door lightly as Erdal started the engine.

"It was my pleasure, Uncle Jason!" he said. "I hope you don't mind me calling you uncle? My father loves you like a brother." He winked and drove off.

"We'll see you on the other side!" he yelled, closing the truck window.

It was nearing eleven at night.

• • •

After their first real nights' sleep and well into the next morning, Jason and Bobby finally woke up to some commotion in the warehouse. Erdal's brother was back. His eyes bloodshot, his clothes wrinkled. He had slept in them, with lots of tossing and turning. His wrinkled shirt looked like a road map, with all highways, roads, and side streets well marked.

"Breakfast is ready. Everyone get up. Time to eat, otherwise I'm eating it all." Erdal's brother coughed the words out. He then set the food down and went to brew some tea.

Jason got up, washed his face, and changed his shirt. "Where have you been, my friend?"

"I was at a hookah bar, then a party, and then this dude's house till three in the morning. With a group of his university friends and my Johnny Walker bottles. They all finally fell asleep around two a.m., after which I picked his pocket and got the perfect ID card. I thought it would take at least another day or two to befriend them, but the liquor closed the deal."

"Great!" Bobby said, grabbing the ID card, "Sounds like you had fun."

"Fuck no. I hate smoking cheap tobacco and the guy was a dumb ass. But not all was lost," he said smiling, showing Bobby his new iPhone. "I found this lying around. It should pay for my time and whiskey."

He then tossed Jason a set of car keys. "And here is your car, straight from the airport parking lot."

Jason looked at the ID card. It was a damn good match for Bobby. He then went to inspect the car. He popped the hood, looking over the engine. He turned it on, inspecting it in more detail, checking the fluids and such. Closing the hood, he checked the tires, the spare and the undercarriage. He came back for more food and some tea.

"How does it drive?"

"It drives great. Pulls ever so slightly to the right, but has great pickup, great brakes, and the clutch and gearbox are smooth. I tried to get the newest common car I could find. You have to dirty it up a bit."

"The road we're taking will give it all the dust it needs." Jason sat back down, sipping his tea, reaching for more bread and cheese. He was famished.

Bobby washed up and joined him for breakfast. Erdal's brother passed out on the couch and never touched his breakfast. Jason pulled out the map and went over the route with Bobby.

"It looks like we won't get to bond like we thought. Now that we have everything, we have to get going. I'm sure we can chat on the drive," Jason told Bobby as he stared at the map.

"We need to get to *Piranshahr*, where we're spending the night. Then we'll cross the border into Iraq and work our way to Erbil. The first leg will take us about ten hours, and the second leg about four hours. By tomorrow evening, we'll be at the embassy in Erbil. And, the best part is this kebab joint half way there, in *Zanjan*, with the best food I've ever eaten."

"Then what?" Bobby asked.

"Then you'll order food and we'll eat, man!"

"Seriously, then what?"

"Then we'll get you home on a flight, and all will be good." Jason filled his teacup with more tea, hoping it would really be that easy.

After breakfast, they loaded the car with food for the road, the toys; a suitcase filled with their local garb and placed two full twenty-liter gas tanks in the trunk. They woke Erdal's brother up for a quick goodbye. He got up with his eyes bloodshot and his head throbbing, to wish them luck. He then walked over to the desk, took out an envelope and gave it to Jason.

"Baba-Jan asked me to give you this, some money for the road, to bribe or to buy your way around things." He then collapsed back onto the couch and was out for the count.

Jason and Bobby got in the car, said their goodbyes to the last brother who was working on a truck engine and started their drive, leaving Tehran for the border.

• • •

In the car, Jason divvied the money, giving some to Bobby, hiding some around the car, and placing the rest in different pockets. He had planned their route carefully, sticking to the busy main roads. The trip would take them toward Turkey on Highway 2 and, once in *Tabriz*, they would cut back over the mountains and down to *Piranshahr*.

"In another hour or so, Erdal and gang will be at the Turkish border. We'll call them and see how things are. You study the map for now." Jason handed the map to Bobby.

"I've marked all the stops, the main road, the secondary roads, and major landmarks. Memorize. Then tear it up and throw it out the window."

"On the way to Tabriz, we are merchants. You are my apprentice and we're going to *The Grand Bazaar* to purchase materials, cloth, and cotton inserts, to make teddy bears. On the way down from Tabriz, we just sold our teddy bears and we're going to visit relatives."

"Keep it simple. Less is better. And, if you don't know what to say, just point to me and say 'ask my boss.'"

"Don't *you* wish?" Bobby whispered with a smile as he began to study the map.

• • •

Slightly over an hour into the drive, Jason took out a cell phone and called Erdal. He wanted to know where things stood if all was well and if he had to make any drastic changes in his plans.

"*Salam!*" Erdal answered on the first ring.

"*Salam Alaykum, Erdal Khan, khoobie?*" Jason replied, suffering a long pause as he listened to the conversation in the background.

"OK …" Erdal finally got back.

"The customs guy was collecting our paperwork. He was standing at my window when you called."

"How are things with you and the crates?" Jason asked.

"The crates are all good. We checked on them two hours ago, and nothing had shifted or broken. We're twentieth in line for inspection. They're definitely looking hard this time around."

"Will you be OK?"

"Not too worried," Erdal said.

"The Turks don't care about people coming through because they know everyone moves on to Europe. So all they look for is drugs, using dogs, and we're clear on that note."

"As for the Iranians," he continued, "They're only worried about people and don't care about drugs leaving the country. All they look for is people, the driver, all passengers, and anyone who might be hiding in nooks and crannies, but they are way too lazy about moving heavy crates around."

"I'm more worried about you," Erdal said. "Have you seen the daily *Kayhan* newspaper?"

"No," Jason said, "We were on the road early this morning."

"On the first page, there is an article about three men, two pictured and one described, having kidnapped a little girl. The girl is the niece of an unnamed local *Mullah*. It is a very sad story! You should read it."

"So, they're looking for the girl and three guys. That would be you guys." Jason joked.

"Shit! You're right. I didn't think about the numbers, just the picture of the two guys!" Erdal suddenly became worried.

"Thanks for the heads up. Call me when you get through."

"I'll call in a couple of hours. If I don't call you, call Baba!" Erdal nervously finished and hung up.

• • •

"How are they?" Bobby asked.

"Good. But, I have bad news." Jason said, thinking of everyone's predicament.

"What bad news?"

"You're all over the news. Apparently, you and some other dudes kidnapped some cleric's daughter."

"What the fuck?" Bobby said sitting straight in his chair.

Jason retold the news story he had heard from Erdal. He then educated Bobby on facial recognition and the psychology associated with recognizing people. Mistaken identity was so common, with the main reason being poor encoding at the time of initial observation. That's the first time someone sees you or your picture, as compared to seeing you the next time. And mistakes are inevitable when comparing two people, mostly because the circumstances for comparison were different; low lights, far away, different hair, and dozens of other reasons. Finally, human nature causes faulty memory all the time. He ended with one basic rule.

"When people think they've seen you or recognized you, the only definitive and final confirmation is the way you react to their gaze. So, stare back at them as though you've never seen them and are happy to meet them for the first time. Never look away, look shy, or look nervous."

• • •

Nearing the outskirts of *Zanjan*, Jason sat straight, pointing at a road sign. "Good, finally we're getting near one of my favorite eateries. I'm starving."

Jason came by this restaurant on one of his visits, years back. Acting the tourist, he was to meet an asset at the *Laundry House Museum*, for a tour package, which included lunch. The lunch was a short walk away from the museum where he ate the best food he had ever had at a restaurant in Iran. A man, his wife, and four children ran the restaurant, a family affair all around. The food was fresh, made with love, as though they were feeding family and friends at a wedding. The ingredients were of the best quality, for a public restaurant. Jason took the *Zanjan – Bijar* exit and drove into town.

"Bobby, tear the map and toss it out the window now. It's time to go local, all the way. Are you ready?"

Bobby tore the map up into stamp size pieces, opened the window looking for a clearing, and then tossed the confetti out the window.

"I'm ready!"

Jason, working from memory, took a wrong turn, then two or three more, but found his way to the restaurant. Parking right across from the restaurant, they got out, stretched a bit, and then entered. They found a table near the window. The tables were clean and empty. As they sat, a waiter loaded the table with water, bread, greens, raw onions, and an assortment of fresh *torshi*, Persian relish. There were no menus.

"*Salam, Khosh Amadeen.*" The waiter welcomed them, giving them a rundown of the days' offerings, and asked for their order.

Jason responded in kind, ordering several starters, two main meals, and two carbonated *dooghs*, a popular yogurt-based drink. He sat back, casually taking stock of his surroundings. The place was as busy as it was last time, with families and young couples occupying most of the tables, and solitary elderly men filling the remaining tables. The place was thick with the aroma of great Persian food, intermixed with that odd cigarette or two that people still smoked at the table.

Jason eyed a man sitting several tables away reading the *Kayhan* newspaper. He did not want to ask for it but tried to peek at the article below the fold with pictures of the kidnappers. Noticing his gaze, the man politely offered to give him the paper once he was done. Jason tapped his chest in a gesture of thanks, and started on his bread and greens, waiting for the main dishes.

Bobby and Jason were both ravenous. Looking down at their plates, they ate their starters and the appetizers, never looking up. They were making small talk and Bobby was practicing his Farsi. Unexpectedly, a man tapped Bobby on the back, handing him the paper, with his picture facing up. Nearly choking on his food, Bobby stood up, looking the man straight in the eyes, and took the paper, thanking him.

"Please sit," the man said, pushing Bobby back down, "Are you folks from around here?"

"No," Jason said, "My apprentice and I are on our way to Tabriz to buy merchandise. We always eat here on our way up and down. What about you?"

"I work at the museum down the street. Have you ever been?" he asked warmly.

"Oh, yes, several times. It is quite interesting, and beautiful inside. Would you like to sit?" Jason stood up as he offered the man a chair.

Bobby's eyes widened, looking stunned. He stared at Jason as if that was the dumbest question he'd ever heard. The man politely refused, wished them luck on the journey, and left the restaurant. Bobby looked at Jason, with that ever so popular millennial WTF look. To which Jason whispered.

"You must make *tarof*. Didn't your mom and dad teach you anything?"

In the Persian culture, it was customary to make *tarof*, the art of offering something even if you didn't mean it, and to do so at every turn in your daily routine. The polite response was to refuse, at the start. Then, the game began. One hoped the other did not accept, and the other hoped the first did not stop offering. It was a dying custom, but still very prevalent among the elderly. If done poorly, or not at all, it marked you as rude or culturally unaware, none of which would be helpful.

Bobby was slowly reading the paper. Jason did not care about the story which was a fabrication, but he was very interested in the pictures. They were sharp, clear, and recent. It was definitely a picture of Bobby. He grabbed the paper from Bobby, turned the photographs face down, and waited for his lunch. The meal arrived within minutes. They ate fast. They talked briefly. They finished the meal with a cup of tea. Paying, they took the paper and left.

Back on the road and quite full, they both felt sleepy. A few minutes into the drive, while staring at the beautiful scenery, Bobby passed out into a deep slumber. Time slowed to a crawl. Jason's mind was full of misgivings and worry, the only thing keeping him awake. The sun was warming up the car nicely as they reached cooler weather in the mountains.

• • •

Erdal was now number one in line. They directed him into slot #44 and ordered him to open the rear doors. The customs area was crowded with bearded, armed guards. A forklift moved behind the truck. A man jumped in the back, comparing inventory to the manifest. He marked a bunch of pallets with red chalk and then jumped out. He ordered Erdal to remove all the marked pallets. Erdal complained, just enough, about the inconvenience, the timing, the delays, and moved into his salary, his wife, and his kids. He then topped it off with how this delay would make everything worse. He couldn't complain too much, but just enough to show dismay. They yelled at him and barked the orders again.

Having removed the pallets, Erdal stood by as two men jumped back in the truck and looked at his inventory sheet, asking questions about the contents of various pallets. They opened one pallet, with a crowbar, then another, and then a third. All seemed to be as written in the manifest. One man jumped back out, looking over the offloaded pallets. While the other stayed behind staring at the back of the truck as though something was amiss. Erdal didn't want to interrupt as that may cause suspicion, so he caused a bit of commotion with the man inspecting the pallets on the ground.

"Are you now going to open these too? They're in the sun. Let me at least put them back on the truck, and then you can open them," raising his voice with every sentence.

The first man jumped out. "No need to yell. We're just doing our job. Now, stand by your truck and be quiet."

The customs officer then walked in front of Erdal and his brother, staring at their faces as he looked at some photos on a clipboard. Satisfied, he barked his final orders.

"Load it up and get the hell out of here!"

Erdal quickly loaded the pallets. The Iranian side was completed and his paperwork stamped. Now to the Turkish side. He drove through to the Turkish side. They quickly weighed the truck, inspected the paperwork, and directed them to one of twelve lanes. This time around, Erdal was number seven in line. Fortunately, his paperwork was marked with the Open Inspection and Open Crate stamps, which made the Turkish side a little faster. In no time he pulled into his stall, driving over an in-ground walkway used to carry out undercarriage inspections in search of Afghan heroin.

• • •

Afghanistan was responsible for nearly 87% of global heroin production. The region between Afghanistan, Pakistan, through Iran, to Turkey, known as the Golden Crescent, was where a very large portion of that heroin traveled. Nearly the entire supply of heroin in Europe got there by way of Turkey.

There were several men with bright lights looking for hidden compartments, places where heroin and opium could be stored, tapping truck parts as they moved. Meanwhile, with the truck doors open, a drug-sniffing dog and handler jumped into the back. Erdal's brother remained in the cab with his radio on to mask any noises that might emanate from the secret compartment. The dog jumped onto the pallets, smelling many odors but none that triggered any alarms. There was no barking and no alerts from the dog. The handler jumped back out followed by his dog. The underground crew signaled OK, by turning on their green light. Everything had passed the tests and Erdal was given the go ahead. He got several more stamps on his paperwork. Leaving the border area, they began the drive to *Ankara.*

• • •

Twenty minutes away, Erdal made a call. Jason and Bobby were jolted straight when the phone rang. Bobby woke up so suddenly, he hit his head on the side window, slurping a bit of drool from the edge of his mouth.

"*Salam!*" Jason picked up.

"Can you speak?" Erdal asked in Farsi.

"Yes," Jason responded in English.

"We made it through both sides. We're good, safe, and unharmed. We'll be dropping off our cargo in two days. I'm going to call Baba with the update. How are you?"

"We're on the upside of our mountain trip. We'll be there late afternoon, hopefully," Jason replied happily, repeating the news to Bobby.

"OK then, be safe, and be careful Uncle, and may God be with you. Keep us posted." Erdal hung up.

• • •

Bobby was happy for the girl and her father, but looking around he recognized nothing.

"Where are we?" he asked.

Jason told him he had slept for nearly two hours, and that they were over an hour away from *Tabriz*, after which they were going to drive down towards the Iraq border. Bobby was glad to have napped. His ribs were hurting from overeating and from his beating at the Center, but the nap helped relieve some pressure. "I never knew Persian food could hurt so much!"

"Wait till it comes out!" Jason said as they both laughed away some of their worries.

"Ouch! Please don't make me laugh," Bobby begged.

35 | TAKE OUT

Henry had already prepared a detailed email, specially created for the FBI's San Francisco regional offices. It contained all the pertinent information regarding the startup. Before sending it, he had to confirm the exact name and number of the person responsible. An expedited email was necessary. The normal channels would be too slow. Henry contacted Warren Spencer, who was now well on his way to Iraq. He called to confirm the FBI contact information and timing. He got the information and the go-ahead.

With the direct number in hand, Henry called the FBI offices. "This is Special Agent Gonzales. Who is speaking?"

"I'm calling on behalf of Jason Caius," Henry replied, in his most polite tone and with proper vocabulary. Controlling his expletives was torture for him. It made him speak slower, sounding a little stunted, a little retarded, as his friends would say.

"How did you get this number?" Agent Gonzales demanded angrily. As if getting personal information, in the digital age, was a difficult task. Any teenager with half a brain can search for or buy someone's phone number on the internet. Spencer just saved Henry time and trouble.

You FBI are so fucking stupid. I found it on a toilet wall, with … 'for a good blowjob call …' Henry so desperately wanted to say.

"I was given this number by Deputy Director Warren Spencer and told to call with the address of a warehouse holding weapons-grade biologicals, a warehouse about which you were informed," Henry calmly forced the words out.

The pain, the suffering one must endure while speaking without expletives. He thought.

"I don't know what you're talking about. Why don't you come to our offices, and we can chat about this Jason Caius and warehouse situation," Gonzales added.

Henry lost it.

"Listen, fuck face, I don't have time for your fucking bullshit and fucking games. You know what the fuck I'm talking about, so pay attention. We've confirmed the warehouse has biohazards. And, we've confirmed they're working on a dispersal system, also at the warehouse. Be ready to take it down. I'll call you on your cell within the next 12 hours with the exact address. Got it?"

"Got it! Can I have your cell …?"

Henry hung up.

• • •

Gordon had been checking encrypted emails at Mike's house on a daily basis. If not himself, he had Mike check first thing in the morning and the last thing at night. Finally, there was an email from Baba. It simply read:

JASON AND BOBBY NEAR THE IRAQ BORDER. FATHER AND DAUGHTER IN TURKEY. SAFE. WILL KEEP YOU POSTED.

That same day, Henry got a call from Baba on his cell phone. They too knew each other well. Baba could not stand Henry's crassness, yet he had the utmost respect for his friendship with Jason. They exchanged and discussed their plans, giving each other quick updates on everyone's whereabouts.

Henry, Baba, and Henry's man in Denver were all on the same page. The plans were in place to eliminate the minders.

• • •

On a sunny day in Palo Alto, Silicon Valley was buzzing with excitement, as another group of kids became paper millionaires. Each happy having made money by selling yet another useless, cloud-based service, another dating app, photo sharing app, another candy crush wannabe app, or a massive multiplayer app where a button pushed thousands of times over many months killed zombies and vampires.

The minder was sitting in his master bedroom checking his emails. The automatic coffee maker ground coffee and then dripped water into the fresh coffee grounds, making for an aromatic morning. A nice dark French roast with a hint of hazelnut was inviting him to come downstairs.

He jumped in the shower, a seven-headed affair, three outlets each on opposite walls and one on the ceiling, all pushing out even streams of water. This much water was a luxury during the California drought, but one he felt he deserved. He was only a couple of minutes into his shower when the house alarm blared loudly. He jumped out, quickly wrapping himself in a towel. Walking to the side table by his bed, he took out his fully loaded Glock pistol. He looked at the alarm pad above his bed. The zone 5 light blinked brightly. That was the side door, downstairs, in the kitchen. The phone rang. It was Bay Alarm calling for an identity check. The minder gave the operator the password and after a quick chat hung up. He put on his robe and went downstairs with his handgun in the ready position.

He began his search.

• • •

The Denver minder was in the underground parking structure at Mike's company, having followed Mike that morning as part of his daily routine. It was late in the morning. He checked his messages and email, still waiting for his daily status confirmation. None had been forwarded, a bit unusual, but not alarming. Three or four-day communication delays from Iran happened, occasionally. He didn't give it much thought.

He stepped out of his warm car, to get himself a fresh cup of coffee. Mike's office cafeteria served coffee better than what Starbucks offered. He liked this job, surrounded by rich and educated people, with an easy target to watch, in a nice area of town. He had become accustomed to the lifestyle. The cafeteria was just a short walk away. Food would be a welcome addition to his coffee. So, food and coffee it was.

• • •

It was nighttime in Copenhagen. Baba's fourth son, Aslan, and a cousin were sitting in their car, watching a car parked across from Yasmin Akbari's house. The Copenhagen minder was in it, engine running, sipping something from a small silver flask, rum perhaps. They had been following him for several days and were comfortable with his routine. The minder didn't think Yasmin was much of a threat and acted accordingly. Once her lights were out, he would take off for his home.

From a distance, they saw Yasmin's kitchen lights go out. Before the minder could drive off, they drove towards his neighborhood, parking several houses away from where he would arrive. The cousin got out; along with a dog, she had borrowed from a yard nearby, down the street a few days before, a small Dachshund. The dog was old, quiet, and a bit shaky, perfect for the job. The cousin stood near a tree, leaning in, waiting for the minder to arrive. The minder finally arrived. She began her walk toward his house.

As he was getting out, she was nearing the front of his driveway, slowly following the dog with her fist in a plastic bag, getting ready to pick up after her old pet. She stopped in the middle of the driveway looking away from the minder and his house. She was a beautifully formed woman in her twenties, with long black hair, perfect skin, and dark blue glimmering eyes. She looked gorgeous under the street lamp. Walking towards his house, he stopped midway to look at her.

"This is the third night in a row I've seen you and your dog. It must be karma," he said, looking down the driveway.

She didn't understand a word of what he said, but she didn't need to. She knew the influence she had on men. She looked back ever so slightly, smiling at him. She turned away and re-focused on the dog. He walked down to the bottom of the driveway.

"Are you new to the neighborhood?" the minder asked.

"*Ja!*" she said in Danish, again looking at the dog.

The minder moved around, facing her, asking her name.

"*Mit navn er Adrianna!*" she said, hoping it was the last question he would ask. That was all the Danish she knew.

Finally, the dog did his business. She smiled and lifted the blue poop bag covering her fist. She moved forward towards the dog who was standing between her and the minder. He was looking down at the dog, not looking at her. She lifted her hand farther. Two silenced .22 caliber bullets popped through the plastic bag, into the minder's forehead. He dropped where he stood. There were no exit wounds. The bullets just ricocheted inside the skull until they stopped, making mush of the brain.

Aslan quickly drove to the base of the driveway. The girl let the dog loose, hopeful it would find its way home. They loaded the body into the car. They both got in and drove around the block to wait, listening for sirens. There were no sirens, which meant no calls and no witnesses. After a safe interval, they drove back to the house, parked across the street, opened the trunk, and went through the dead man's jacket pockets for his house keys. Aslan walked to the house carrying a small backpack. At the door, he knocked, waiting. No one answered. He unlocked the door and walked in. He found a laptop and a desktop in the office. He took an electric magnet out, plugged it in, and zapped the hard drives on both devices. He looked through the desk, finding a folder with pictures of Yasmin along with related documents. He grabbed those, all the flash drives and CDs, shoving them all into his backpack. He did another quick search around the house but found nothing. Stepping out of the house, he left the door open, walking back to the car.

They began their drive to the train station. Driving over a bridge, they tossed the gun, house keys, and the minder's cell phone into the river. Dropping off the stolen car at a long-term parking lot, they inconspicuously dropped the minder's wallet in a homeless man's lap and caught a train back to Hamburg. Soon after, Baba got a text message.

We dropped off the package!

Baba called Erdal to give him the news. Erdal then passed the phone through a sliding hatch behind the headrest to the father in the secret compartment.

"You can call your wife now. She too is safe," he shouted back.

. . .

As the minder had learned, Mike's construction company had one of the best food services around. The offices were far from downtown restaurants, and the nearest diner was over five miles away, so they had to have good food to keep the employees happy and close to their work. A professional chef and her staff created the menu, with a forty-five-day rotating plan. Their breakfasts were superb, the tea and coffee selection fantastic.

The minder ordered his coffee, large and black with a hint of caramel syrup. He then ordered an egg sandwich to go. Two eggs fried, on a French roll with crushed pepper. He paid and then stood to the side waiting for his order. Looking over the free newspapers, stacked ten high, he took one. In the kitchen, his meal was prepared. They poured his coffee and loaded his takeout box. Henry's man too was in the kitchen keeping watch.

"Order #27 is ready," a young woman called out as she looked around for a taker. The minder walked over, still reading the paper, and took the box, barely looking up.

"Thanks," he said, turning and walking away, carrying his food on top of his newspaper.

Using an underground tunnel, he took a minute to stroll back to his car. With practiced diligence, he looked around as he walked, eyeing people he had seen before, making sure no one was following him. He got to his car, looked around once more, checked the inside, and finally got in. He placed the box on the seat next to him. Opening the takeout box, he breathed in the scent of fresh coffee and egg sandwich. He took a sip of his coffee, a little hot. He placed it back and started on his sandwich. Crunchy bread, easy to bite, and the eggs made perfectly. He devoured the whole sandwich before taking another sip. The coffee was now a perfect temperature. He sat back and enjoyed his coffee, checking his phone every so often for updates.

• • •

Bright lights were all around the parking lot, making a stealthy move impossible. Gordon and Henry's man were in the stairwell, waiting. Henry's man took a walk. Taking out his car keys, he started towards the back wall with gusto, as though he was in a rush and knew exactly where he parked his car. As he got closer, he glanced at the minder's car, seeing him hunched over the steering wheel. He kept walking and then dropped his keys. As he picked them up, he maneuvered himself to the aisle in which the minder had his car. He moved around and behind the minder's car. He kept looking and waiting. A minute or so went by, nothing moved. The drugs had done their job. He sent Gordon a quick text and then moved to open the car door. The front driver's side was unlocked. Before opening it all the way, he reached in and grabbed the minder's gun and car keys.

Gordon pulled right in front and parked. He popped the trunk open and made sure no one was watching. The two men loaded the minder in the trunk, binding his legs and hands, duct taping his eyes and mouth. Gordon got back in the car and drove off. Henry's man got into the minder's car and followed.

Watching over the CCTV cameras in the security office, seeing the whole action, as it unfolded, was Mike. Once the two cars had left the property, he looked at the only other person in the room, the chief of security, a friend.

"Erase everything from cameras two and fourteen for the last 15 minutes." He watched as the chief deleted the files for both cameras.

"It's done!" the chief said, as Mike started back to his office.

• • •

Gordon and Henry's man ended up at a warehouse belonging to Mike's company, a place where older construction equipment and sub-standard materials were stored while awaiting proper disposal. Few had access to the facility. It rarely had a visitor. Opening the gate, Gordon drove through, the other car just behind. Gordon locked the gate again, and they drove toward building K. Gordon backed the car to the door. They both got out and dragged the bound man, who was stirring awake and struggling. Once inside, as the man kept thrashing around, they dropped him to the ground.

Henry's man got the mix of sodium hydroxide, sodium nitrate, and salt drums ready. He chose the nearest two from a dozen in the storage facility. These were chemicals used in major renovation projects for the sewage cleaning process, with a great side benefit. They were perfect for getting rid of bodies.

"Gordon, you can leave. This part isn't for you to see," Henry's man said while dragging the bound man closer to the drainage area.

"I'm going to have to cut him up. Otherwise, he won't fit into the plastic drum barrels." Upon hearing this, the man on the ground screamed, shaking, and trying to get free.

"Aren't you going to kill him first?" Gordon asked.

"No, why waste a bullet. Besides, the chainsaw will kill him, anyway." Now the man really screamed and gyrated on the ground.

Henry's man placed a face shield over his head, slipped into a painter's body suit, and pulled on the starter cord. Seven or eight pulls into it, the saw roared. He moved towards the man. Gordon stepped forward, interrupting Henry's man from the side, being careful not to get close to the working chainsaw. He drew a gun from his belt and pointed at the bound man's head.

"I can't let him suffer like this," Gordon yelled over the chainsaw.

"I have my orders," Henry's man yelled back, pointing the chainsaw at the man on the ground.

"What orders?" Gordon said, holding him back.

"Mike's," he said. "He told me to make him suffer."

Before Henry's man could take another step, Gordon shot the minder in the heart twice and once in the head.

"Mike will never know."

Henry's man nodded, casually. He really couldn't care either way. The body was then properly quartered, and placed into two half-filled forty-gallon plastic drums filled with one of the best bio-cremation liquids available on the market, Drano. The process would take some time, but time and privacy were two things this facility provided in abundance. The cutting and submersion process, including the cleanup, took two hours.

Having disposed of the body, they inspected the man's car for any incriminating bits and pieces that might lead back to Mike or his family. They took both cars and parked the minder's cleaned vehicle in a seedy part of Denver, the kind of place where a careless person might disappear. Then they drove to the minder's house, a converted loft on South Broadway, to clean up there. Gordon dropped off Henry's man a block away and then headed back to Mike's house. Henry's man used the minder's keys, entering the building lobby, and taking the elevator to the third floor. He was soon in front of the minder's apartment door. Looking for the man's door keys, he noticed a particular key fob, the kind used not for a car, but for a security system.

He unlocked the door, and once opened, the security system triggered a thirty-second timer. He walked in, clicking the fob near the reader by the door, stopping the timer. He spent the next hour removing the hard drives from the computers, collecting all discs and flash drives, gathering all printed evidence. He did a superb job, leaving the place in pristine condition, seemingly untouched. Once finished, he walked out of the building, and down the street past several bus stops. He caught a bus at the third stop. By late afternoon, Gordon and Henry each received a text.

ALL IS GOOD. ALL IS CLEAN. I'M GOING HOME.

Early that evening, Henry's man got on a Greyhound bus back to Los Angeles.

• • •

The California minder carefully made his way downstairs to determine why the alarm had gone off. He walked straight for the closed and locked kitchen door onto the back yard. He briefly stepped out, looking left and right. He inspected the lock jam, finding no signs of forced entry. He looked at the specialized anti-picking lock and saw no scratches. He came back in, re-locking the door, and continued searching the house. He inspected all the rooms and finally went back upstairs. He searched the upstairs rooms as thoroughly as he had those on the first floor. Once satisfied, he went to his office. Nothing was out of place. He carefully laid the gun on his desk and went to finish his shower.

Before long, he was back downstairs, with a freshly brewed cup of coffee in hand, leaning against his granite counter top, reading his Wall Street Journal. He hated that Rupert Murdoch had bought and sullied the WSJ brand, but his was a company-paid subscription. He was less than a third of a cup into reading when his legs buckled. He tried to brace himself against the counter, but he couldn't, and quickly fell. Emerging from the door to the garage, now standing above him was Henry.

"Yes, maybe you guessed it. I spiked your coffee with a neurotoxin!" Henry said with a smile.

He dragged the fully awake but completely limp body to the couch in the breakfast nook. He rolled up the minder's sleeves and took out a syringe and a large vial of liquefied heroin from the shaving kit he had brought. He injected the man with a full load and added a collection of puncture marks to each arm whilst adding more heroin, supporting a bad habit. He left the gear behind as evidence, along with a lighter and some cigarettes.

"What? No questions? No drawn out chit chat like in the movies?" the minder asked in a sleepy tone.

Henry then placed a small device on the kitchen counter, closed all the windows, and severed the gas connection behind the stove. Before leaving the house, he walked by the coffee table in front of the minder and left a nice farewell card, positioned so that he could read it. It simply read,

BOOM. A HOUSE FOR A HOUSE.

The actual kill method was a gas explosion, but he had to make sure the accidental overdose scene was set just in case the explosives didn't work and he would not go back in to check why it didn't work.

Henry was back in his car, half a block away, and waiting for the gas to collect in the house. With a small, handheld scope, he kept an eye on the house and could see the top of the minder's head, as he lay on the couch, high as a kite but conscious.

Thirty minutes were almost up. He drove by the house, triggering the timer on the device. A block away, he heard the explosion, followed by a concussion blast. He pulled over and stopped the car as everyone else did. Getting out, he looked in the general direction, acting shocked and frightened. The house, the minder and any evidence were on fire.

• • •

Henry called Agent Gonzales. Once he had his full attention, he gave him the address where the startup was located. Simultaneously, he triggered an email, with all the details as attachments. He then mentioned the Palo Alto explosion as part of their plan.

"Tell the story any way you like, but this terrorist had to go, *our* way."

"Who are you people?" Gonzales asked, angrily.

Henry again hung up on him.

Henry then started his drive back to his house, to meet up with his wife and to share the good news with Jason's wife.

• • •

That same night, after a long hard day, Henry was back home in his lounge chair. He had his Budweiser, waiting for the ten o'clock news. All three were sitting around having pizza and chatting when finally the news came on. The top story was the raid on a startup in Silicon Valley. The raiders had uncovered a cache of highly dangerous biohazard materials, along with dispersal equipment. The videos showed the entire area blocked off, with hazmat-suited people walking around collecting things. FBI agents arrested three Iranians in the raid, one a Stanford graduate, and two other local residents.

"Wait," Henry said. "I think there might be more."

Half-dozen commercials later, Henry yelled, "Here it comes. Pay attention everyone. Pay attention." The wives refocused on the television.

"In related news, also in Palo Alto, there was an explosion at a house, so powerful that windows were shattered several blocks away. It took firefighters several hours to put the fire out. Sadly, there was one casualty, the owner of the house. We will release the name after notifying the next of kin. The FBI and local authorities attribute the explosion to a gas leak."

Jason's wife looked at Henry. "So, was this the man?"

"Yup, this was the man, and now he's gone from your life, for good," Henry said, smiling at her.

Leaning back in her chair, finally free of fear, Amitis looked at Henry, smiled, and raised her bottle towards him.

"Thank you," she said softly.

She closed her eyes, a tear slowly moving down one cheek.

Where are Jason and Bobby?

36 | THE MOUNTAINS

The road across Turkey combined rolling hills, deserts with little plant life, rock formations sometimes smooth and sometimes jagged, intermixed with large stretches of lush green vegetation. None of which could be seen from the secret compartment in Erdal's truck. The father and daughter would have to stay in there until they pulled into the embassy compound in *Ankara*. Random inspections were a high probability. In the wrong part of Turkey, missing or inadequate paperwork, or insufficient bribe money, could mean a prison sentence. The father and daughter seemed to be happy sitting in the back, after a long and satisfying telephone conversation with Yasmin, the wife, and mother. They were looking forward to freedom and safety, which they could regain within days.

• • •

Jason and Bobby were only halfway between *Tabriz* and *Piranshahr*. The mountainous roads to *Tabriz* were gorgeous, busy, but fast. After *Tabriz*, they had to drive down a mountain, around the base of yet another mountain, across a barren flat plain, around a lake, and finally up the *Zagros* mountain range to *Piranshahr*. The back roads and passages were mostly winding two lanes, not well paved, filled with bad drivers, road hogs, and gun-toting outlaws, with any semblance of law sparsely scattered in between. Western *Azerbaijan* was the thorniest part of the trip and infamous for being lawless. The people in this region were mostly *Kurds* and against the Iranian regime, be it a monarchy or theocracy. Jason had traveled this road several times, since the first gulf war, and for many reasons, this trip felt more dangerous. Perhaps his responsibility for Bobby had something to do with that.

In *Naghadeh*, an hour away from *Piranshahr*, they filled the car and both reserve gas canisters in the trunk. You never knew if a mountain gas station would be out of gas or unwilling to sell at a reasonable price. Snow covered the mountains, and the air was chilly. They got provisions, including food, water, snow chains, and blankets, in case they had to spend the night in the mountains or if they became stuck. They were an hour away from their final stop in Iran and hoped to find a place to sleep. They were not going to a tourist destination and had no real reason to be in that town at all. They had to be very careful.

37 | THE FIRE PIT

The Center was reeling from the explosions and fire. Center agents had yet to take stock of the full damage. A small group had established a temporary residence in the Revolutionary Guards' HQ. In the parking lot, they had two mobile sites, portable surveillance trucks filled with the latest in tech, used to take the intelligence collection apparatus closer to the more challenging targets visiting Iran, such as the diplomats, who required 24/7 scrutiny.

Rezadad spent most of his time in these trucks. He could not stand the Revolutionary Guards' HQ. The smell, and the religious nature of everything, all made him sick. Deeply unsettled by so much loss, he was trying to reconstitute communications, or at the very least to manage the workforce, most of whom now worked from their own homes. The only agents working outside their homes, or who had temporary spaces, were those dedicated to the immediate situation, and the existing critical vectors were in play. As for the Mossad, that was an entirely different intelligence division's problem.

An analyst sitting at a monitor interrupted Rezadad. "Sir, we've just received a report from Parvaresh's house."

"What did they find?" Rezadad asked.

"He wasn't home and they've checked all his hangouts. Someone had ransacked his place and his car was found at The Center parking lot."

"He'll show up soon enough if he's not dead. What about the data backups and data recovery?" Rezadad demanded. Parvaresh was not really an issue at this point.

He was happy, at least, that this might end the vector he so hated to execute. Maybe, the prisoner getaway was for the best. Besides, he had to get The Center back on its feet. One vector meant nothing compared to the decades of work, research, intelligence, and all the coordinated effort that went into building the group.

"The report should be in shortly." The analyst had pinged all onshore and offshore backup sites, requesting immediate updates. Within minutes, he received the updates, which he printed and handed to Rezadad.

The updates started out with technical jargon about the backup process, schedules and timing, encryption key sequencing and rotation, and a series of steps the backup sites had executed for a partial restoring of the system. But all the necessary final set of steps had failed. Rezadad handed the page back to the analyst. "So what exactly does this mean?" he asked.

The analyst looked at it more carefully, reading it over several times, answering cautiously. "It basically says we can't get our data back!"

"Why not?" Rezadad asked, perturbed.

"All the data was re-encrypted. And, we don't have the key," the analyst responded nervously.

"Who has the key?" Rezadad demanded, now furious.

"Whoever sent the order to re-encrypt sent it from The Center the night of the fire."

"Oh my god." Rezadad stood nervously, realizing what had occurred. The intruders could not read the data. They could not move the data. They could not delete the data. All three were impossible, given the limited time and logistics. Their only remaining option was to re-encrypt the data, using the existing security features.

• • •

The hunt for runaway guests went suddenly from routine to critical. Now he was angry about the story around the kidnapped cleric's niece. What a stupid idea. When you create a story like that, you set the stage for what people perceive. In this case, three men, and a girl, with the focus being the girl, the least valuable of the bunch. If they couldn't see the girl, then nothing else mattered, even if the other three men were standing right in front of them.

Rezadad immediately snapped a string of orders. He had a 'most wanted' alert issued with a reward for Bobby and only Bobby. Rezadad then ordered a complete re-encryption of the lost data. He was assuming the data was lost to him, and thus should be lost to anyone who might go after it.

The duty analyst quickly sent a full-spectrum encryption order, followed by a broadcast message, each on a special government security channel. The message carried photos of Bobby and a simple text: Most Wanted/Reward Offered for any Information. The message instantaneously went to seven thousand locations encompassing all police stations, police cruisers, military bases, airports, bus stations, train stations, border crossings, and banks, newspapers, TV stations, government blog sites, and information kiosks at every school and university. This security channel could only be used in unique cases when there was an imminent flight risk for a person of interest, or if the public was in immediate danger. To Rezadad, this was definitely one of those situations.

The hunt for the encryption key was paramount. One of two groups had it, Bobby and his rescuers, or the Mossad. Rezadad got out of the mobile unit and went back inside the Guard HQ, to see if another round of family therapy was necessary for the captured agents. He took the elevator to the basement, and went to the offices where his people were located, for a fresh update.

"The email servers and the ERP systems are all back up. Also, we have the last six months of project data back on our temporary servers," an analyst said to Rezadad's surprise. He was standing near the door half expecting to get more bad news.

"Where did that data come from?" Rezadad happily asked.

"Apart from our data streams that are sent to backup sites every month, we create and store rolling six-month disks of all project data and infrastructure system files nearby," the analyst cheerfully replied.

"Good," Rezadad responded, thinking from now on he'd have to pay closer attention to what the techies were doing and saying. He then asked for a report on all assets and their whereabouts. In short, an immediate check-in, with updates every half-hour.

Before leaving for the basement hospital ward to visit the Mossad agents, he left more instructions. Certain data searches had to be made and certain voice files located while he was with the prisoners, all in a particular order.

The basement had a trauma center, with trauma doctors and a cardiologist on hand around the clock, and equipment to manage many related emergencies.

You don't want them to die on you while they still had some value.

Rezadad walked into the ward. The prisoners had now been separated into small rooms. Checking in with the ward staff, he found the wounded agent had died. That left only three to interrogate. Rezadad began in Gideon's room. They had handcuffed Gideon to the bed, with an IV tube in one arm, heart monitor electrodes on his chest. Visible and random muscle contractions shook the bed from time to time. He looked up at Rezadad.

"How are my men?"

"They're being taken care of," Rezadad answered curtly, not mentioning the death.

"I'd like to ask you some questions, in a civilized manner," Rezadad said. He recapped the information they'd collected already. He added more, that they already knew or had extrapolated, making the collected intelligence seem like a great deal more than it was.

"As you can see, your team has been very helpful. And, I appreciate their cooperation." He assured Gideon that, if he too cooperated, he could go home to his family as part of a planned prisoner swap.

"My men will never speak out of school," Gideon whispered.

"Your faith in your team is admirable," Rezadad said, "But, for now, I'm interested in only one thing. Who, in your group, is your computer and systems expert?"

"All of us. None of us," Gideon replied in a weakened voice.

Rezadad walked over to the phone on the wall. He dialed a number and softly spoke. "Kill the wounded Mossad agent, and bring his body here when you're done." He then coldly sat back down.

"I will ask you only two more times. Who is your computer and systems expert?"

Gideon turned away, staring at the wall, thinking it was a bluff. He had played the same game before, interrogating Palestinians for the Israeli Defense Forces.

Minutes later, the door to his room opened. A nurse rolled in a gurney with a body. It was Gideon's colleague and friend.

"Bring it closer to the bed," Rezadad ordered. "And now go to room #4 and wait for my call."

"I ask you again…," Rezadad said, in his most calm voice.

"Fuck you," Gideon shouted.

Rezadad got up and walked to the wall phone. He dialed and again softly spoke his orders, "Kill him and bring the body over to this room. But first, make him suffer." He hung up and sat back down.

This time, he said nothing, just waited. A man screaming down the hall shook Gideon to the core. The man was in pain, in deep agony, suffering. Every so often, you could hear his muffled and unclear voice, yelling in Hebrew. Gideon did not react in any way. Rezadad got up and picked up the phone. He dialed again.

"Please begin on the next one. Thank you." Before he could hang up, Gideon begged him to stop.

"I will as soon as you tell me what I want to know," he said as the screaming continued, from two directions.

"Now, who is your computer and systems expert?"

Gideon offered a name. Thankfully, it was not the dead man.

"What level of expertise does he have? And what was he tasked with?" Rezadad asked.

Gideon explained their entire operation inside the building. He started by detailing his colleague's technical expertise, nothing close to that of a high-level cyber-hacker, but enough to get around. He then explained their mission, to find the much-rumored Center and damage the facility, primarily to slow down or set back their operation.

The background screams continued unabated.

"Please stop," Gideon begged.

Rezadad got up, making a call, ordering the stop. He sat back down.

"Please tell me more."

Gideon detailed every second of their time inside the Center. At the end of the conversation, Rezadad thanked him and walked out pushing the gurney with the dead agent, leaving him in the hallway for pickup. He visited each of the other Mossad agents. They all asked anxiously about the screaming and yelling in Hebrew. Were the others okay?

"Everyone is doing fine," Rezadad reassured them all.

He made one final stop in the room with his people, to thank the analyst for the great torture soundtracks.

They had worked wonders.

38 | THE INN

By dusk, Jason and Bobby had made it to *Piranshahr*. They spent another thirty minutes driving up and down the three main boulevards to get their bearings and to look for a place to sleep, a hotel, an inn, or anything resembling one. The dreary town seemed to have no hotels, just inns with poor signage. Most were converted homes, open on the whims of their owners. The only reason for anyone to be in the town was that they were born there, or were on their way in or out of Iraq. This was one of many cities, on either side of the border, considered by locals to be part of the borderless nation of Kurdistan. Jason settled for the second largest square away from the main city center, a large traffic circle with a two-story shopping mall, several restaurants, and two inns.

He parked the car near the first inn and then told Bobby to wait while he got out and walked to the second inn. He knocked on the door and waited and waited. Eventually, an old man opened the door about an inch or two, squinting out with one eye. He was wearing traditional Kurdish clothing, baggy pants and shirt, a black cummerbund around his waist, and a beautifully beaded and embroidered skullcap. A thick white mustache with years of tobacco stains bristled under his nose. He asked in Kurdish. "What do you want?"

Jason replied in Farsi, "A room for the night."

"Are you coming or going?" the innkeeper asked, switching to Farsi.

Jason decided to tell him the truth but not the destination. "We're coming, and on our way to Tabriz."

"Well, the rooms are 100,000 *tomans*. I only have one left. How many are you?" He said looking around and behind Jason, with the door now half-way open.

"Me and my nephew," Jason replied.

"That'll be 150,000 *tomans*. Pay now!" He said, extending a hand that bore the signs of decades of toiling in the fields, growing whatever would feed his family.

Jason dug through several pockets and put together the money. "All I have is 140,000. Would you take it?"

Bartering was a must no matter what.

The man paused briefly, shaking his head in disgust. He opened the door all the way and grabbed the bills. Counting the money, he began to walk. He showed Jason to a room halfway down a hall.

"This is your room. It has two beds and a washbasin. The toilet is down the hall."

Jason leaned in and looked the room over. "This will be fine. Where can we get something to eat around here?"

The man pointed in the direction south of the house. "Several buildings away," he said, "you can get good *ash*."

Jason thanked him, telling him he would be back after dinner.

"Don't be too late. I can't open the door once I'm in bed sleeping. I'm an old man. Bad hearing you know?"

Jason smiled as he left the house. He made his way back to the parked car. He knocked on the windshield, waving Bobby out of the car. They walked in the direction of the soup kitchen. It was a short block away, tucked into the corner of a building that housed an industrial workshop. The sign, in Kurdish, read simply 'breakfast-lunch-dinner,' no name. They walked inside and sat at a table near the window, a drafty spot, but better for keeping an eye on the street. As the two men had entered, the other eaters gawked. The staring went on just long enough for people to decide if the arrivals were known, and if not if they were interesting, or more importantly if they might be dangerous. Then, perfectly synchronized, they all went back to whatever they were doing, eating, playing backgammon, smoking water pipes, and some just staring at the old black-and-white TV perched on a shelf in the corner.

A young man pushed a makeshift kitchen on wheels over to them. Under a wooden shelf were two rusty gray gas canisters and on top, two burners, one with tea brewing and the other holding a huge pot of *ash*, a popular Persian soup. This soup was rich and bursting with greens, meats, vegetables and thick noodles, a cold weather favorite. The waiter ladled two bowls of soup, poured tea for two, and covered each bowl with a fresh piece of *sangak* bread. He then extended his open hand.

"That will be 10,000 *tomans*."

Jason reached into his pocket and gave the young man the money. As the waiter pushed the cart away, both travelers lunged towards the warm, inviting bowls, dipping in their freshly baked bread to soak up the juices, taking bites in between each spoonful. Bobby was inhaling his food. Jason loved this dish and remembered all the times his wife made it, and how wonderful it was on cold winter days in Colorado. The men ate everything within minutes.

Leaning back looking through the window, taking a sip of his tea, Jason staring absently at the reflection of the TV. His eyes nearly popped when he saw a full-screen picture of Bobby, with a telephone number and message. When he turned to read the message, he noticed the waiter taking a picture of the screen with his cell phone. He quickly turned back around to study the room in the window reflections. The waiter was looking back in their direction, staring at Bobby. Then he took a second picture.

"Bobby, you've been made. We have to go. But slowly!" Jason whispered.

Bobby finished what remained of his tea. They both got up. Bobby left first, without looking at anyone. Jason turned around and politely said thank you and goodbye. They walked toward their car. Jason got in, and while collecting all the hidden money and the teddy bears, he studied the waiter staring at them from the restaurant entryway. The waiter was on his phone. Jason got out of the car and opened the trunk. He took the suitcase from the trunk and he and Bobby walked towards the nearest inn. As they got closer to the door, the waiter went back into the restaurant. Jason looked around and once they weren't watched, they ran to the other inn. They knocked incessantly until the innkeeper finally opened the door. The innkeeper was mumbling about something, but neither man was paying attention. Eventually, he mumbled his way back to his own room.

"Bobby, go to the room and get into layers of warm clothes," Jason said, pointing down the hall. Jason peered out the window, looking in both directions, waiting.

Where was the waiter calling?

Moments later, Jason went back to the room, and he too put on layers of clothing. They each filled different pockets with money. Jason took out the handgun from his waistband. It was loaded, checked and replaced. He took the remaining ammo from inside a teddy bear and put it in his jacket pocket. He then took off his Breitling watch and gave it to Bobby.

"This watch has a personal locator beacon. Pull this integrated antenna out and it automatically starts the signal. It runs for twenty-four hours but use it when and if you are within an hour of needing a rescue. Got it?" He stepped back out of the room and walked to the window.

He looked across the circle and saw a police jeep with two policemen looking around and inside Jason's now abandoned car. Standing nearby was the waiter. One policeman walked towards the nearby inn and banged on the door. Five minutes of banging later, the door opened. He pushed his way in. Within minutes, he came back out. Walking straight to the waiter, he slapped him hard. A heated discussion ensued, arms waving around, with more threats of violence. The waiter looked across the street. Tapping the angry officer on the shoulder, he pointed to the other inn. The policeman paid no attention and looked through the car once more. The waiter shrugged and walked toward the other inn by himself. Jason waited and watched.

Soon, the waiter was at the door. Before he could knock and wake the innkeeper, Jason pulled the door open and dragged the waiter in at gunpoint, pushing him to his room. Bobby closed the door behind them. As the door shut, Jason put his arm around the waiter's neck in a sleeper hold, pressing until the waiter went limp. They tied him up, filled his mouth with a sock, and shoved him under the bed.

Bobby was more frightened than he had ever been, even at the Center. They were in deep trouble, without a car and the police on the lookout. Bobby sputtered and spoke, in English, forgetting where he was and what the rules were. Three or four sentences in, Jason told him to shut up. They covered the bed, making sure they hid the waiter well. Jason tore the satellite phone out of the last teddy bear. He made a quick call, leaving a date, time and some numbers as a message. He then placed the phone in his jacket pocket. They were fully dressed for the cold night and a long walk in search of another car. They needed a new plan for getting across the border. Jason opened the bedroom door. Standing outside were the innkeeper and two younger men. Each was pointing an AK-47 in Jason's direction.

"I am a sleepy old man," the innkeeper said, "But my sons are not, and they have great hearing."

They pushed their way into the room. "We heard you speaking English. Are you Americans?" the innkeeper asked.

Before Jason could answer, a loud banging erupted at the front door. The old man handed his rifle to one son and walked out, closing the door behind himself. He went to the main door, yelling in Kurdish.

"Who is it and what do you want?" He opened the door slightly as before. This time, the two policemen forcefully pushed their way in.

"We're looking for a suspect," they said in Farsi. They were not Kurds. Most police and military in that region were not. It was a matter of control.

"And, we're looking for a waiter who came in here moments ago."

The innkeeper told them the waiter left a while ago, and that there were no guests here. He then went on a rant, complaining about how bad business was, how the inn across the street was stealing his entire livelihood, that they were thieves, and dealing with many unsavory businesses. Finally, why were the police harassing him? He drowned the two policemen in his misery, despair, and bitterness. The two left the inn, laughing at the old man, apologizing for disturbing him. They took another cursory look at the abandoned car, then got into their Jeep and drove off.

The innkeeper returned to the room. Seated on the floor, with hands on top of their heads, were Bobby and Jason. In front of them on the floor, were Jason's pistol, ammo, and phone. The old man closed the door and sat on the bed. He looked around a bit, and then under the bed.

"So, there is the waiter they were looking for! Is he dead?"

"No. Just sleeping," Jason said.

"Good for you," the innkeeper responded.

"I would hate to see you kill one of our young men," he said, telling them to put their hands down. They looked silly like that.

"So, are you American? British? Where are you from?"

Jason spoke in Farsi. We are not Americans, but Iranians who grew up in America, and were visiting relatives in Tehran where we got into trouble.

"Was it drugs?" the old man asked. "Or, was it spying?" Either one is punishable by death he explained. "Or, was it something completely different?"

Jason did not want to answer yet. He needed to know where they stood with these Kurds. Instead, he asked why they did not turn them into the police. "Why not let the police deal with us no matter what we did?"

"Because, you are in Kurdistan, our country, our laws," he said proudly, standing up.

"We deal with our problems, in our own way."

The innkeeper's sons pulled the waiter out from under the bed. The larger of the two sons slapped the waiter in the face, waking him up, as the other untied him. Eventually, the waiter got his senses back, looking around nervously. Pointing at Bobby, he rattled off what he had seen on TV. Pointing more emphatically and repeating himself, he got louder each time. Now the innkeeper slapped the kid, hard.

"Where is your pride, boy? Didn't you learn anything from your father? You don't call the police. You call the elders."

The waiter sobbed, apologizing, railing about money woes. He needed the reward money for his family, for medicine. He admitted to calling the number on the news bulletin and, fumbling for his cell phone, showed them his photo of Bobby taken from the TV screen, which included the message and call-in number.

"You were definitely not involved in drugs. I can tell from how you made the news you did something a lot worse," the old man said, smiling at Jason.

"You hurt the government, and that, my friend, makes you our friend."

The innkeeper handed Jason his gun and satellite phone and offered to help. However, he said they had to move from the inn to another house. Most importantly, they had to blend in better. The city clothes had to go, even the cold weather gear, to be replaced with typical Kurdish clothing. He sent one son to bring some of his boys' clothes, and after Jason and Bobby changed, the five men drove to another house on the outskirts of town, closer to the border. At the same time, they also stealthily moved Jason's car to another, safer location.

• • •

Rezadad was ending his grueling day, sitting inside one of the mobile centers, reviewing the last of the asset and Center status reports. It was a blend of good and bad news. Several key assets had not reported. In one case, an entire vector asset group had gone dark. For now, the hunt for the encryption key and apprehending Bobby were his crucial top priorities. But it was past midnight, time to go home for a bit of rest.

On his way out, an analyst stopped him with yet another bulletin report. He looked at the printed page and saw a cell phone snapshot of Bobby sitting at a table. He read the details and knew immediately that he'd have to rest later; it would be a long night. He sat back at his desk, calling in Ali Najafi, the project manager responsible for Bobby, ordering him and a dozen agents back to duty. There had been a photo-verified sighting of Bobby, along with an unknown subject, near the Iraq border.

Rezadad called the Revolutionary Guards' 5th Division, stationed in *Tabriz*, to send a patrol to *Piranshahr* ASAP, faxing them clear photos of Bobby made at The Center and the photo sent to them on the tip line. Within the hour, the military patrol was on the road and four hours out. Rezadad then dispatched Najafi and several other agents to be on the ground in *Piranshahr* immediately.

Najafi scheduled a military flight to land at the municipal airfield near *Piranshahr*, putting them there before the Guards' patrol. They called the *Piranshahr* police station, receiving no response, very typical of outlier police stations, with minimal service and lazy, corrupt officers. Rezadad knew the fugitives were making a run for the border. Once at the airfield, the agents would have to wait for the military patrol to pick them up and escort them into town, strength in numbers being the best way to squash resistance and cut through local politics and corruption.

• • •

It was dawn. You could hear calls to prayer all around *Piranshahr*. Bobby was just waking up. Jason was wide-awake, thinking, planning, keeping watch. He had a firm grip on his handgun, hidden under the blanket, pointed at the door. He'd only slept an hour, taking catnaps here and there. Then, a quiet knock on the door. One of the innkeeper's sons came in telling Jason, and the slowly awakening Bobby, that everyone was getting ready for prayers in the living room. It was a subtle invitation.

Bobby and Jason looked at each other. "Well," Jason said kicking at Bobby's feet. "Get up and go do your prayers."

Bobby got up and started for the door. "I'm going to tell them you're a Jew," he whispered with a smile as he left the room.

In the living room, Bobby knelt down over a large water basin for *ābdast,* the ritual washing steps before prayer. They then invited him to stand by the host. Next to him were the elder's two boys and, behind them, the wife and daughter. The Kurds began their prayers, reciting their *Surah's,* with a slight gaze now and again checking on Bobby. Bobby performed flawlessly.

After prayers, the men went to the kitchen, sitting on the carpet around a table setting. The wife and daughter served them breakfast, rushing around serving tea, all the while eating their own food standing by the stove. Jason joined them halfway through breakfast.

"Please sit and join us," the innkeeper asked.

"Thank you," Jason said. He then apologized for missing prayers.

"I am very tired and have been traveling for days. I combined my prayers into two *rakaats* and did them in my room so as not to disturb your family."

"Very good!" the innkeeper said, patting Jason on the back. "It's good to know you have not forgotten your prayers, living in America."

While they ate, plans were discussed. Nearing the end of breakfast, several more men dropped by the house, all carrying rifles and side arms. They too sat to eat, and immediately the women hovered, pouring tea, and bringing in more fresh bread, cheese, and nuts. The men brought news to the table. Plans had to change, again.

The military had two patrol trucks with a dozen men in each at the police station. Another group of men landed at the airport early that morning. They were not military but looked more official than the military. Taking a scrap of newspaper, they drew what looked like a sophisticated long-range drone, presumably their eye in the sky. These men from the airport were quite organized and a great deal more professional than the soldiers who accompanied them.

"Well, it seems we have to make other plans," the innkeeper said matter-of-factly.

The original intention had been to take the less traveled crossing several miles north. The local Kurds typically used that road due to their long-established relationship with the well-bribed border guards. Most likely, they would have closed that crossing. Moreover, the road had little room for a forced breakthrough, with terrible roads on the other side. The innkeeper suggested sending Jason's car with two men in that direction, while two other men, transporting Bobby and Jason, would use the main border crossing. The plan, using Jason's car as bait, meant that the timing had to be just right.

Before they left the house, someone appeared with a new report. One truck filled with army men had moved to the upper crossing while the other one remained at the main crossing. The men from the airport had split evenly across the two, with Najafi's group at the main border crossing. The plan could still work, but now would be more dangerous.

Jason's stolen car, the bait, started out first. Jason, Bobby and the other two, in the second car, would wait several kilometers away from the border. Jason and Bobby were in the back seat of the second car, when Jason tapped Bobby on the shoulder and told him to pull the antenna out of the Breitling watch, starting the homing signal.

The bait car, with two men dressed in city clothes, drove past the police station several times until they finally got the attention of one lazy policeman sitting smoking in his patrol jeep. A chase ensued, followed by a call to the main station. Within five minutes, the drone was above, following the chase. The bait car took the chase toward the upper border crossing. The driver in Jason's car made his move upon receiving a cell call, the trigger. Both border crossings became very active. The military truck at the main crossing left the border to catch the bait car from behind, closing off any escape back. The truck at the upper border crossing moved off and down the road to head off the bait car. The drone, from above, was covering the bait car. Najafi and a handful of agents at the main border crossing were watching the drone feed on a portable monitor. The car Jason and Bobby were in was on the move to the main border crossing, now with slightly better odds.

· · ·

The U.S. embassy compound in Erbil was chaotic as usual. It supported thousands of embassy personnel, of which many hundred were CIA employees. Life there was a combination of daily chores and complex military and policy planning and execution. In one office, Warren Spencer had been waiting for news of Jason. His people updated him on the status of the minders, and the arrival of the father and daughter at the U.S. embassy in Ankara. He was on his fourth cup of black coffee when a marine ran in with a report.

"Sir, Jason's locator signal. It's on."

"Where is he?" Spencer demanded.

"He's on the move, two clicks away from the Iraq border, and about to cross."

"Get the search and rescue crew in the air, ASAP, along with a support Apache," Spencer ordered.

39 | THE MAD DASH

The Kurds drove the second car closer to the border, with Jason and Bobby in the back seat. During fall and winter nights, the border patrol would close the border and then open it again the next morning on an entirely random schedule. Most people did not show up until noon. Border crossers waited until they had news about the weather, snow cover, and accidents, all of which would delay them, or worse, force them to turn around, except for buses. Buses usually ran on schedule. Only under terrible weather did they stop.

Jason and Bobby's car was waiting by the side of the road, near a gas station. The first morning bus drove by, right on time. They moved behind the bus and tailed it as if being towed. The bus neared the border crossing, honking its horn fifty feet out. The gate did not open as usual. The bus stopped, with the car bumper-to-bumper right behind. The Kurds, in the car, were fully armed and ready to shoot, the driver with a handgun and the other with an AK-47. They could hear talking and banter in the distance. The Kurd, on the passenger side, peeked out of his window, leaning out. He saw an Iranian border guard getting on the bus with a clipboard.

"They never stop buses, unless they're looking for someone," the Kurd said.

The search was fast, probably because there were few on the bus and clearly none looked like any person of interest. After getting off, the guard lifted the gates, on both sides. The bus moved, with the car close behind.

"OK, this is it," the driver said, "Get ready!"

The bus made it past the gates with the car moving in sync. The Iranian border guard was still standing by the side of the road, writing on his clipboard, checking off boxes, noting the time, and the bus number. Jason's car passed right in front of him. The guard glanced up, seeing something different, but not reacting immediately. The car passed the second gate, the Iraqi gate, also open for the bus. Realizing what he saw, the Iranian border guard jerked forward toward the alarm button by the gate. Pressing it, he set off a super loud siren. The Kurd behind the wheel downshifted and swerved around the bus, tires squealing.

The alarm was loud, blasting on both sides of the border. Najafi and the other agents jumped out of their seats and ran out of the guardhouse yelling at the guard to find out what was happening. The guard pointed toward the dust kicked up behind the stopped bus. Breathlessly, he explained that a car was tailing the bus, and as the gate opened for the bus, it took off. The car had four people in it, all Kurds, from what he could see. On the other side of the border, an Iraqi guard started his jeep, others jumped in, and a pursuit began. Najafi jumped into his car with his agents, and they too roared into Iraq.

The chase was on.

• • •

Thirty minutes had passed since Bobby pulled the antenna out of the Breitling watch, triggering the location signal. Jason's car was ahead by nearly a kilometer, with the Iraqi jeep closing in, and not far behind The Center agents. The chase took the three cars through a small, yet busy and populated village. Because of the civilians on both sides of the road, this was the safest section. After the village, it would be open season on them. The roads became mountainous, with steep cliffs on one side with tight turns, slower and far more dangerous, forcing the driver of Jason's car to slow down. The Iraqi and Center cars cut the gap in half. The Iraqis' leaned out of their open car and shot every chance they got. Coming hard into every curve, Jason's car seemed next to the Iraqis, inviting machine gun fire from the Iraqi soldiers. Najafi and his agents were shaking their heads each time the soldiers fired their machine guns.

"We want them alive, you dumb shits!" Najafi was yelling.

The Iraqis were getting closer. Najafi was right behind, not wanting to pass. He couldn't risk a friendly fire incident. He stayed on the Iraqi jeep's tail. Ten minutes of sheer mayhem later, one of the Iraqi bullets hit a front tire, swerving the car towards the drop-off at the edge. The driver over-compensated, pulling the car in the opposite direction, hitting the side of the mountain, and sending it into a ditch. The car came to a full stop.

Jason and the Kurd with the AK-47 jumped out of the doors on the right. The ditch blocked the other doors. Jason yelled at Bobby to get out and to stay in the ditch in front of the car. The Kurd waited for the Iraqi jeep to get closer and, as it did, he shot, stopping the jeep in its tracks. Jason, with only one extra magazine for his pistol, held his fire. The Iraqi soldiers jumped out of their car, with the Iranians right behind them. The only people shooting were the Iraqis. They were riddling the ditched car with bullets. By now, everyone in Jason's car was crouched in front, protected by the engine block. The Iraqis moved toward the ditched car, shooting, yelling in Arabic and broken Farsi for the intruders to give up.

As they got closer, Jason grabbed the AK-47 from the Kurd, checked the magazine, and asked for more bullets. The Kurd shook his head, signifying no more bullets. Jason counted ten in the magazine, one in the chamber. He propped the rifle on the edge of the ditch and, with two shots, killed the two Iraqis in the lead. The rest scattered, as did The Center agents. Taking cover, the Iraqi soldiers shot at the car again. The Center agents too shot and were much better shots. They shot the Kurdish driver in the shoulder. Jason shot another Iraqi, wounding him. Everything slowed down. More time passed between shots. Jason had emptied the AK-47, and then his pistol. They were out, like sitting ducks.

Najafi and his agents moved towards the car. The two remaining unwounded Iraqi soldiers reloaded and moved past Najafi and his people, intending to kill everyone. Najafi tried to stop them but got a gun barrel in his face. He backed off, looked at his Center agents, nodding an order. The Iraqi soldiers aimed their guns forward, walking faster. They were less than fifty yards away. There were no more shots from Jason's direction. The Iraqis felt confident. They were happy to kill the criminals who had killed their comrades. They took several more steps. Suddenly, two shots echoed through the air. Both Iraqis dropped to the ground dead. Behind them stood Center agents, pistols held at head level, a wisp of smoke floating away from each barrel.

The agents moved in. They were forty yards away. Jason placed Bobby in between himself and the car, pushing him down low.

"Sorry, son. I tried my best. You're a great kid."

The Kurds, one wounded and the other staring at him prayed. Jason placed his hand on the shoulder of one, thanking them, apologizing for their predicament.

Twenty yards away, The Center agents were about to move around the car, ready for the capture and a triumphant return to Iran. Jason felt they were seconds away from death. Suddenly, a whizzing sound went by above their heads, and the Iraqi jeep disappeared in a blinding flash. Jason recognized the signature sound of a

Folding-Fin Aerial Rocket. Looking back, he saw the AH-64 Apache, the revolving barrels of its 30-millimeter cannons blazing. He covered Bobby's body as a barrage of shots streamed down at the approaching Center agents. Just yards away, pieces of road, rocks, dirt, and body parts flew into the air with each round that zoomed just over the heads of Jason, Bobby, and the Kurds.

Less than a minute later, all who had been standing were dead. The Apache shot another rocket at the remaining vehicle and then climbed straight up, opening airspace for an Army UH-60 Black Hawk to come in for a pickup. A soldier rappelled down with a hoist. Jason pushed Bobby forward, and the trooper fitted the harness around him and signaled the operator to take him up. The hoist came down again. The soldier pointed at Jason. Jason shook his head and pointed at the wounded Kurd. The two Kurds were lifted one after the other, and then Jason, with the soldier going up last. The Black Hawk tilted and turned, moving back toward Erbil. The Apache pilot made another sweep around the area and then followed the Black Hawk.

Minutes later the two helicopters were side by side. Jason grinned as he looked at the Apache, seeing his son Sean, with his helmet visor raised, smiling back, joyfully showing the thumbs up sign.

• • •

On the ride back, everyone was quiet, with one U.S. soldier treating the Kurd. Apart from some abrasions, all the rest were fine.

Bobby looked at his wrist. "So, do you want your watch back?" he asked Jason.

Jason smiled. "No, you keep it. I'll have your dad buy me another."

40 | INTELLIGENCE

After a quick stop at the Erbil U.S. embassy, a military transport airlifted Jason and Bobby to the Ramstein Air Base, for checkups and debriefings. Earlier, Mr. Akbari and his daughter flew in from Turkey. They were all about to sit through debriefing sessions with Warren Spencer. Followed by a succession of other intelligence officers, each of whom wanted a go at one of the biggest intelligence leaks out of Iran.

Before the drudgery began, they had breakfast as a group for the first time free and safe. Breakfast began with hugging, tears of joy, and an emotional father thanking Jason and Bobby again for saving his daughter's life. During breakfast, they reminisced about the entire experience, focusing on the positive, the funny, and the human side of it. It was a two-hour breakfast, with eggs, bacon, sausages, fruits, German pretzels and jams, and freshly brewed coffee. It was good to be together, to be safe again.

"Oh, I brought your laptop back," the little girl said suddenly, as she ran to her room to fetch it.

She handed the computer to Bobby, then he and she went to a side table and talked as Jason and the father remained at the table and went over the debrief process. Jason urged the father to be as clear and complete as possible in everything he remembered. He and his girl would be back home soon.

"Your wife, Dr. Akbari, would also have to be debriefed and answer for her deeds," Jason finished. She had been arrested earlier that day in Copenhagen.

The father nodded in resigned agreement. After breakfast, they were escorted to the all-day de-briefing. The first round was one-on-ones, with later rounds involving smaller groups and, finally, the whole group together.

• • •

Each of the four started in separate rooms. In each room were at least one member of the intelligence team, one psychologist, and one person from the military establishment who would be part of later inquiries into the rescue mission. The father and daughter offered up all they knew, which was little. In their case, Yasmin Akbari was more culpable and responsible. However, the story told by these two could help persuade others to be lenient with her.

The debriefers were grilling Bobby hard, but Jason had prepped him well in the days preceding the rescue. Jason instructed him to keep the encryption key to himself and specifically, to be quiet about the key's whereabouts. Other than that, he was to speak the truth, as he remembered.

Jason's room, unlike the others, was filled with many more people, all of whom he assumed were there to find out about The Center and its intelligence gathering operations. Jason's de-briefing began with people asking questions all at once, out of order, and talking over each other. Chaos filled the air, with everyone wanting to know about the Center. They wanted to know how it might affect their groups. The rest be damned, politics over facts.

"One at a time!" Warren Spencer shouted.

Jason waited for calm to reign before he began. He started by first requesting that all repercussions and actions against him and his cohort be waived. To which he received a quick negative and assurances that that judgment would have to be made later. Jason nodded. He knew in the end, he held the key to his ultimate clearing.

He told the story. Everyone took copious notes even though the video recorder operated the entire time. They asked many questions repeatedly. Each answer brought more questions. For some questions, Jason had no answers, and he would not answer. Hence, his dilemma with governing laws be they U.S. specific, given what they did in California and Denver, or international, given what they had done in Europe.

• • •

Hours into the debriefing, the intelligence team recapped the entire story several times, broke it into pieces, revisited parts, tested, and challenged every fact. Eventually, they determined that the story was complete. Or as complete as they would get. However, they were still annoyed by not knowing the whereabouts and condition of the minders. They wished they could have captured them alive, to be interrogated. Most importantly, they were curious about the data download and its location. It was then that Jason began his negotiations.

"One last thing, about the data," Jason said. "There were two locations, as I mentioned, for which I have IP addresses. Along with the employee list we took from their ERP system, we re-encrypted the data with our own key, all of which we stored in the cloud."

"What do you want in return for it?" Spencer asked.

"I want complete and all-encompassing immunity for me and all others who helped me, from any country-specific or international laws, just as I mentioned this morning!"

The group on the other side of the table talked quietly among themselves, and eventually, Warren said they agreed.

"And it has to be in writing, signed by the U.S. Attorney General," Jason finished.

By late that afternoon, everyone had had enough of the debriefing. They all left Jason's debrief room except one, Warren Spencer. He waited for the last person to leave and moved to turn the recorder off. He then made a cell call and placed the ringing phone, in speakerphone mode, on the table. Picking up the phone at the other end was Mossad's Director of Political Action and Liaison.

"Hello, Warren. Is he on?" he said.

"Yes he is, and we are alone. Ask him whatever you want," Spencer whispered, letting Jason know who was on the line.

The Mossad director asked detailed questions about the four Mossad agents who had helped Jason, and if he had any news about their circumstances and location. Jason had little to offer other than what he believed happened to them and how supportive they had been.

"Thank you, Jason. Oh, one last thing," the Mossad director continued. "The last satellite message we received from them said they were in a data center that was being destroyed and that the U.S. had access to the data. Can you elaborate?"

Spencer quickly picked up the phone, taking it off the speaker and walked out of the room. He finished the conversation away from Jason. Jason was now out of the loop.

• • •

Back in the U.S., Jason's attorney reviewed all the paperwork for the agreement and emailed him a copy for final approval. Two days later, still in Germany, satisfied with the legal proceedings, Jason emailed Warren Spencer the IP addresses for the two offshore data centers, Qatar and Turkey, The Center employee list, and the 256-bit AES encryption key.

For Jason, it was now finally over. He could go home.

41 | THE HOLIDAYS

Three weeks later, a holiday gathering took place at Mike's house.

This celebration went beyond the normal Christmas festivities. Mike wanted to gather all those who helped in re-uniting Bobby with his family, to thank them in person. He had purchased first-class tickets for Jason and his wife, for Henry and his wife, and had even offered to bring Baba and his family to Denver, to which Baba regretfully replied that now a visit to the U.S. would not be advisable.

The house was decorated beautifully for the holidays. Mike's wife had prepared a great feast, and the house was brimming with joy, as the family and guests all sat around sipping eggnog, listening to classic Christmas music, and enjoying the warmth of the fireplace. Jason was happy to be in a big house since he and his wife were still in a hotel waiting for the final insurance check to be delivered, letting them start the search for a new home. Mike was back to his jovial self, hugging and kissing Bobby every chance he got.

"It's about that time," Mike's wife whispered. At which Mike jumped up and fetched a gift from under the tree. It was a small box, wrapped beautifully.

"Okay, everyone, gather around, gather around," Mike yelled over the music as he took another sip of his eggnog.

He got everyone into a group, making sure that Jason and Amitis were in front. He then handed Jason the box, telling him it was in appreciation for all he had done. Jason, as was customary, refused, handing back the gift to Mike. Henry quickly intercepted the box and announced he'd take it in Jason's stead.

"No, seriously Jason," Mike said. "I want you to have this. It's just a small token of my appreciation." With some effort, Mike pulled the box out of Henry's hands.

Jason, eyeing the small box, assumed it was a new watch. A watch much like the one he'd given Bobby during their escape. He accepted and slowly unwrapped and opened the box. Inside was a key, a simple nickel-plated brass key. Jason picked it out of the box and looked inquisitively at his wife, and then at Mike.

"Open the envelope that goes with it," Mike smiled.

Jason looked deeper into the box to find a small envelope. Inside was a picture of a house.

"It's your new house!" Mike's wife screamed, having waited long enough for the surprise.

"What new house?" Amatis, asked, bewildered.

Mike took the picture and handed it to Amatis. "This is your new house. We thought about all the times you and Jason told us about your wishes for your dream house, — rooms, property, all the little details, and found a house that best fits that vision, in a gorgeous part of Monterey, overlooking the bay."

Jason's wife held the picture, with tears in her eyes. She got up and gave Mike and his wife each a long hug, all the while crying. Jason stood up, shaking Mike's hands and thanking him. He got a bear hug back, and a tearful Mike blubbered uncontrollably over Jason's shoulders.

Bobby got up to separate the two, also teary-eyed, saying, "OK dad, it's not like he saved the world. Let the man go!"

Henry too stood up. "Where's *my* house?" he joked while grabbing another Budweiser, a drink that had never and would never again see the inside Mike's house.

This would be a great holiday for all.

42 | 3RD DATACENTER

As the group of friends and family in Denver celebrated the holidays, thousands of miles away another group was working around the clock.

In the outskirts of Kuala Lumpur, dozens of technology experts sat in a warehouse, hunched over their computer keyboards. Behind them were rows and rows of towering servers, with interconnected cables, lights blinking, fans humming. At a loading dock at the end of the warehouse, trucks were being unloaded with more servers, more cables, more of everything to build out a large data warehouse. Outside, several fuel trucks were filling up the underground storage tanks that fed the generators. The immense power consumption would otherwise become a red flag for the local utility company, causing scrutiny and other problems.

In Malaysia, the third offshore location, data recovery was up and running at full speed. The data backup was clean and only one week out of sync. As the site was upgraded, its intently working staff sent the data back to Iran, to a new and more secure location.

• • •

Local national forces, with the urging and full support of the U.S. government, had taken down the other two sites outside Iran. Once local counter-terrorist forces arrived, they found the places emptied of all people. Taking the data servers back for analysis, they found it further re-encrypted and rendered useless.

• • •

Unknown to them and U.S. intelligence community, Vector #188 had just been initiated.

The hunt was on for whoever destroyed The Center facilities.

Other Books

"Autarky" (Book #2)

(To buy: Go to bit.ly/boroumand)

M. Max Boroumand
DIGITAL DARKNESS
A BROKEN COUNTRY

About the Author

Max Boroumand is a seasoned and experienced technologist and management consultant. His career spans over two decades, with clients in the Fortune 500, Governments, and non-profits, as well as many technology startups. His work and life have taken him all over the world, from the Middle East and North Africa, to Europe and the Americas, and to Asia.

He is now the CEO of a holding company, whose portfolio includes several software companies, and most recently a publishing and media company supporting his new passion, writing books: The first in the collection, 'The Minders', was published in 2015, followed by "Autarky" in 2016, and "Digital Darkness" in 2018.

www.boroumand.com